DISTANT

Annette Keen

Published by Sunbird Publishing

A CIP catalogue record for this book is available from the British Library.

ISBN 978-0-9574080-5-0

Cover design by Strumpet Design

Prepared and printed by:

York Publishing Services Ltd
64 Hallfield Road
Layerthorpe
York YO31 7ZQ

Tel: 01904 431213

Website: www.yps-publishing.co.uk

For all my cousins

Annette's TQs:
AP, PK, JJ, RC, LD, SB, JK, CW,
for all your help and support.

SJR at Strumpet Design, for the cover artwork.

PC, CB, NS & all at YPS, for making my vision a
reality.

AG, for allowing me to use the photo of your dad.

And the beautiful city of Cape Town,
for inspiring me.

Love,

Annette

x

DISTANT COUSINS

FEBRUARY 11th 2010

As they picked up speed at long last, Walter wound his window up a little to cut out the motorway noise. The traffic in Cape Town had been heavier than usual due to an accident on one of the approach roads, and diversions had forced them to take the long route home, but now that the build-up was moving along on the N1 he started to feel more comfortable. He disliked driving through the city, more than ever at that time because there were road works everywhere – all part of the city's preparations for the football World Cup. It was almost 10.30pm by then, a warm evening after a hot and airless day.

'Your mama looked well,' Walter remarked to Anneline. 'Cheerful'.

'But we both know that no matter how she looks she's *not* well. She would be so much better if she came to live with us.'

'Annie, you know she won't do that. And anyway, where would we put her? There's no room.'

'If we could get a bigger place... then maybe she'd come.'

This was a variation on a conversation they'd had many times. But there was no chance of them having a bigger place, and the five of them were squashed in the apartment at Ocean View as it was, leaving no room for a sixth person. Walter didn't reply to his wife. There was nothing he could say that hadn't already been said.

Ahead of them a rusty old car chugged along belching out fumes, its exhaust hanging just above the road surface. Walter's finger hovered over the indicator. He checked his mirror but instantly changed his mind about overtaking and instead, pulled back. Coming up at speed in the outside lane was a convoy of sleek, black cars, headlights on full and blue lights flashing. Sensing Walter's unease, Anneline turned to look as the unmarked cars drew level with them, and cruised past. Tucked in the middle of a line of security vehicles was a long, black limousine with tinted windows bearing the number plate RSA 1.

Walter jerked his thumb across to it.

'And I doubt if we can rely on him to help us get a bigger place,' he remarked.

Anneline turned back to look out of the windscreen as the presidential convoy sped away. She clicked her tongue impatiently, and for a moment Walter wasn't sure if her disapproval was aimed at Mr Zuma, or at himself for making the comment.

'All those children of his that he never even sees...' she said, shaking her head.

Walter relaxed. For the moment it was the president in her bad books.

* * *

Kate was restless, and channel hopping. She'd started watching a film, but then realised it was one she'd seen before. Another click on the remote and a current affairs programme came up on screen with a report from South Africa, but this didn't catch her interest at all. Then she found some stand-up comedy from a festival somewhere, which was more promising but finished two minutes after she found it. Nothing else grabbed her.

The heating had already gone off and the big, high-ceilinged room was getting chilly. Kate clicked the

TV onto stand-by, and went round switching off the table lamps in her sitting room and plumping up the cushions on the sofas. Pulling the curtains back a little at the French windows, she peeped out to see snow still falling onto the white expanse of garden beyond, and shivered.

* * *

In a comfortable air-conditioned bedroom at his official residence in Acacia Park, Jacob Zuma slept soundly, and snored. After watching the recording of his State of the Nation Address (which he was pretty pleased with) the president had a few drinks before retiring, then fell immediately into a dreamless, trouble-free sleep.

Out on the peninsula at Kommetjie, Walter and Anneline Maketa passed a restless night in their Ocean View apartment. It was hot, and even with the window open there was no air circulating. Anneline lay awake worrying about her mother's failing health, and Walter tossed and turned on his side of the bed, worrying about Anneline.

And six thousand miles away, in a pretty Surrey village, Kate Hatchman lay huddled under her duvet, hearing nothing beyond the muffled silence of a heavy snowfall. She wondered sleepily, but without much hope, if the snow would clear by the weekend so that she could get down to Sussex as planned, and meet up with her cousins.

THE HATCHMAN FAMILY TREE

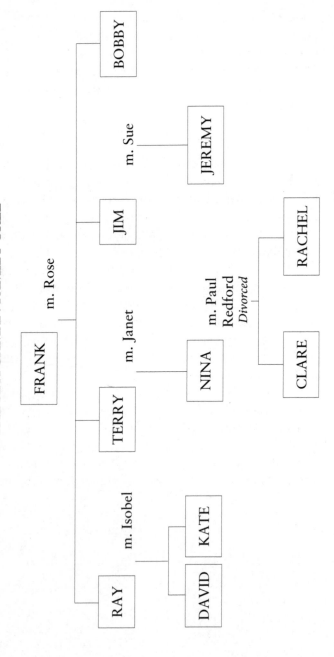

CHAPTER 1

APRIL 2010: ENGLAND

Rachel Redford stood on the steps of the hotel and checked her watch again. Her usual confident air had temporarily deserted her thanks to a hasty, last-minute attempt at repairing her make-up which hadn't worked terribly well. For once she'd forgotten to bring a brush with her, and had to resort to finger-combing her hair. Now, to make matters worse, it was drizzling with rain and she'd left her umbrella on the tube earlier on in her rush to get to the hotel.

Behind her, the huge revolving glass doors enveloped an elderly couple and silently swished them into the lobby. The doorman, spying Rachel's approaching taxi before she did, walked down the steps and held the door open for her.

'The Little Starlets Nursery, Knightsbridge,' she said as the door closed. Then she leaned back in her seat, shut her eyes and sighed.

Oh my God, what am I doing? she thought, not for the first time.

She looked again at her watch, put her head forward into her hands and a curtain of blonde hair fell forward, hiding her face. A tear slid down her cheek, and she brushed it away and flicked her hair back, instantly annoyed with herself.

The taxi idled in a queue of traffic.

I'm going to be late, Rachel thought. Please, don't let me be late.

Her phone beeped, and a text came up. 'u r gr8 lol jason xx'

She stared at the phone, contemplated replying, then changed her mind. She would call him later, once the children were asleep. He'd be on the train by then, heading for Manchester, away for four days.

The taxi jerked forward a few metres, then stopped again.

I could lose my job, she thought. I'll lose everything if I'm not careful. Why am I being such a fool?

And then Rachel did what any girl needing reassurance and a few loving words would. She phoned her mother.

* * *

They'd already been in the restaurant long enough to drink about half the bottle of wine, and still there was no sign of Kate. A waitress brushed past Jeremy, carrying garlic bread and a dish of risotto. He breathed in the aroma as if it might keep his hunger on hold a little longer, and glanced at his watch.

'I'll have to order soon, Nina. Got to get back home then up to London for a gig,' he said, picking up the menu again.

'Yes you're right, we can't keep waiting – if I drink any more wine on an empty stomach I'll never get myself home.'

Nina looked around and caught the eye of the nearest waitress.

'We're still waiting for someone,' she explained, 'but we'll go ahead anyway.'

Nina's phone rang as Jeremy was ordering pizzas for them both. She pulled it out of her bag on the fourth ring.

'Hello darling, how are you?' On a bad line, her daughter said something she couldn't make out. Nina put her fingers against her left ear and spoke a little louder.

'Sorry, Rachel, I missed that. I'm having lunch with the cousins in a restaurant in Tunbridge Wells. Jeremy's here already and we're supposed to be meeting Kate – if she turns up. What was that you said?'

Rachel's voice, small and miserable, broke through the static.

'Oh... oh, nothing Mum. I just wanted to say hello, that's all. Give them my love.'

'OK, yes I will.' There was a pause. 'Rachel, are you all right?'

'I'm fine Mum. I just...'

But the line was breaking up again, and when it went dead Nina flipped her phone closed and put it back in her bag.

Jeremy looked up from his wine glass. 'Everything OK?' he asked.

'Mmm. Well, to be honest I don't really know. Just between the two of us, I've been a bit puzzled about Rachel lately.'

'Oh? Surely not a problem with the family she's working for?'

'No, I don't think so. It's the dream job she always wanted – who wouldn't want to live in luxury in SW1?'

'Then what?' he asked. 'A man?'

'Nobody I know about,' said Nina, fiddling with her knife and fork. 'Maybe it's nothing, but my maternal antennae, as the girls put it, are up. I just have the feeling something's not right there.'

'Ask Clare,' Jeremy ventured.

'Maybe I will when they're down next weekend. I'm probably just being hyper-sensitive. Both of them have always told me when something was worrying them and I like to think that just because they live away from me now that hasn't changed.'

'I'm sure you're right about that. But there must be times when those kids play her up – maybe she rings you on days when she's had enough of them and needs an understanding adult to talk to.'

'Yes, that's probably it.' Nina looked at her watch. 'Where on earth is Kate?'

'Perhaps she forgot,' said Jeremy.

'No,' said Nina, gesturing behind Jeremy's head as Kate flew in through the door, hesitated for a moment as she looked around, then picked her way over to their table.

'I'm so sorry,' she said breathlessly as she struggled to unwind a scarf from her neck. 'Traffic coming into town was at a standstill – motorcyclist collided with a car – have you ordered yet?'

'Only just,' said Jeremy, pouring Kate a glass of wine. 'We were starting to get worried about you.'

'Sorry, I should have texted... I'll have whatever you're eating,' she added.

No you won't, thought Nina, you never eat pizza. So when the waitress re-appeared at her elbow she ordered the salad that Kate always had, then turned to face her with a smile.

Kate finally extricated herself from her scarf, and bent to air kiss her cousins, first Nina, then Jeremy. They glanced at each other and exchanged a smile as Kate turned to put her bag down, then unbuttoned her jacket. This pseudo-kissing was something they never did, preferring a big hug instead. But Kate had always been the more distant of them, Nina thought, even when they were small. Out of the four cousins Nina and Jeremy had always been closest, and Kate never quite made it into their inner circle. It wasn't as if there was a big age gap either – one year younger than Nina and two older than Jeremy, she should have been comfortably cocooned in the middle of them. But somehow it was never like that. Maybe it was something to do with her branch of the family – Kate's older brother David was even more withdrawn and had never really had much to do with any of them, including his own sister.

And yet, thought Nina, the family still ties us three together.

Looking at Kate now, her looks so totally at odds with theirs, one dark head against two fair, Nina could see that a stranger would not have thought them related at all.

Takes after her mother, she thought, in looks and temperament, whereas we're both so like our dads.

Behind Kate's back the Gaggia machine hissed and gurgled and Nina wondered if she'd ask for another table away from the noise, one of the many things Kate had been known to complain about, gently but firmly, on other occasions when they'd met for lunch. Kate liked things to be just right. A request to move tables at that time would certainly have been tricky as the restaurant was filling up quickly, but to Nina's relief the Gaggia seemed to have got away with it that time.

'So, how's everyone?' Kate sipped her wine and leant back in her chair, just as the garlic bread arrived on their table – to Jeremy's delight. 'How are the girls, Nina?'

Nina shot Jeremy a warning look. The last thing she wanted was Kate getting wind of her anxiety. Like a terrier with a bone, she wouldn't let it rest.

'Oh, you know. Busy with work and their social lives in London. They see each other quite a bit, which is nice.'

It was some time since Kate had seen Nina's daughters, and she couldn't picture them living independent lives in the big city.

'I still think of them as little girls with ponytails and matching dresses,' she said. 'So sweet.'

'Uncle Bobby turned up at Mum and Dad's recently,' said Jeremy, stepping neatly into the breach and pulling the focus away from Nina. 'He never lets them know he's going down to see them, just arrives with a suitcase. Anyone want more garlic bread?'

'He drives all the way to Exeter?' asked Kate, declining the bread with a raised hand.

'Train. He doesn't have a car.'

'What if they were away?'

Jeremy shrugged. 'Suppose he'd turn round and go straight back to London. I can't imagine him booking into a hotel.'

None of them could imagine Uncle Bobby doing anything much. A determined bachelor, he was the wild card in the Hatchman family. Always invited to family gatherings, the chances of him actually turning up to anything were a constant source of speculation within the family. He made it to Kate's first wedding, just in time for the reception, but failed to arrive at her second. When Nina got married he was there for the church service but disappeared again as soon as the photos were over. He was generally considered to be an oddball.

'Paul thought he was hilarious, always guaranteed to say something inappropriate. He sent me a card when our divorce came through,' said Nina, 'and wrote inside "To Paul and Nina, probably all for the best." How weird is that?'

'Well, that's Bobby for you.'

'And I hesitate to ask, but what about David? Any word from... wherever he is now?' asked Nina, turning to Kate, who shook her head.

'But there's a new baby boy,' she replied, 'that much I know for sure because the latest Mrs. Hatchman sent a birth announcement to his girls in America. It appears that they're living somewhere in north London now...'

'Chicken Caesar salad?' asked the waitress, from behind Nina's shoulder.

Kate indicated the empty space in front of her without missing a beat.

'... but I've had no direct contact with David since Mum's funeral, and that was six years ago. His kids get in touch with me very occasionally, or I wouldn't even have known he'd married again. Poor girl.'

'It's a free country – she didn't have to marry him,' Jeremy ventured.

'She's the same age as his eldest girl. Wonder if he ever thinks of that,' Kate mused, grinding black pepper over her salad.

'Yuk,' said Nina, at the same time as her pizza arrived. 'Not this,' she smiled up at the waitress, 'this will be delicious. That yuk was heading for a different target.'

The waitress returned Nina's smile uncertainly, her level of English not up to the exchange, and moved away.

'And how are you, Kate?' asked Jeremy. 'How's the beauty business?'

'Busy. Very, very busy. We launched a new product range last month and it's been hell on wheels ever since. I've been working terribly long hours, but thankfully sales are picking up now after a slow start. How's the music going?'

'Yeah, not bad, a fair bit of work coming in anyway. I'm playing in Chelsea tonight at the 606 – why don't you both come? Come back to my place and we could all go up together.'

He knew Nina would. She liked going to Jeremy's gigs, liked the jazz atmosphere and hearing him play. He knew Kate wouldn't.

'Well,' she said, 'I don't know. It'll make it a very late night by the time I get home.'

'It's Sunday tomorrow, Kate. No work,' said Nina.

'No office, but there are still things I should be doing from home. I don't know. Chelsea, you say? Well, it's only just over the river... I'll think about it.'

Jeremy glanced at Nina, who raised an eyebrow then went back to her pizza.

'I went to your exhibition, Nina,' said Kate, sipping her wine, 'and I was very impressed.'

'Did you? Were you?' Nina was surprised, and showed it. 'You didn't say you were going, I never really thought you'd have the time...'

'Well the gallery is quite close to the office – and anyway I wanted to see what you'd been up to. Your photos were definitely the best there. The others were all a bit too dark and obscure for my taste. Anything good come from it?'

'Yes, a couple of really nice commissions from magazines, one for a series that could run over a few months. So it was worth doing, and it's given me the courage to float some ideas with a couple of commissioning editors for book projects.'

'Ah, you see there may not be many of us Hatchmans...' said Jeremy.

'No thanks to you Jem – unless you get your skates on David's new baby will have sole responsibility for keeping the name going,' said Nina. Jeremy ignored her.

'... but we haven't done too badly in our careers.'

'Well, we've worked hard,' said Kate.

'Yes, but let's face it, we're just *hugely* talented,' added Nina, poking fun at them all.

Jeremy and Kate laughed.

'Anyway, here's to us,' he said, and lifted his glass.

* * *

It was busy in the 606, a Saturday night crowd out to enjoy themselves. With all the tables booked Nina had to sit in the bar, but she didn't mind. There were plenty of people-watching opportunities and there was the club atmosphere to soak up, plus she had an elevated view across the heads of the diners to the tiny bandstand. At the end of the first set Jeremy picked his way across the room and joined her.

'I love this band Jem! It's a really exciting sound. Could this turn into a regular gig for you?'

'Sadly no, I'm just depping while their usual pianist's in the States. But you never know what else might come from it. And I get the chance to do three other gigs with them before he comes back. Shame Kate didn't come – what do you suppose she's doing now?'

'Sat in front of her laptop I should imagine, unable to bear the thought that the company might just function without her constant attention. Kate's always been a workaholic – she's probably not going to change now.'

Jeremy got them both drinks, and introduced Nina to a couple of other musicians from the band.

'My cousin Nina Redford,' he said, 'but more like my big sister really.'

And as people always did, they remarked on how alike Nina and Jeremy were, before heading off in the direction of the bar and the rest of the band.

'I just wish Kate would lighten up a bit,' Jeremy said when they were on their own again. 'It's like there's nothing else in life that interests her, and I find that really sad.'

'Well, I just think Kate's life didn't turn out the way she wanted and in the absence of a family the business has taken over and filled the gap.'

'God, I hope we never get like that.'

'I won't. And I don't suppose you will either,' Nina said, smiling up at him. 'Although I know what you musicians are like. You're all so...' she paused, searching for the right word.

'Committed? Dedicated? Barking mad? All of the above?'

'Probably! But not driven in the way that Kate is, thankfully. I think you're far too laid-back for that.'

Jeremy turned at the sound of his name from the other end of the bar.

'OK, we're back on – see you at the end.'

And then he was gone.

* * *

Kate was right about one thing – it was a very late night by the time Nina and Jeremy got back to his cottage, and then she'd driven on down to Brighton. She let herself into her flat soundlessly and headed straight to bed.

Poor Kate, she thought, missing out on so much. Success had come to her, but with a hefty price tag attached. I must try to get her out more, she thought sleepily. Get her down here for a weekend, maybe, in the summer. She yawned. Yes, that's what I'll do. But the thought got lost in the fog of sleep and by the next morning Nina had forgotten her resolve.

It was two days later, having walked the short distance to her mother's flat, that it came back to her.

Janet Hatchman, at eighty-three years old, was sprightly and independent. Selling the family house after her husband Terry died, she indulged herself by buying an expensive apartment in a block right on the seafront, with an old fashioned lift and a concierge to bring up the post and the milk. At first, thinking she might miss a garden, she grew flowers in pots on her balcony, but as her social life expanded she discovered she couldn't be bothered with them and bought wooden steamer chairs to put in their place. Her flat was often full of groups of friends, playing bridge, having supper and planning holidays – but even so it was a comfort to her that her only daughter lived within walking distance, and their relationship was close and warm.

'Now tell me about the girls,' she asked Nina, as they stood together in the kitchen. 'Did that last project of Clare's work out OK?'

'Yes, she said it went very well and I know she put a lot of work into making it a success. They'll be down at the end of the week so you'll be able to ask her all about it then. Rachel's got the whole weekend off work so they're coming Friday evening and going back Sunday afternoon.'

With her mother, Nina didn't feel like expressing any vague concerns about Rachel. Janet was a woman who, faced with real problems and real emergencies, was sensible, capable and totally supportive, but she wouldn't give the time of day to airy-fairy fanciful dilemmas. Nina could just imagine her response: 'Nonsense, dear, it's just your imagination.'

Janet took the cellophane wrapper off a battenburg cake and started to slice it while the kettle boiled. As a young housewife in the frugal fifties she'd made all her own cakes – everyday, birthday and Christmas – but these days was far too busy having a good time to blow the dust off her cookery books and baking tins.

'I had lunch with Jeremy and Kate last Saturday,' Nina said, carrying the tea tray into Janet's elegant living room. 'I feel I should be a better friend to Kate, she's such a loner. It's all work with her.'

And so Nina's late night plan of inviting Kate down to Brighton popped back into her head as she told her mother about their meeting.

'She was always such an anxious child,' said Janet, cradling her teacup, 'a bit too eager to please. David bullied her of course, the same as he bullied you and Jeremy whenever he thought there were no adults watching. Horrid boy.'

'He's got another baby, a boy this time.'

'Oh dear. Poor little chap.'

'I thought I might ask Kate down here one weekend,' said Nina, peeling the yellow marzipan off her slice of cake and splitting up the pink and yellow sponge squares.

'Would she leave the business behind for a whole weekend? Still, it's worth a try, I suppose. I'd like to see Kate again. We could all go out to dinner somewhere in town – it would take the pressure off you a bit,' said Janet, realising straight away that no matter how well-meant the idea was, in reality it was likely to be hard going for Nina.

'I've got a few assignments coming up soon, so it wouldn't be till the summer I don't suppose,' said Nina. 'She went to my exhibition, you know, in London.'

'Did she? Well that was kind.' Janet poured more tea.

'It's funny, isn't it – Kate continued to use her maiden name professionally and I didn't, but every time I see her it strikes me that she's less of a Hatchman than either me or Jem, in both temperament and looks.'

'Well, that's because she's got Isobel's colouring,' said Janet. 'You only have to look at pictures of her mum when she was younger to see that.'

She indicated the family photos on her sideboard but before either of them could pursue this line of thought, the phone started ringing and Janet eased herself out of her chair to answer it.

'Have more battenburg,' she instructed Nina. 'They were three for two and I bought six, so you won't be leaving me short.'

Only my mother, thought Nina, could consider six battenburg cakes a bargain buy. She must have a bridge evening coming up.

But Nina, who never normally bought, made or ate cake, did take another slice, looked across to the Hatchman photo gallery and leaned back in her armchair with a small sigh of something that she supposed was contentment.

CHAPTER 2

JUNE 2010: SOUTH AFRICA

Walter Maketa folded back the Cape Argus newspaper and shuffled the pages into line. He was a man of few aspirations, most of which were being satisfied at that particular moment. Home a little earlier than usual from the garage where he worked as a mechanic, Walter had claimed his favourite chair and turned to the sports pages of the local paper, with the accompanying background sounds of Anneline preparing supper in the kitchen. Maize and beans, she'd said, with a beef stew. The warm, meaty smell drifted out to him, and for a moment or two Walter experienced the perfect peace of a man who asks for little in life, yet most of the time has trouble achieving even that.

The door to the apartment opened, and crashed back against the wall. A tall, gangly youth in jeans and a hooded sweatshirt strode into the living room, and ruined Walter's five minutes of serenity. Dropping his college bag down on the floor, he stepped over Walter's outstretched legs, reached across for the remote control and jerked the TV into life.

'Hey,' he said, pulling out earpieces and flopping into the nearest chair.

'Whatever happened to "hello"?' asked Walter, his voice rising over the sound of a television soap. 'A perfectly good word, used all the time by civilised people. I can't understand why your generation has so much trouble with it.'

From the kitchen, Annie called out, 'Sele, is that you?'

'Possibly,' Walter called back to her, 'or it could be an alien. I can't tell the difference.'

He made a great show of flapping and folding the Cape Argus, but if Sele noticed then he chose to ignore his father, instead clicking through the TV channels. The early evening news popped up on SABC 1 and Walter lowered his paper, but after less than half a minute Sele had swiped it away and another soap – equally as bad as the first – was immediately in its place.

Annie bustled into the living room. Filled with so much furniture that it required some careful manoeuvring to travel across from kitchen to front door, the room fulfilled many functions in the Maketa household. The children had done their homework there when younger, and Sele was occasionally still found studying a book at the table. It was where they all watched television and had family discussions, where Annie did the ironing, Walter read the newspaper and everyone ate meals. Squeezed in between the wall unit and four open shelves were two pictures – one of Nelson Mandela, and next to it something that one of the children had painted at school years before.

Annie negotiated the furniture with a practised ease, placed two covered dishes on the dining table, and turned to kiss her son on the top of his head.

'Hey, Mama.'

'Wash your hands, Sele. Supper's ready. Come – now.'

'The girls home yet?'

'Late night shopping at the mall,' said Annie.

Mandisa and Elana, the twins, and Walter's two perfect jewels, both worked in the shopping mall. On late nights Annie, Walter and Sele ate without them. She nurtured a hope that these evenings might be an opportunity for some father and son bonding, but there was little evidence so far of anything like that happening.

Parental conversations regarding Sele usually followed a well-rehearsed format, as happened later that evening after he'd gone out in search of his Ocean View friends.

'He's got no ambition,' said Walter.

'He's a clever boy,' said Annie. 'His teachers all say so, clever with computers and numbers.'

'He's nearly twenty, and he's got no ideas of what to do when he leaves college next year. He seems to think something will just turn up.'

'Something will. He'll be just fine.'

'Oh? And how will that happen? Nothing will turn up if he doesn't make some effort to let people know he exists. Employers won't come knocking on our door, he'll have to start applying for jobs if he wants to get one. Instead, he just hangs around with those idiot boys...'

'He hasn't been in any trouble for a long time now. He's grown up.'

'Huh! He hasn't been caught recently, you mean.'

'He'll probably find a job with computers, that's what he's really good at.'

'He drives me mad,' said Walter, signalling the traditional end of the exchange.

With the start of the World Cup less than a week away, Annie's hopes of male bonding in the Maketa household rested firmly on the four weeks of football that would engulf the host nation. There, at least, was some common ground. The sound of vuvuzelas being blown had become commonplace around Ocean View, although Walter had banned Sele from bringing one into their apartment.

'It's like having mosquitoes trapped inside your ears,' he commented.

Even Sele laughed at that.

On the eve of the opening ceremony, they sat together in front of the television and watched Jacob Zuma, a national scarf around his neck, his round, shiny face beaming to the nation.

'South Africa is rocking!' the President enthused. 'South Africa is cool!'

Sele prised the tops off two bottles of Castle beer and handed one to his father. Walter seldom drank, but feeling a certain sense of impending occasion he was prepared to make an exception on this evening. Annie, looking on, smiled approvingly and placed a small dish of biltong between them.

Everything's going well, she thought. Everybody's happy. It's OK.

* * *

Less than a week later, as Walter and Sele settled down to watch their team get thrashed by Uruguay, the phone rang. Annie, less interested in the football than the sight of her menfolk sharing the experience, answered it, thinking it was probably for one of the girls.

'WHAT?' she shrieked into the handset, causing both Walter and Sele to turn away from the television, thereby missing the first near-goal of the match.

'WHAT? Are the police there? Mama, don't upset yourself, go and lie down. We'll come...'

'What's happened?' asked Walter, seriously alarmed. Mandisa and Elana, hearing their mother's voice, appeared in the living room doorway.

'Has there been an accident?' asked Elana softly, waving her hands around because Mandisa had just finished painting her nails.

Annie spoke soothingly to her mother for a few minutes then replaced the receiver and turned to face her family.

'Somebody's been killed,' she said, 'murdered... and right outside Grandmama's place, in the street, blood streaming everywhere. She borrowed a cellphone from her neighbour's son to call me. The police are there – Walter, we have to go to her. Her heart...'

Sele, his attention temporarily prised away from the football, struggled to get the picture straight in his mind.

'What was it – knives? Guns?'

'How should I know? Isn't it bad enough that a murdered man is lying at your grandmama's feet?' said Annie, impatient and snappy in her concern for her mother.

'We have to go to her, Walter,' she repeated.

Walter knew he didn't stand a chance.

'Well... OK. I'll get my jacket.'

'And we can't leave her there. She'll have to come back here with us.'

He opened his mouth to speak, but decided there was no point. Later, when everyone had calmed down, then he'd try reason and logic. At the moment it was out of the question.

Almost three hours later, they were back in Ocean View. Sele was out, and the vuvuzelas were silent. The twins were watching a film that was punctuated every few minutes by adverts. They looked up as their parents came in.

'Didn't you bring her with you?' asked Mandisa.

Annie went directly to the bedroom, and closed the door behind her.

'She wouldn't come,' said Walter. 'In any case the murder wasn't in front of her place, it was three streets away and until a neighbour knocked on the door to tell her about it she had no idea that anything had happened.' He unzipped his jacket and sat down at the table. 'Your grandmama likes a drama, and your mother falls for it every time.'

'But a man *was* killed – that's not a good thing for her to hear about,' said Elana, who was very fond of her grandmama. 'It's such a shock at her age.'

'It's a shock at any age,' said Walter. 'But it's not as if it's never happened there before. She's lived in Gugulethu all her life, she should be getting used to it by now. And she wants to stay where all her friends are, she doesn't want to live anywhere else. It's your mother who thinks she should move away.'

'Well I think Mama's right,' said Elana. 'She should come to live with us, where things like that don't happen.'

'They happen everywhere,' said Mandisa, with a rare flash of insight, then adding, 'but it's nicer here.'

'And where would we all sleep?' asked Walter.

The girls were silent for a moment.

'Someone would have to sleep in here,' said Mandisa, indicating the already cramped living room.

'Yes, that's what I'm afraid of,' said Walter, pulling himself to his feet and heading for the bedroom, where he confidently expected to have a similar conversation with his wife.

* * *

A local doctor had come to see Annie's mother while they were there, given her tranquillisers, and drawn her daughter and son-in-law to one side for a private chat.

'You know about her heart condition?' he asked.

'Of course we know!' said Annie, affronted.

'Ideally, she needs peace and rest.'

'We know that too. This neighbourhood isn't the best place for her to get that.'

'Could you...?'

Walter sighed deeply.

'We've thought about it. It wouldn't be easy.'

'For a short time, perhaps?'

Annie moved towards the bedroom alcove, where a curtain hung across the opening in a flimsy dividing wall. 'I'll help her pack a few things,' she said.

But Annie's mother was stubborn. She wouldn't go. In the end, Annie gave up.

'I know you worry about her,' Walter said on the drive home. 'But you can't help her if she doesn't want to be helped.'

Annie sighed. 'I know, but Mama knows how difficult it would be in our apartment – I think that's why she's determined not to come.'

'It *would* be difficult, we know that. But we can't afford a larger apartment on our money, unless one of us gets a big pay rise and I don't think that's going to happen.'

'I could talk to Mrs Leighton.'

Annie's employers, for whom she cleaned each morning, were white, rich and generally very good to her. She'd been with them for years, taking the workers' taxi into Simon's Town every day except Sundays and walking up to their big house on the mountainside, never asking them for anything in all that time. She'd watched the Leighton children grow, picked up toys they'd thrown on their bedroom floors and washed and ironed the discarded clothes they'd trampled underfoot. Mrs Leighton had given their cast-offs to Annie's children, and there was always a sandwich lunch in the kitchen for her, every day. Mrs Leighton had an elderly mother, too. She would understand the problem, Annie thought. She would help.

Back at home, the more she thought about it the more it seemed possible. Annie cheered up a little. There might be a way out.

* * *

It was another three days before the opportunity arose to speak to Mrs Leighton. For all of that time Annie had been worried and distressed – upset with her mother for exaggerating the situation and then digging her heels in, upset with herself for dragging Walter (whom she loved dearly) all the way over to Gugulethu for nothing, and furious with both the murderer and the victim for causing so much upset.

When the much-anticipated and rehearsed conversation with Mrs Leighton finally happened, it didn't go to plan.

'Anneline, I hope you know that we would help if we could,' said Mrs Leighton in a voice that left Annie in no doubt of the 'but' that was on its way. 'But the truth is that with all the children away at university now I don't really need you every morning. I haven't for some time, to be honest, but I kept putting off telling you.'

They were in the kitchen at the time, and Mrs Leighton poured them both a coffee. Annie's hands shook, and it was all she could do to take the cup without spilling coffee all over the newly washed floor.

'But I've been asking around – and a friend of mine would love to have you on one of the days you don't come here. So you see you'll hardly lose anything.'

But I certainly won't gain anything, thought Annie.

'Thank you, Mrs Leighton,' she said quietly. 'Thank you very much.'

When Walter got home later that evening Annie was in the kitchen, peeling sweet potatoes and chopping cabbage. He could see she'd been crying the moment she looked up at him, and knew before she told him that a pay rise from the Leightons wasn't going to materialise.

After dinner, with Sele in front of the television, the girls out somewhere, and Annie working her way through a basket of ironing, Walter slipped quietly out of the living room.

From under the bed he retrieved an old shoe box, lifted the lid and took out a dog-eared, folded sheet of paper, which he smoothed out on the bedcover. He knew every word by heart, but still he read it again. He sat for a few moments with the paper in his hand, then re-folded it on the same creases, replaced it in the box and tucked it away under the bed again.

Annie was putting the ironed clothes away when the football match reached half-time, and it gave Walter a chance to speak to his son.

'Sele – I need you to help me with something. It's just a bit of research on the computer, it'll be easy for you but impossible for me. Can you do that?'

Sele's mouth fell open in amazement.

'What?'

'And there's no need to mention anything to your mother about this at the moment, let's keep it quiet for now. So, can you do it?'

'OK...erm...OK. I can use a computer at college in the lunch break. But what's this all about?'

'I expect you'll need to write down some details to get started. We'll do that after your mama goes to bed,' said Walter, turning back to the second half of the match, while Sele continued to stare at him.

CHAPTER 3

AUGUST 2010: BRIGHTON

What had started out as an invitation to Kate for a weekend by the sea was rapidly turning into a family reunion. Both Clare and Rachel were coming, and though it was the middle of the jazz festival season Jeremy had checked his gig list and was sure he could make it for a late lunch on Sunday.

'Could the girls stay with you, Mum?' Nina asked. 'Probably better that Kate has my spare room than yours.'

'Oh, that'll be lovely, dear. They haven't spent a weekend with me since they were both at school and we were in the old house – and your Dad was still alive,' said Janet, glancing across at her husband Terry's photo on her sideboard.

And then the six threatened to become eight, as Jeremy's parents thought they might come up to Sussex and stay at his cottage for a few days so that they could travel down to Brighton with him on the Sunday. Janet was very enthusiastic about this latest extension to the party, more so than Nina who was beginning to feel the pressure of being the instigator, organiser and host.

'I can't remember the last time I saw Jim and Sue,' Janet said. 'We don't even talk on the phone as often as we used to... it's dreadful to get so blasé about one's family. You think they're always going to be there – but of course they aren't.'

'All we're short of now is Uncle Bobby,' said Nina. Janet looked horrified.

'You're not really going to ask him, are you?'

'No, Mum. That was a joke.'

* * *

Clare and Rachel were the first to arrive on Saturday afternoon, in a taxi from the railway station.

'Parking here's almost as impossible as it is in London,' said Clare, putting down her weekend bag to give her mother a hug. 'We thought train was best.'

'I assumed you'd go straight to Grandma's flat. You don't mind that you're staying with her do you?'

'Course not,' said Rachel. She handed her mother a carrier bag and some flowers. 'These are for you, we thought we'd drop them off first, then walk round to Grandma's.'

Nina was glad that they were there before anyone else. She didn't get much time with her two daughters and knew that most of the weekend she'd be sharing them with the rest of the family.

'Let's have a coffee together first. Kate won't be here for an hour or so. To be honest,' said Nina, 'I'm beginning to wonder why I started this whole thing. It was just Kate at the start, now there'll be eight of us for lunch tomorrow.'

'Righto Mum, we get the hint! We'll just have that coffee then head back to London,' said Rachel, placing two bottles of wine in the fridge. 'Come on, you know you love it when everyone gets together! Consider yourself lucky we're a small family, I've got friends who have to hire a hall for family reunions.'

Nina unwrapped the flowers and found a vase to put them in, passing it to Clare to fill with water as she was nearest to the sink.

'So can we assume David won't be coming?' Clare asked, cutting at flower stems and tweaking off the lowest leaves. In her hands the flowers went where she wanted them to. For Nina they would certainly have flopped over to one side, as they always did.

'Definitely not, he wasn't invited. He's married to a gold-digging bimbo.'

'Mum! You don't know that!'

'I know she's about the same age as you two, and David was never exactly the stuff of romantic daydreams. But guess what? He's loaded. So draw your own conclusions.'

'Hmm. You have a point there,' said Clare.

Relaxing in the sitting room with her girls, Nina started to calm down. She was used to living in an ordered, minimalist setting, an organised home and work space which she kept tidy and streamlined. Now, with all her china out of the cupboards, including the stuff she normally never used, and extra dining chairs borrowed from her neighbour, there was an expectant, buzzy feel in the flat that felt quite alien.

'I'm out of the habit of entertaining,' she said.

'You should have asked Clare to take it on,' said Rachel.

Clare, an events organiser, was used to dealing with parties and functions on a grand scale.

'Too domestic for us,' she said, laughing. She ran a hand through her long, blonde curls and drew her legs up under her on the sofa. 'Give me the O2 and I can handle it, but if I had to start going through Mum's kitchen cupboards then sorting out her unmatched napkins I'd be in a panic too.'

They had almost an hour together before Kate arrived. Surreptitiously on the lookout for anything unusual in Rachel's behaviour, because she still hadn't quite shaken off the idea that something was wrong, Nina made more coffee and let the girls talk on about their friends and work. But Rachel seemed just the same as always, leaving behind no clues or jangling alarm bells in her conversation that might put Nina on red alert.

When Kate arrived at Nina's door she was loaded down with a weekend bag and presents for everyone.

'I hardly ever see you – at least let me spoil you when we do get together,' she said, handing all three of them Selfridges perfume carriers. And she'd brought a box filled with sample bottles of creams and lotions from her company's latest skin and beauty range, for them to share out.

'This is something for Aunt Janet, when I see her later,' she said, placing a small, elegantly wrapped package on a side table. 'Don't let me forget to take it, will you?'

Nina had been grateful for Janet's suggestion that the five of them should go out for dinner on Saturday evening. It offered her the opportunity to slip out of hostess mode, a role she didn't inhabit very comfortably, and took the pressure off everyone else. Kate, notoriously ill at ease out of her familiar work-orientated environment, could wind down on neutral ground, and three generations of the family could just concentrate on enjoying each other's company.

A small, unpretentious Greek restaurant around the corner from Nina's flat seemed like a good place to get everyone relaxed, and it was. The evening was fun, with everyone wondering aloud why they hadn't done it sooner, and meaning it.

'I'm paying,' said Kate, reaching across for the bill when it arrived.

'You are *not*,' said Janet, bending down to get her bag.

'We're all emancipated women, Kate,' said Rachel.

'We pay for ourselves. Anyway, we can't do it on a card. Clare wants to go up to the bar with a stack of cash because she fancies the waiter and while he's counting it she can gaze longingly at those eyelashes.'

'Well, he is rather cute,' said Clare, as everyone piled their money onto the plate. Kate looked around.

'I hadn't really noticed him,' she said. 'Oh yes – you're right, he's gorgeous.' She sighed. 'Oh, to be twenty again!'

'Don't let that stop you,' said Rachel mischievously. 'Lots of young guys prefer older women.'

'There's even a website where you can get a toy boy,' said Nina, 'I heard about it on the radio. Perhaps we should look it up when we get back to the flat, Kate!'

'Well be sure to let me know if there are any seventy-year-olds on the lookout for older women, dear,' said Janet. 'I'll book an appointment at the hairdresser's.'

Outside the restaurant they parted company, the girls and Janet going in the direction of the seafront and her apartment block, and Nina and Kate heading away from them, back to her flat. Kate threaded her arm through Nina's.

'You're so lucky, Nina, to have your family. They're just lovely.'

'They're your family, too.'

'Yes, but you know what I mean. I see you and the girls together, and I envy you that closeness. I wish they were mine. Well, not them of course but others like them. Kids of my own.'

'Kate, it was nobody's fault, it just didn't happen for you. Sometimes it's...'

'I still think of him you know, my beautiful little boy. I had him for such a short time but I can still see those tiny fingers and miniscule nails and his head covered with soft, fluffy down. And I remember how he smelt. Is that weird?'

'No, I don't think so. A baby is always precious, especially one that you lose so soon. He arrived much too early.'

'He was the only one I was able to hold, and even then I didn't get to keep him.'

They reached Nina's flat and she opened the street door to the building.

'And your mum, she's such good fun,' Kate added as they climbed the stairs. 'I didn't have a relationship like that with my mother – I'm the first to admit we were a bit distant with each other, though I never quite understood why. I wouldn't have talked about toy boys in front of her!'

Nina led the way into her flat, putting on lights as she went. Kate's mother, Isobel, had been stricter than her own, but the children always knew where they were with her and didn't cross the line. In an unexpected flash of memory, Nina remembered one particular day at the seaside, a holiday in Dorset she thought. Swanage floated into her mind, and got lodged there as a picture postcard view of the bay on a hot day in summer. The children were all attempting to do headstands on the beach while Janet and the aunties chatted and organised a picnic lunch. Suddenly Jeremy overbalanced, crashed down onto his back and burst into a noisy wail, and while his mum picked him up it was Isobel who told the others off for not helping him, the smallest child. And Nina remembered that David – unseen by anyone but her – had pushed Jeremy over. She'd been too scared to tell on him, because she knew he'd pick on her next.

It was something she hadn't thought about in years, having consigned it to the dim past and then forgotten the whole incident. And where were the dads? she wondered suddenly. They weren't in her mind's eye picture, and she had no recollection of them being around at that moment, but they must have driven the cars that got them all there. Gone off to find a pub, she supposed, or to play at pitch and putt or something.

'I was a bit wary of your mum when I was little,' she said, 'but as I got older I liked her a lot. She was a feisty woman. And your dad was a sweetheart.'

'Yes,' said Kate, 'apparently so.'

While Nina made coffee, Kate disappeared into her room and came back into the kitchen clutching an envelope.

'I didn't want to mention this with the others around, but... have a look at this in a minute and tell me what you think of it.'

When they were sitting down in the living room Kate opened the envelope and handed Nina a letter, written in blue biro on cheap lined paper.

"*Dear Miss Kate Hatchman*", it began. "*I hope you will not mind receiving this letter from someone far away from your country, who you do not know, but I believe we are related.*"

'It's a scam,' said Nina as soon as she'd read that far. 'I used to get these all the time by email, usually from Nigeria.'

'This is from South Africa,' said Kate. 'And I sometimes got those Nigerian ones too. But this is different and I think it could be genuine.'

'Kate, you could hardly have South African relatives! Black, I'm assuming.'

'Actually he's not very black,' said Kate, passing a photo across to Nina.

Walter gazed up at her, smiling just a little, and

wearing a collar and tie. The picture seemed to have been taken in a photo booth.

Nina read on, her eyes widening.

"*You will want to know what evidence I have of this. My mother, Grace Ntoko Maketa, just before she passed on, gave me a letter she had kept since before my birth. It was given to her by a Royal Naval sailor from the ship HMS Comus. The ship was leaving Simon's Town on the following day, and in the weeks it had been in port the sailor had formed an attachment with my mother. When he left he did not know that she was expecting his child. I was that child, and the sailor's name was Ray Hatchman. I believe, Miss Hatchman, that your father and mine were the same man.*"

Nina let the letter fall into her lap.

'He could have got this information from anywhere. All you need these days is access to a computer.'

'Maybe. It was sent to me at the office, and as company CEO I do have an online professional profile. But Nina, this is all so personal. Look, he gives me his home address, not a post office box. The Nigerian scam-mongers don't do that.'

'And where is this place he supposedly lives...' Nina looked at the top of the letter, '...Ocean View?'

'It's a township near Cape Town. I looked it up on the internet but I couldn't find out much about it.'

'So he lives in a shack? Kate, this man is after your money...'

'No, I didn't get the impression it was a shanty town. Just a district that was built for coloured people originally – mixed race as opposed to black.'

'Yes, well I don't think that meant quite the same then as this man has in mind with the parentage he's claiming. And what about this other information? Was Uncle Ray in...what's this place, Simon's Town?'

'He was certainly in South Africa, I can remember him talking about it a little when there was all that news coverage after Nelson Mandela's release. And I know he was on the Comus at some time – Mum had the band from his cap, along with some from other ships he was on. I still have them at home amongst the stuff I cleared out of her house after she died.'

Nina looked back at the letter and turned to the second page.

"*I would be very happy to receive some news of you and I would like to know a little about you and the rest of your family. I believe that Mr Ray Hatchman sadly passed on some years ago, and his wife also. Please understand that I do not wish to cause you any embarrassment but if I am correct then we are half brother and sister and this knowledge comes as a great joy to me. I have enclosed a copy of the letter given to my mother by Able Seaman Mr Ray Hatchman.*"

'He's done his homework, I'll give you that,' said Nina.

'Exactly – and why would he target me if this wasn't true?'

'Because you can't easily prove it isn't true, I suppose.'

Kate handed Nina the copy letter. The original had faded, and consequently the photocopy wasn't easy to read, so she moved closer to a table lamp to look at it. The writing was scrawly and indistinct but there was no mistaking that at the top it said "*AB R.Hatchman, HMS Comus*" and at the bottom "*Your ever-loving Ray*". It was a love letter to Grace, a letter of parting, and of a parting that would probably be forever.

'Does this look like your dad's writing?'

'It's hard to say, everyone was taught to write in the same way in those days. I compared it to something he wrote not long before he died, and there are similarities, but there would have been a forty year gap between the two.' Kate shrugged. 'I can't be certain. I think only a handwriting expert could be.'

Nina handed both letters back to Kate then sat back in her chair. She kept Walter's photo in her lap, and looked at him again.

'He could get all of this from the internet. Search engines, ancestry sites – it's all there to be discovered. And he found you so he would also have found David,' she said.

'I thought of that too, if he's got hold of a family tree then he would obviously know about him. But David's been in the USA and Canada for years, and only in the last year back in England, so he might not be able to locate him. *I* don't even know his address. I tried to find a profile for him online and there wasn't one. In any case if Walter had sent a letter like this to David I shouldn't think he would have read beyond the first sentence before it went in the bin.'

Nina picked up Walter's photo again and leaned forward to hand it back to Kate.

'Can't see any family resemblance,' she said, but Kate missed the irony.

'He looks nice though. He hasn't asked for anything beyond contact with me and I don't think people running scams usually send out pictures of themselves, do you?'

Nina had to admit that it seemed unlikely. As she looked at Kate there was something in her face she hadn't seen before, a glow of excitement that was quite unlike her usual cool demeanour.

She's already made up her mind, Nina thought. Kate wants this to be true, because she's found what she's been longing for all these years – a family of her own, a cause she can claim as hers alone.

'Be careful, Kate,' she said. 'There's probably going to be money involved in this sooner or later.'

'We don't know that.'

'Don't we? Black family living in South African township find they have a British relative who happens to be the CEO of a successful company? What do *you* think?'

Kate, folded the letters and put them and the photo back in their envelope.

'I think I'm going to give Walter a chance to prove himself to me,' she said.

'Will you say anything to the rest of the family?'

'Jeremy, definitely – tomorrow if there's a chance. The others, well let's see how this develops first. I don't want to upset your mum or Jim and Sue – but they might actually know something about it for all we know.'

When they finally switched the lights out in the living room and went to bed, Kate drifted off straight away into a contented sleep. Nina, on the other hand, tossed and turned until the early hours, chasing thoughts of Uncle Ray and his South African sweetheart around in her mind, with Walter's mild, affable face an ever-present backdrop.

* * *

It wasn't until the following afternoon that an opportunity presented itself for Kate to talk to Jeremy. Contrary to Nina's fears, Sunday lunch was problem free, and enjoyed by everyone in spite of – or maybe partly because of – the cramped seating arrangement around her dining table.

By the time they'd finished, the mid-afternoon August sun was still hot.

'We're thinking of a couple of hours on the beach,' Clare announced. 'Anybody want to join us?'

'I wouldn't mind a walk along the seafront,' Kate said, and both Jeremy and Nina agreed that would appeal to them more than baking on the beach.

'Then why don't we three walk back to my place,' Janet suggested to Jim and Sue. 'We can sit on the balcony and have tea. I've got plenty of cakes for later, not knowing quite how the arrangements would work out.'

'You always were enthusiastic about baking, if I remember rightly,' said Sue.

'Date and walnut,' said Jim. 'Terry's favourite I believe, and mine too. There was always an iced date and walnut cake when we came round to your place. I used to look forward to that.'

Janet pulled a face. 'Well I hope you're not looking forward to it today, Jim. I don't bake these days.' But Jim, happily contented after a few glasses of wine, showed no signs of minding too much.

So the party split up temporarily, and Kate, Nina and Jeremy set off together.

It didn't take long for Kate to bring up the subject of Walter and the letter. Jeremy shared Nina's concern that there was likely to be a financial motive at the back of it – even if everything Walter claimed was true.

'You could just ignore the whole thing,' he said.

'No, I can't,' said Kate. 'It's out there now, I can't pretend it isn't.'

'Then at least don't part with any money till you've been over there to see him,' he said.

Kate stopped dead in her tracks and Jeremy turned to face her.

'What did I say?' he asked, hands outspread.

'You think I should go to South Africa?'

'I think you'll have to in the end, if you're going to take this seriously,' he replied. 'And ask him if he'll have DNA testing. That's the only way you'll be certain and if he agrees to do it that'll be a good sign.'

'I hadn't thought this through to the point of actually meeting him...'

They walked on in silence for a few minutes, surrounded by lots of other walkers but isolated in their own thoughts.

'Would you come with me?' Kate said suddenly, taking them both by surprise. 'It wouldn't have to be for long, a week maybe or ten days. I don't think I'd want to go alone.'

'Well,' said Nina, 'I guess so, if it was at a time when I didn't have much work lined up.'

'Jem, what about you?'

'Yeah, maybe, I've got a quiet period at the end of November. I can't remember the last time I had a holiday and I might even pick up a gig or two over there, you never know,' he smiled, not seriously thinking that he would.

'Look – I'm not sure it'll even come to that Kate,' he added. 'You need to do a bit of digging around yourself before you seriously think of setting off across the world. He found our family tree, you must be able to find his too. Just make sure that the facts at his end check out, as far as you can.'

'Yes, good point. And I'll write back to him and see what happens next.'

* * *

Clare and Rachel found a spot of beach that suited them both, stripped down to their bikinis, slapped on some sunblock and settled down for a couple of hours.

'Rach, I need to ask you something.'

'Mmm?'

'D'you remember Becky James?'

'Sure'.

'Last Tuesday afternoon she was in the St Martin's Hotel for a job interview. And she saw you come out of the lift and then go out to a taxi.'

There was a silence. Clare sat up and looked down at her sister.

'And she saw the guy you came down in the lift with.'

Rachel said nothing, but her hand gripped the edge of the beach towel.

'And she thought I'd know who it was, but I don't. So Rach – what's going on?'

CHAPTER 4

SEPTEMBER 2010: OCEAN VIEW

It was more than two months since Walter had posted his letter to England. For the first month it was hardly off his mind, and he came home from work each evening expecting to see an envelope waiting for him. Then as time went on his hopes faded until, by the beginning of September, he had reluctantly let the thought slide to the back of his mind.

There were plenty of other things to occupy his thinking. Ocean View had had a difficult winter. Public sector workers' strikes in August affected a lot of the people living in the township, and many of his friends and neighbours went on protest marches. The vuvuzelas Walter hated so much had been brought out again for use at noisy demonstrations, and President Zuma was on the defensive.

'You're lucky you're not caught up in any of this, Walter,' his immediate neighbour, a bus driver, had said to him at the height of the unrest. 'When their cars break down people will still need to have them repaired. And see how good we are to you? We're keeping the buses off the roads so they *have* to use their cars!'

Walter was good at his job. He knew the intricacies and foibles of motor engines better than any of the other mechanics at the garage, and his employers valued his knowledge and experience. His friends and neighbours, many of them in poorly paid public sector jobs, were already bringing home smaller wage packets due to intermittent strike action. A union welfare office had been set up in Ocean View to help the most needy families. Spirits were low generally, and Walter's weren't much better.

At home, the effect of Annie's reduced hours was beginning to bite. Mrs Leighton's friend, so apparently eager to take up some of the slack in her hours, had changed her mind and Annie's wages had been cut in half, overnight. They were managing, but only just. It wouldn't take much of an increase in rent, food or utility bills to push them over the edge.

So when Walter came home one cool and cloudy spring evening at the end of September, his mood was not an optimistic one. As he opened the door, Annie was almost right behind it.

'Who's this, Walter Maketa, writing to you from England? What is it?'

She waved an envelope in his face, and Walter stopped in his tracks. With his heart trying to punch a way out through his ribcage, he took the letter gingerly from Annie, as though it might crumble to dust if handled carelessly.

'It's something I need to explain to you, Annie,' he said.

Sele, in his usual position in front of the television, looked up at him and was about to speak – but one look from Walter changed his mind. They hadn't discussed the matter since Sele's computer research had turned up the information Walter needed. Sele didn't have the full story, and didn't particularly want it, but he was smart enough to have guessed what was going on.

'Yes, I think you do,' said Annie, intrigued by the turn of events, but at the same time distinctly put out that her husband had been up to something behind her back.

'But first I want to read this,' he said.

Walter put the letter on the table, took off his oil-stained work jacket and hung it in its usual place, on a hook by the door.

'And a pot of rooibos might be nice for all of us,' he added. 'The girls will be home soon.'

Annie went out to make the tea, although as she left the living room her gaze was still on the unopened letter. The door to the apartment swung open, and Elana and Mandisa stepped into an atmosphere they could almost reach out and touch.

'What's happening?' Mandisa asked her father, who by then had sat down at the table and was opening the envelope with a dinner knife.

'Your father's getting international post these days,' Annie called from the kitchen. 'He's a very important man.'

The twins sat side by side on the sofa and looked across to Sele, but he was, as ever, unreadable. Annie brought everyone a mug of tea, and then squashed in next to her daughters. All eyes were on Walter as he unfolded the letter, smoothed it out on the table and put his reading glasses on. He read silently to himself, taking his time, unperturbed by the watching eyes of his family.

"*Dear Walter, I must say that your letter came as a surprise to me, but once I had recovered from the shock, not an unpleasant one.*"

This was a good start, and some of the tension slipped from Walter.

"*I hope you will not mind that I shared your letter with my cousins, who are as close to me as a brother and sister. On their advice I have been doing some research of my own...*"

Walter's shoulders tightened again. What if she wasn't the right person – or worse, what if Ray Hatchman wasn't the right sailor? No, Sele had checked it all out – but how reliable was he? What if Sele had got it wrong?

"*I have consulted a graphologist...*" Walter looked up.

'Sele, a graphologist – remind me what that is?'

'Erm, it's someone who studies handwriting, I think.'

Walter nodded. That made sense, he thought. Miss Hatchman was a clever woman, she wouldn't just take the word of a complete stranger.

"*... but he was unable to be 100% certain that my father had written the letter. All he would say was that it was 'not unlikely.'*"

'Yes,' Walter said aloud, nodding his head. 'Yes, of course.'

The girls looked at each other wide-eyed, and shrugged.

Walter sipped his tea, and read the rest of the first page, which he then turned face down on the table as he started on the second. Sele shifted in his seat and wondered if his mother would be angry with him for colluding with Walter. He glanced at her, but her eyes were fixed on his father. Walter read down the page, at what seemed to his waiting audience in the silent room, slower than a snail's pace.

"*I would be very happy to hear more about you, as it seems likely that we are in fact related and family is very important to me, as I feel sure it is to you also.*"

Walter folded the letter along the original creases, and placed it carefully back in the envelope. He took a mouthful of tea, and put his mug back down on the table.

'Well?' said Annie. 'Tell us!'

Turning around, he took off his glasses and Annie could see that there were tears in his eyes.

'What is it, Walter?' she said softly.

'I have just found my half-sister,' he announced to his astonished family.

* * *

When the excitement had died down and Walter had sworn them all to secrecy 'just for the time being', Annie went into the kitchen to cook dinner. Walter sat in contemplation for a while, then followed her.

'I don't think we should say anything to your mother, Annie, not until we know more,' he said quietly. 'We don't want to get anyone's hopes up.'

Annie, frying onions on the stove, turned to him and pointed an accusatory wooden spatula in his direction.

'Get our hopes up? For what? You aren't going to ask her for money, are you? That would not be right, Walter. Not right at all.'

'But you saw the letter, Annie – she says that family is important to her. I may not need to ask her,' he replied, taking a small step backwards and folding his arms across his chest.

The smell of onions catching on the bottom of the pan took Annie's attention away from him for a moment, but she was soon back on the case.

'Is that the reason why you started this now, at this time?'

Walter nodded. 'I couldn't think what else to do,' he said.

'And if she can't or won't help us? Then what?'

'Then I don't have any more ideas.'

The twins were very excitable over dinner. In their room they had discussed their new aunt and the lifestyle they supposed she had, and now they wanted to try out their ideas on the rest of the family.

'She must have a big house, she probably has dogs to guard it – and perhaps she keeps horses as well,' Elana speculated. 'What's the name of the place where she lives?'

'Surrey,' mumbled Sele through a mouthful of rice.

'Can you look on the computer tomorrow and find out what Surrey looks like?' asked Mandisa. 'I wonder if it's near London.'

Sele, suddenly and unexpectedly the pivot on which his family's fortunes may be about to turn, was finding that he liked his new status.

'Of course I can,' he said nonchalantly. 'There are ways of looking right into people's streets, I might be able to find her house,' he added, full of self-importance.

'I hope that's allowed,' said Annie. 'Don't do anything you aren't supposed to do, Sele.'

He laughed an indulgent sort of laugh. 'No Mama,' he said, 'it's OK, people do these things all the time. Maybe she's looked at our apartment.'

'Could she? Is that possible?' asked Annie, turning to Walter for an answer but finding none, because like her Walter was out of his depth with anything involving computers.

'If they've sent the filming cars round here,' said Sele, realising he had everyone's attention now, and enjoying the respect his superior knowledge was bringing him. 'But probably not, who would want to see this street?'

'Miss Kate Hatchman might,' said Elana.

* * *

Sele arrived home next evening with more information. A powerhouse of facts and figures now that his skills were finally receiving the credit he felt they deserved, he held court over the dinner table, answering the family's questions patiently, in the way that a teacher might.

'Surrey is a province, like the Western Cape, so it's not just one place but lots of towns and villages,' he began. 'Miss Kate Hatchman lives near a town called Guildford.' Sele pronounced it with a hard 'd' in the middle, Elana repeating it after him a couple of times until she'd said it to his satisfaction.

'Yes, that's right. It's quite a big town.'

'Bigger than Simon's Town, or Muizenburg?'

'Of course, man. It's an important place. There's a university there and everything.'

'As big as Cape Town?'

'Erm, no, probably not. Cape Town is like London and I don't think Guildford is as big as that. It's more like...' but Sele was running out of towns he'd been to, and he couldn't name any that might compare in size to Guildford. 'Well, it's in between Muizenburg and Cape Town,' he finished lamely, deciding then to move on swiftly.

'The village where she lives is this place, Fordham,' he said, jabbing a finger at the address label on the top of Kate's letter. 'And you know what? I walked along the High Street in Fordham!' Sele smiled broadly when he saw how this was received.

'What's it like?' asked Mandisa, her eyes wide. 'Is it pretty?'

'Oh man, yes, it's very English,' said Sele, an expert now.

'And did you find the house?' Elana asked.

'Yes! It's big, there are two garages and a garden at the front.'

'How could you see over the wall?' asked Annie, intrigued in spite of herself, and having no real conception of how Sele had achieved this miracle.

44

'There isn't a wall, Mama. No wall, no gates. There's nothing at the front but some grass and flowers.'

The family considered this for a moment in silence.

'So she *must* have dogs,' said Elana, who would have liked a dog herself, 'to keep her safe.'

'The houses we drive past in Bishopscourt, when we go to Grandmama's – is it like them?' asked Mandisa.

Sele was stumped for an answer to that one. He'd never really had a good look behind the security gates of any of those houses, just an occasional brief glimpse as they drove past if one of the gates was just opening or closing. But he knew that Mandisa hadn't either, so he bluffed it.

'Some of those houses are very big indeed and it's not really huge like them, but very, very nice. English houses aren't like the ones we have here. They're mostly old, you see.'

Walter, quiet up to that point, felt he should step in before Sele got too carried away with himself. He had a hunch that some of the detail flowing out of his son owed more to imagination than internet.

'I don't think we should worry too much about Miss Kate Hatchman's house, the lady herself is more important than where she lives. After all, she is our relative, one of the family.'

Then noticing that Sele looked a little crushed by his comment, he added, 'But it's wonderful that you were able to find all this information, Sele. When I write back I will certainly tell her how clever you are with computers.'

Later, after their kids had all gone out, Walter and Annie sat together to watch the news. President Jacob Zuma was in Durban, explaining to the nation about his fact-finding mission to visit the best and worst government facilities.

'We promise the South African people that they will see change,' he said.

Walter turned to Annie and took her hand in his.

'I know you feel uneasy about Miss Kate Hatchman,' he said, 'but we can't wait for Zuma to change our lives because his change may come too late for this family. We have to do it for ourselves. We're very lucky, because we have this chance, and we must take it – for Sele and the twins, and your mother, we must do it. Do you understand?'

Annie nodded her head slowly. 'I understand,' she said, then looked up at Walter and added, 'but I don't like it.'

CHAPTER 5

OCTOBER 2010: ENGLAND

Walter's reply dropped through Kate's letterbox, along with a few other letters, one chilly day at the beginning of October.

Kate was home from the office early that day, intending to drop off her laptop and briefcase before driving in to Guildford, where House of Fraser had informed her that they had an order for matching bed linen and accessories ready for collection. Kate's bedroom had just had a make-over by a local interiors company, and the goods awaiting her at the store would complete the new look they'd created. She hadn't stopped for lunch and was feeling hungry, so she scooped the post up from the mat and took it through to the kitchen, where she dumped it on the worktop while she put some coffee on and looked in her fridge. There was nothing much there. Kate, used to business lunches and eating out, wasn't good at maintaining a store cupboard. In the end she pulled out the remains of a tub of cream cheese, and a bagel, reminding herself that she must get something out of the freezer for later.

She put her meagre lunch on a plate and carried it, the coffee and the pile of letters, to the breakfast bar. Perching on a stool, she flicked through the letters: credit card bill, bank statement, service due reminder from the garage, and then Walter's letter. Leaving all the others on one side, she slit the envelope open with her knife and took out two folded sheets of notepaper.

Walter's excitement in their new-found relationship beamed up at her from the page. He told Kate about Annie and the children, and about his job as a car mechanic. He said that Sele had found her village, and that the girls were worried about security at her house without a gated perimeter wall. He didn't mention Annie's mother, and he kept to himself the fact that Annie's wages had halved recently and they were struggling financially.

In her original letter to him Kate had suggested a DNA test and Walter understood the reason perfectly well, although he admitted he had no idea how the process was achieved or how conclusive the results would be. He trusted her to make the arrangements and he would, he insisted, see it through.

"I am happy to take a DNA test," he had written. *"I don't think either of us should have any doubts."*

Kate had made it clear that she would arrange and pay for testing. But before organising this she wanted to talk to Janet, Jim and Sue to find out what, if anything, they knew. She knew her Aunt Janet and Uncle Terry had always been very close to her parents, and there was just a chance that her father had taken Terry into his confidence and that he had then confided in Janet.

She also needed Jim's consent to take tests too.

'How can they test for paternity without the father's DNA?' Nina had asked, in one of their many phone conversations. Since Walter had emerged from nowhere, and Kate's cousins had become her confidantes, she'd got into the habit of ringing Nina regularly. Jeremy escaped, because Kate presumed that he was out on a gig in the evenings, even though that often wasn't the case. He had specifically not put her right on that point.

'It doesn't have to be paternity,' Kate explained. 'They can do half-sibling and aunt and uncle tests. So I need Uncle Jim's agreement, too. I'm hoping to get down to Exeter next weekend to talk to them.'

'And Mum?'

'Yes – she won't need to be tested of course, but I don't want her to find out about this in a phone call from Sue.'

'I don't mind talking to her,' said Nina, 'to save you a trip down here as well. She can ring you if there's anything to report back.'

Kate's evenings had changed. These days her laptop was in use less for work and more for personal research. She'd signed up as a subscriber on an ancestry site, spent hours finding out about South Africa and the Western Cape, and discovered that Sele was right – the Google street map people hadn't driven around Ocean View. She peeped into Cape Town museums, found out where the best shopping areas were and compared seafront restaurant menus. From the comfort of her luxurious sitting room, she travelled the Garden Route and just for fun looked at a selection of hotels between Hermanus and Port Elizabeth. Then she went onto eBay and bought a copy of Nelson Mandela's 'Long Walk to Freedom', and a CD by Ladysmith Black Mambaso. She never for a moment considered the possibility that the DNA tests would come back negative. For Kate, it was already a done deal.

Since the news was now spreading out among the family, Nina took it upon herself to put Clare and Rachel in the picture. She'd seen both of them since the family weekend in August, but not together. When she asked, it seemed they hadn't seen each other either, but she knew that Clare had a lot on at work and put it down to that. Neither mentioned to Nina the conversation they'd had on the beach that hot afternoon.

'Come on, Rachel, I can guess most of this,' Clare had said, in the face of her sister's defiant silence.

'Good, then you won't need me to tell you, will you?'

'Well, let's just see how close I can get. The St. Martin's Hotel isn't what you'd call a dump, so that must mean he's rich, and if you went there on a weekday afternoon I'd bet money that he's married...'

Rachel said nothing.

'And this arrangement doesn't seem to be bringing you much joy...'

'Oh? And what makes you say that?'

'Because these things never do, Rach, and because you obviously haven't been bursting to tell me about him.'

Rachel sat up and looked at Clare. 'I didn't think you'd want to know,' she said. 'And I can see now that I was right to keep quiet, because straight away you've gone into big sister telling-off mode.'

'I'm not telling you off. I just don't want you to be the one who gets hurt when all this comes out – and it will, you must know that. So, who is he? Not the guy you work for, surely?'

Rachel lay down again on her back and crossed her hands over her stomach.

'I'm not that stupid.'

'Then who?'

Rachel didn't answer. Clare lay back down too, and they both looked up at the cloudless blue sky, a tension between them that they hadn't experienced before and neither liked. Rachel shuffled her feet.

'A friend of mine nannies for the family.'

'So you met him at their house?'

'No, at my house. They're close friends of my family. Neighbours.'

'Oh, Rachel...'

'OK, OK I know, doesn't look good for my job prospects does it?' Rachel snapped.

Neither spoke for a moment. Then Clare broke the silence.

'Is that really all there is to it? Just a romp with an older married man?'

'What more do you want?' Rachel said, defensively. Clare turned her head in Rachel's direction, and thought how unhappy she looked.

'You're not pregnant are you?'

'No, I'm bloody well not!' Rachel stood up and started gathering up her beach towel and other bits. 'You're so clever, *you* work out the rest. And I'd rather you didn't mention this to Mum,' she said as she started to move off up the beach, crunching her way over the pebbles.

On the train going home, Clare tried to make peace without referring specifically to the spat they'd had that afternoon. But Rachel had closed in around it. To most people she wouldn't have seemed much different to usual, but Clare knew better and could see through her defence shield. It was an uncomfortable journey back to London for both of them.

Clare hadn't told Nina any of this. But she couldn't say she'd seen Rachel when she hadn't really, so she invented a few extra projects that her team was working on, so as to sound extra busy, and Nina seemed to accept it. She had to watch her step each time they spoke on the phone, though.

'You're home early,' Nina said one evening in October, when Clare answered on the first ring. 'I was expecting to leave a message and talk to you later.'

'Well, we were all a bit jaded after so many late nights. Sometimes you just have to walk away,' Clare said, gathering her curls up at the nape of her neck and twisting them into a loose ponytail. How did I get drawn into this deception? she thought.

'Well it's great that you can do that every so often,' Nina said. 'Too much work and not enough play...'

'Yeah, I know, Mum. So, what's the latest news?'

'Well, something rather unexpected, actually...'

And so Clare, and later on Rachel, discovered that they may have another set of relatives.

* * *

It was years since Kate had been to Jim and Sue's house in Exeter, and they were more than a little surprised when she rang to ask if she could come down for the weekend.

'I've been researching the family tree,' she said. 'And I thought I'd just see if you could help me out with a couple of things.'

Jim put the phone down to her and remarked that Kate must have found something mighty strange if she was coming all that way, after all those years.

'Maybe because we all met up in the summer,' said Sue, 'she started to think more about her mum and dad. I think it's nice, anyway.'

'Oh it's nice all right. Just a bit queer,' Jim replied.

Driving down, Kate remembered holidays in Devon with her parents and David when they were both still at school, many years before Jim and Sue moved down there. The drive used to take up most of the day and in order to get off to an early start her dad would wake them all up in pitch darkness, at about 4am. They took Thermos flasks, piles of sandwiches, apples and chocolate biscuits in Isobel's big shopping bag, and watched the sky lighten gradually with the rising sun until the street lights were finally switched off and the new day began.

The names of the towns and villages they drove through were imprinted on Kate's mind. Ray was a member of the AA, and a devotee of their door-to-door routes, which someone read out to him while the others kept a look-out for signposts. Usually Isobel read the route, but sometimes she let David do it. Kate never got the chance, but the place names had stuck with her: Alton, Alresford, Ringwood. When they reached the New Forest they stopped for a late breakfast of bacon sandwiches, while wild ponies tried to nose their way in through the opening at the top of the car windows. At Dorchester, where they usually had a toilet stop, Ray's car had once refused to start again and a garage had to be called out to it from a phone box in the town centre. Then it was on to Honiton, which was always busy and made for slow going through the High Street before they reached the layby where they always stopped for a lunch break. Their AA route was not the quickest way to reach the delights of the South Hams, but the first time they went Ray had requested the scenic drive and he never thought afterwards to vary it.

Kate smiled to herself as she sped down on dual carriageways that weren't there when the family visited the West Country. Her route didn't take her anywhere near the places she remembered, and in a way she was sorry for it, but reaching Exeter was more important to her that day than the journey.

Surprisingly, Jim and Sue took the news of Walter pretty much in their stride.

'You've got to remember,' Jim said, 'that the Navy took these men away for many months at a time. It was only natural that they found other girls when they were in dock. It doesn't mean he thought any less of your mother, sweetheart.'

Kate was touched by his concern.

'You don't have to worry,' she said, 'I'm not in any way upset by this, Uncle Jim, I just wondered if you knew anything that could verify Walter's claim. Did Dad ever talk to you about a girl in South Africa?'

Jim thought back, fixing his gaze on the blank television screen as though the answer might suddenly pop up there.

'No, I can only vaguely remember him being in South Africa,' he said finally. 'There was one time when he and Bobby were on the same ship, though I don't know if it was on that posting – have you spoken to him?'

Kate hadn't known, or had forgotten, that there had been two sailors in the family.

'I would be a tiny bit reluctant to go and see Uncle Bobby.'

Sue laughed. 'Not surprised at that,' she said.

'But I suppose he'll have to know about this sooner or later.'

Jim pursed his lips and tried the television screen again for inspiration.

'No,' he said, shaking his head. 'No, I don't think I can help you, love. And you know what, with five years between Ray and Bobby they probably didn't share confidences of that kind anyway. When your mum and dad got married Bobby hadn't long been out of school so they wouldn't have had much in common. How old did you say this Walter is?'

'Fifty three,' said Kate. 'The same age as David.'

'Good thing your mum's no longer with us in that case,' Jim commented.

'Very strong woman, your mother,' said Sue, 'but even she would have been knocked sideways by this.'

'Of the four of us, your dad was always closest to Nina's dad,' said Jim. 'There were only three years between Ray and Terry and they spent a lot of time together as they grew up. If anyone had known I wouldn't mind betting it would have been Terry – pity he's not alive now to tell us. I suppose you haven't asked Janet yet?'

'Nina was going to speak to her. Uncle Jim, I need to ask you something else,' Kate said, 'something you can do to help me with this, if you're willing.'

* * *

Nina did indeed tell Janet the news, the following Sunday afternoon. It wasn't something she felt they could talk about over the phone, so she walked round to Janet's flat and passed on as much of the story as she already knew. It wasn't long before she wished she hadn't offered to do it, because although Janet couldn't come up with any further information she was strangely indignant at being asked. Behind Nina, but in Janet's line of sight, a parade of family photos eavesdropped silently from the sideboard. In one of the pictures were Ray and Isobel, side-by-side with Terry and Janet, their arms all linked as they walked together along a seaside promenade somewhere towards an unknown photographer.

'I certainly didn't know anything about this, and I can't imagine your Dad did either. If it's true, which I doubt, then it's hardly something Ray would have mentioned to anyone in the family, is it?'

Janet was less than thrilled at the prospect of an illegitimate nephew suddenly popping up in the family, and made no effort to disguise it.

'He'll be after her money,' she said. 'You wait. Why else would he want to get in touch with her after all this time?'

'I thought that at first,' said Nina. 'But now I'm beginning to wonder. He seems completely genuine – and Kate is over the moon with finding him. It's certainly given her something other than work to think about, and that can only be a good thing.'

Janet considered this, but only for the briefest moment. The whole concept of trusting an unknown black South African man was a very big leap of faith for her, and welcoming him into the family simply too much to contemplate.

'There'll be tears before bedtime,' she said, finally.

The following day, she rang Nina with news that had clearly taken her by surprise.

'Kate wants Jim to take a DNA test!' Janet was in high dudgeon, as if she was the one Kate had asked.

'Yes, I know. It'll prove it one way or the other. They're having half-sibling tests too, but they aren't conclusive, they only indicate probability. How does Jim feel about it?'

'Well, he's all for it! Maybe he's hoping it will prove to Kate that this Walter is a fraud,' said Janet.

'Did he say that?'

'Not in so many words, exactly, no. Sue thinks it's all terribly exciting. Mind you,' Janet continued, 'they probably don't have much going on down there in Devon, so they'll be dining out on this story for years to come.'

'Well if there's not much going on they'll only be dining with each other,' said Nina, who was surprised by her mother's hostility. 'Loosen up a bit, Mum. If Walter does prove to be Kate's half brother, which seems quite possible, the world won't end. But if he doesn't,' she added, 'Kate's world just might. At least be happy for her if you can't feel positive about it in any other way.'

Janet huffed at the end of the phone, and was then silent.

'I was very close to Isobel,' she said finally, 'and Ray, too. *If* this turns out to be true I think Kate owes it to them to just quietly deal with the man, and then discourage any further contact, because if he were alive that's probably what Ray would do. A large cheque in the post – and she can afford it – should be all it takes. Perhaps Kate ought to be thinking more about her parents in all of this, and less about herself.'

Nina rolled her eyes impatiently, cross with her mother for being so negative.

'This is Pandora's Box, Mum. Walter won't just go away and it's too late now to pretend he doesn't exist – and what's more Kate doesn't want to. It can't hurt Uncle Ray and Aunt Isobel now, whatever happens.'

'It does no good raking up the past,' Janet said, 'and sometimes things are best left unsaid,' and the subject was closed as far as she was concerned.

Nina knew that nothing she could possibly say at that moment would change Janet's attitude. Once the idea has had time to settle with her, she thought, she may see things differently. On the other hand... Janet could be very stubborn at times. It could go either way.

1956

CHAPTER 6

JANUARY 1956: SIMON'S TOWN

They got their first good look at Simon's Town one hot Thursday afternoon. The sun was beating down on several groups of ratings as they left HMS Comus and wandered ashore through the East Dockyard Gates, pausing there at the junction with the main road to get their bearings. With the Comus due to be in dock for many weeks undergoing repair and refitting work, the crew were well aware that Simon's Town was somewhere they would get to know rather well.

It was a town that was used to servicemen. Many thousands of them had passed through it since the far off days of the Dutch East India Company, and Simon's Town took them all in its stride as it always had. The current crop were not much different to any who'd gone before them, looking a little tentative on their first shore leave, intent on finding out where everything was and how the residents would treat them. They'd had the usual on-board talk about the dangers of fraternising with local girls, and advice about how to deal with the blacks, the gist of which was that they should be largely ignored. Most of the crew hadn't listened to a word. And now here they were, with a few unfamiliar-looking rand in their pockets, the value of which they were still trying to figure out.

Bobby, walking along with five or six sailors of a similar age to himself, was the first of them to spot the Sailors' and Soldiers' Restroom, just along from the Dock Gates.

'Here we are, lads,' he said. 'First stop for a pint?'

They were welcomed into a large recreational centre, with a bar down one side and informal groupings of tables and chairs set out across the room. There was a dart board and a snooker table at the back of the hall – both already in use by sailors from another ship, who seemed completely uninterested in the sudden influx of men and didn't even look round. A battered old upright piano stood to one side and from somewhere behind the bar a radio was playing. The air was thick with smoke and ripe with the smell of alcohol. Before long other groups of sailors from the Comus arrived and a demob-happy party spirit soon prevailed as the drinks flowed. It was a couple of hours before some intrepid sailors moved on but most didn't bother to venture further afield on that first day, preferring instead to prop up the same bar until the time came to return to their ship.

But Bobby was curious. Wherever his ships had taken him he'd always been eager to see as much as he could, so he left the Restroom on his own after a while and wandered along the main street of the town.

It seemed like a pleasant enough place, bustling and cheerful, with shops lining one side of the road leading through and out of the town in both directions. The pavement was busy with locals and servicemen, not only Royal Naval sailors but also some South African Naval personnel, their uniforms crisp and white. The town had a very British feel to it, the Naval Base at Simon's Town still in UK hands until the official handover the following year. Leaving aside the heat, Bobby felt quite at home as he counted five pubs from one end of the main road to the other, plus several liquor stores and cafés in addition to a large bakery and the Criterion Cinema.

Well, he thought, we could be stuck somewhere a lot worse than this for a couple of months.

Ray was not on the current shore leave, being part of the skeleton crew left on board. When his turn came the following day he was one of the men who chose to stay in the Restroom without bothering to take a closer look at the town.

'You go,' he said, waving a cigarette at some of his mates who were about to set off. 'All these places are the same to me.'

'You might see something nice to take home to your missus,' said one of them.

'Or someone nice you'd like better than your missus!' laughed another one.

Ray joined in the laughter. Correspondence between him and Isobel had dwindled a bit recently, and Ray had certainly never been a saint when away from home, but she was six months pregnant with their first baby and he knew it wasn't easy for her at that time with him at sea. His last leave hadn't gone too well, she'd been tired much of the time and they'd been tetchy with each other over the smallest things. And now he was sorry for that, and missed getting her previously regular letters.

'Tell me if you see anything worth leaving here for, and I'll go another day,' he said, turning back to his pint. And later on, when they told Ray about the five pubs, the liquor stores and cafés, the bakery and the Criterion Cinema he decided that he would take a stroll along the main street next time he was ashore.

* * *

Grace Ntoko worked in one of the cafés that Bobby had seen on his first day in Simon's Town. At nineteen, she was a natural beauty with a perfect figure, a girl who turned heads every time she stepped out of the house. One of a family of seven who lived up above Rectory Lane alongside many other black families, Grace took after her mother and, like her, was shy and quiet.

Her job in the café suited her well enough. Most of the time she worked in the kitchen at the back, and didn't come into contact with the customers, but sometimes when they were busy she had to serve at tables, which she did reluctantly. The café owner was a large, mixed-race lady, with a loud laugh and a dubious taste in clothes. Known to everyone as Auntie Betty, she spent her working day moving between the tables, joking with her regulars and welcoming new customers, re-arranging the ashtrays and sugar bowls, brushing crumbs from the tables and generally keeping an eagle eye on everything that went on – especially the girls who worked for her. Her clientèle were mostly sailors and black or mixed-race residents of the town because Auntie Betty's café was at the cheaper end of the scale and not a place white ladies in hats and gloves looking for afternoon tea would venture into. Betty had several chins and an ample bosom, all of which wobbled when she laughed. She was big, bold and brash and the sailors frequenting the café loved her.

Ray and two of his mates found Betty's on their first wander through Simon's Town. They stopped to look at the range of cakes displayed in the window, realised that the shop doubled as a café and, unlike Bobby, they went in.

Auntie Betty sashayed across the room in her purple satin frock and was at their side while they were still deciding where to sit.

'Oh, lovely sailors from the Royal Navy,' she said, taking Ray's arm and guiding them to a free table at the back of the room, 'come to meet your Auntie Betty for the first time! Here, sit, sit!'

The café was almost full, and Betty's two waitresses bustled about carrying pots of tea and plates of cakes or toast. She lifted an arm and clicked her fingers.

'Come here now Gloria, see what we can bring these three sailors, my lovely English boys.'

The girl named Gloria dutifully took their order and all the while Auntie Betty kept up her banter with the men, whilst simultaneously making sure that the running of her café was proceeding as it should. Once she broke off to shout a greeting to a couple of black workers walking past the open door, and another time to chastise the girl selling cakes from the shop window.

'Alice! The gentlemen asked for almond tarts, not almond puffs! Don't you know a tart from a puff yet?' Betty turned back to the room, winked hugely at Ray's group and laughed raucously.

By the time Gloria had brought them a large pot of tea and a plate of warm buttered scones they felt they'd known Auntie Betty forever. They knew they'd go back there; she knew they'd go back there – she'd made another conquest and their business was assured.

Not that they ignored the pubs though, the rand they spent in Simon's Town were distributed evenly, with the British Hotel and the Africa Station Club getting their fair share in the evenings, along with Auntie Betty's during the daytime.

Shore leave started to be something to look forward to. The town had welcomed the boys, and they found the black and mixed-race communities easier company than some of the starchy white residents they came across, most of whom were only interested in the officers from the ships in dock. Skirmishes between sailors from different ships happened occasionally, speedily dealt with by the Naval military police, but by and large life in Simon's Town was proving to be trouble-free.

On the second week that the Comus was in dock at Simon's Town, Ray went alone to Auntie Betty's one brilliant sunny afternoon. He'd just received a letter from Isobel and she'd sounded cool and distant. He thought again that it was probably just the pregnancy getting her down, after all she was alone in the house in Notting Hill, trying to cope with everything and probably feeling a bit cheesed-off with it all at that stage. It was a difficult time for her and they both knew she'd be going through the birth and the child's first few weeks without him. No wonder she was fed-up. He was at a loss to know how to reply to her.

When Ray walked in to Betty's café it was already packed with sailors and a sprinkling of locals. He couldn't see anywhere to sit and had just turned around ready to head off to another café in town when Betty caught sight of him.

'Don't go, lovely sailor boy Ray,' she called out in booming tones. 'I'll find you a place, just let me fetch another chair and make you comfortable...' and she was off, through the back of the shop, her bright orange skirt swishing as she brushed past one of the waitresses just coming through from the kitchen.

Ray stood about awkwardly until Betty returned with a wooden dining chair, which she plonked down at the nearest table, urging the four people already there to shift up a bit. They didn't seem to mind too much, generously shuffling their chairs about to make room for him, and he sat where he was put, facing away from the room.

'Now,' said Betty, clicking her fingers, 'Grace! There's a man here wanting tea and cake! Hurry along!'

Pressed into waitress service from her usual duties in the kitchen, Grace made her way reluctantly to Ray's table, her head bent and eyes downcast. He ordered his usual tea and scone without really noticing her, not then or when she brought them to him. Two of the other occupants of the table were leaving at that moment and as he had fallen into conversation with them there were the usual civilities to observe. Grace did nothing to draw attention to herself; Ray simply noticed as he sat down again that his order had arrived.

Later, as he was getting ready to leave and sorting out money to pay the bill, she came across to clear his table. He had a pocketful of small change and he pressed a few cents into her hand, looking up at her as he did so. Grace, taken by surprise for this didn't often happen, looked straight back at Ray.

And in that instant the breath just left his body.

* * *

The next few times Ray was ashore he headed straight to Auntie Betty's, but Grace was never in the café, although once he thought he caught sight of her behind the counter at the back of the shop. Then he hit on the bright idea of walking along the narrow alleyway behind the shops to find the kitchen entrance.

After he'd loitered nearby for half an hour, Grace came out to throw something in the dustbins. Ray prised himself upright from the wall he'd been leaning against, and called across to her. She turned around and was startled to see a sailor she barely recognised walking towards her.

'Hello,' he said. 'Do you remember me?'

'How do you know my name?' she said quietly, avoiding an answer to his question, because as he got closer she did remember him and wasn't sure if she should admit to it.

Ray jerked his thumb in the direction of the café.

'Betty called you across to serve me the other day.'

'Oh.' Grace nodded.

'I was waiting here, hoping to see you,' he said.

Grace just looked at him with huge dark eyes.

'I thought perhaps...' he tried again.

'I should get back,' she said. 'We're very busy in the kitchen.'

'Would you come for a walk with me when you finish work?'

She looked down, didn't answer.

'Please?'

From the kitchen someone shouted out her name. Grace glanced back at the open door.

'I finish work at six o'clock. I have to be home by seven.'

'So I'll see you here at six,' said Ray, 'and I'll walk home with you.'

'Not here... but maybe I could meet you at St. Francis' Church.'

Then she turned and hurried towards the kitchen door.

'My name's Ray!' he called after her.

He had no idea where the church was, but he was sure as hell going to find out before six o'clock.

* * *

Grace wouldn't let Ray walk her home, instead he left her at the top of Rectory Lane and she insisted on going the rest of the way alone. But in the course of their walk through Simon's Town they'd passed the Criterion Cinema, where posters advertised "Lady and the Tramp", which was showing that week.

Ray had seen the film when it first came out, the year previously. He'd been on leave and taken Isobel to a cinema up West because she'd heard about it and was desperate to see the film before any of her friends did. Apparently it took a while for the latest releases to make it to this corner of Africa.

'We could go to see that one evening, if you like,' said Ray.

'Oh no, I couldn't do that.'

'Why not? I think you'd like it.'

'You don't understand how things are here. I couldn't go into that cinema, especially with a white man,' she said quietly, shaking her head.

Ray was shocked. He knew that things were sometimes difficult here for the black and coloured communities – but he hadn't realised they were restricted in the places they went to in their home town.

'But people in Simon's Town seem to get along pretty well together. Who's going to stop you?'

Grace sighed. 'Maybe nobody would stop me, but all the time the government are making more rules that we have to follow.' She produced a small booklet from her handbag. 'These are my documents; permits and passes. Since last year I have had to carry them everywhere, all the time. White girls don't have these, of course. I would be afraid to go into that cinema with you in case there was trouble.'

'But you live here, and work here.'

'That is allowed, although some people think even that will change one day. It doesn't mean I can do just what I like.'

Ray thought about this for a moment. 'What about Betty? She runs her café the way she wants and everybody seems quite happy with that.'

'Her family have been there for generations, but

even she has to follow the rules. I don't know what will happen to her café if the government do make all the black and coloured people leave Simon's Town and move somewhere else. I suppose it would just close.'

'You need to change your government then.'

'Only white people can do that, we can't vote.'

Ray fell silent. He didn't usually bother voting in elections at home, and for the first time started to think that maybe this was something he should look at again.

Since coming to Simon's Town he hadn't seen any segregation, in fact he'd noticed a few sailors walking about with black or coloured girls. There was no outward sign of the restrictions Grace spoke of, or maybe there was and he just hadn't wanted to see it.

'This is a good place,' said Grace, 'better than most. White people here do not make life difficult for us. We don't have the same problems in Simon's Town as they do in other places – but bad things are happening in this country and wherever you live the laws still exist.'

'Well, OK, not the cinema. There must be somewhere else we can go.'

'There's the church.'

'Is that all?'

'There are one or two bars. Not nice places.'

They sat down on a low wall overlooking the harbour and Ray took Grace's hand in his.

'I suppose we'll have to go to church then,' he said, and she smiled.

'Tell me about that film,' she said.

'Well... it's a musical, a romance, between... erm... two dogs,' he said.

She was silent for a moment, considering this. Then she started to giggle, and the giggles turned into peals of laughter, until she was hanging weakly onto his arm and Ray was laughing with her.

At the top of Rectory Lane they said good night. They didn't kiss, and shaking hands seemed much too formal. For the first time in his adult life, Ray felt completely out of his depth with a woman.

* * *

Whenever he could be ashore Ray dropped into Auntie Betty's café, although he often didn't catch a single glimpse of Grace, and then later he would meet her after work. They now had more time together in the evenings because she had negotiated a curfew extension with her father, but their problem was still where to go. They'd seen other mixed couples going into the cinema, but no matter how hard Ray tried, Grace wouldn't be talked into it.

'You never know who might be watching,' she said, and that was the end of it.

But as lovers always will, they did eventually find their place.

The sky had been full of white-grey clouds all day, and by the time Ray met Grace one evening a couple of weeks later, the first few raindrops had started to fall. It wasn't long before the rain was steady, and the streets began to empty of people. Ray took Grace's hand and they ran to the shelter of a shop doorway.

'We can't stay here,' he said, 'but if we try to make a dash for it you'll be soaked by the time you get home.'

She peered out at the pavement, where rain was bouncing up and the gutters were running like rivers. A young couple with umbrellas rushed past. An occasional passing vehicle swooshed up plumes of spray and the drains gurgled with the effort of taking such a sudden volume of rainwater away. Further along the street the door of a bar opened and a group of four or five sailors shook rain from their caps and hurried inside.

'How about there?' said Ray, turning to Grace.

She shook her head. 'I know some of the girls who go there,' she said, 'but I wouldn't.'

'Then unless you've got a better idea we'll have to wait here until it eases off.'

But the rain showed no signs of easing off and the sky was growing darker.

'There's...' Grace began, then stopped.

'Go on,' said Ray. 'Almost anywhere would be better than this doorway.' She hesitated for a moment, then grabbed his hand and stepped out into the rain. With Ray following close behind her, they ran around puddles, dashed down the first turning off the main road and then along an alleyway until she came to a sudden halt and Ray realised they were at the back door to Auntie Betty's kitchen. Grace reached her hand up and felt along the top of the doorway until she located the key.

Once inside, they shook the rain from their shoulders and giggled together like naughty children as their eyes started to make sense of the darkness.

'Better not put the lights on,' Grace said.

The connecting door was open, a small amount of light leeching through from the street beyond the café.

'The blinds are down in the café – so as long as that door's closed...' Ray stumbled across the kitchen, knocking into something as he went, and a tin clattered down to the floor.

'Shhhh!'

He reached the door and closed it, throwing the kitchen even deeper into darkness.

'Now I can't find my way back to you!'

'I'm here,' said Grace, from right behind him.

Ray turned and wrapped his arms around her, hugging her tight. And then, for the first time in all the weeks they'd known each other, they felt free to kiss.

This wasn't how he'd imagined it would be – in as much as he'd imagined a location at all – surrounded by the stale smell of the kitchen with background scuffling and scratching noises in the darkness. Those noises worried him, the thought of something scuttling around their feet...

'Let's put the light on,' he whispered to Grace, 'so I can see you.'

They needn't have worried about the light, the bulb was so dull that nothing would have filtered out beyond the room. But it was enough for the scuffling to stop, and enough for Ray to be electrified again as he looked into Grace's eyes.

He peeled off her wet clothes, slowly and with infinite care, placing them on the counter top. Grace made no attempt to stop him but, inexperienced as she was, she had little idea of what was expected of her in return.

'I don't know...'

'Shhh, you don't have to worry about a thing. I'll look after you.'

Isobel had been a virgin too, on their wedding night – how different the surroundings had been then, that one expensive night in a hotel room in Worthing. But even with the squalid surroundings of the kitchen around them, Ray knew it hadn't been an experience to match the sweet perfection of making love to Grace for the first time.

Entwined under the dusty light bulb, white skin on black, black on white, their bodies were damp with sweat and their hair still damp from the rain, as they lay together on a couple of empty flour sacks that Ray had found under the counter.

Grace knew, although Ray didn't, that in apartheid South Africa what they were doing was illegal.

***

The repair and refitting work on the Comus was coming to an end. Most of the crew were ready by then to head out of Simon's Town and get back to sea – a couple of months was a long time for them to be in one place and the limited attractions the town could offer had already lost their appeal for many sailors.

Ray was dreading it. He hadn't spoken to Grace about leaving, although he guessed she must know that their time together was coming to an end. The last days dragged on for most of the men, rushed by for him, until he had one final shore leave left, one last chance to see her. He had no idea how he would say goodbye.

They made love that night in a desperate, tear-stained way, clinging on to each other until the very last moment.

Ray put a folded sheet of paper into Grace's handbag as they left Betty's kitchen for the last time.

'I don't want you to read this until tomorrow,' he said, 'but promise me you'll always keep it.'

At the top of Rectory Lane he watched her walk away from him, and it was all he could do to stop himself running after her for one last embrace. Ray had never told her about Isobel and the child she was carrying, but that night he'd said many things to Grace that were the absolute truth. He'd told her he loved her more than anyone else in the world. He'd said she was beautiful and that he wanted to be with her forever. Then he told her a single, big lie.

'One day I'm coming back to you.'

He didn't know it was a lie when he said it, but it wasn't long before he realised it was. The lie sat heavily with him for many years, until one day, eventually, he forgot about it and soon afterwards he forgot about Grace too.

He never knew about Walter, the baby he and Grace had made one night in the kitchen of Auntie Betty's café.

CHAPTER 7

OCTOBER 2010: OCEAN VIEW & FORDHAM

In her lunch break, Mandisa walked along the shopping mall and into the bookshop at the far end, where she looked along the shelves until she found just what she wanted. The book cost her three hundred and forty-nine rand, taken from her savings, and as well as plenty of information for travellers to Southern England it contained lots of coloured photographs.

She sat outside the mall on a low wall facing the car park, unwrapped the book and started turning the pages. Disappointingly, she couldn't find a photo of Guildford, which surprised her as Sele had claimed it to be such an important town. But there were plenty of pictures of village streets and views over farmland and beaches, any of which might or might not have been close to Guildford as far as Mandisa knew. There were maps at the back of the book but the scale was small and turning backwards and forwards seemed like too much of an effort.

Photos of London featured strongly, and these were what interested Mandisa most. She bent closer to pictures of the Houses of Parliament and Buckingham Palace, then turned the page over and saw the London Eye, by day and night.

After a few minutes she was aware of someone at her elbow.

'Hey, you won the Lotto, Mandisa? Don't know how else you're gonna get there...'

Mandisa snapped her book closed and looked up to see one of the girls who had been in her class at school. Also on her lunch break from another shop in the mall, the girl sat down next to Mandisa and reached her hand out towards the book.

'It's a birthday present,' Mandisa muttered, cramming it back into the paper bag and tearing it in her haste. 'I'm not actually going anywhere,' she said, adding 'unfortunately.'

'So if you're staying around, you want to come to a party next weekend?'

'Whose party?'

'Bheki Msonga – you remember him.'

Mandisa did. At school Bheki was always in trouble and Annie had banned both the girls and Sele from having anything to do with him or his family. Since leaving school it was well known that he'd been involved in petty crime and was usually somewhere near the scene whenever a violent incident erupted, acquiring a reputation in Ocean View as a dangerous character. There was no doubt that Bheki had a temper, but he could be charming too, as he was whenever he saw the twins.

'I don't think so,' she said, standing up.

'He'd like to see you there, he told me.'

'I'm busy.'

'You don't know when it is!'

'I'm busy all weekend.'

'Oh, reading your travel book?' the girl laughed and laughed, and Mandisa walked away and went back to work feeling foolish.

She knew Bheki liked her, that much was obvious whenever she saw him, which happened too many times for Mandisa's liking. She had tried avoiding him, walking home a different route each day from where the Volksie buses dropped everyone off, but somehow he seemed to be around too often for it to be a coincidence. Elana was scared of him and clutched Mandisa's arm when she saw him coming. But he had always been polite and never given them any real cause to feel uneasy. And yet, maybe it was just his reputation, but Mandisa did feel uneasy when he came into view. She certainly didn't want to go out with him, an occasional conversation was as much as she could manage.

Hurrying back to work, with the book clutched to her chest, Mandisa hoped they wouldn't see Bheki any evening before the party. She knew he'd badger her to go and feared that if she kept refusing he might lose his temper. Although four years younger, Sele was bigger and probably stronger than Bheki but she didn't want him to get involved. It was her problem, she had to deal with it herself.

Mandisa's book caused a scramble at home as everyone except Annie was eager to look at it. Closer examination revealed two Surrey pictures; one titled Polesden Lacey, and the other Box Hill. They had no idea if these were anywhere near Kate's village and naturally none of them realised that the photographer credited in both cases was Kate's cousin Nina. Poring over the text on the facing page, Sele jabbed his finger at the book in triumph.

'Here! Look, "Polesden Lacey NEAR GUILDFORD"!' he yelled.

'Don't shout, Sele,' said Annie, briskly. 'There's no need for the whole building to know.'

But four heads were already bent over the page, and nobody paid much attention to Annie. It was while the book on England was being scrutinised that the phone rang and Elana, who was closest, answered it.

'OH!' she said, looking startled and sitting bolt upright suddenly. Mandisa thought for one horrible moment that Bheki was calling her about his party, but it soon became apparent (to her relief) that this was a different caller.

'Yes... I'm Elana... yes ma'am, he is...'

By now Elana had everyone's attention. 'Yes... OK...' She passed the receiver to Walter, and as he spoke she whispered to the rest of the family, 'It's Miss Kate Hatchman!'

'Yes... that was Elana... we are all here... all the family...' they heard him say.

In her house at Fordham, Kate was unable to settle in one place and walked about from one room to another with the phone pressed to her ear. Absent-mindedly, she tweaked the curtains in the living room, and straightened an ornament on the mantelpiece. She switched a lamp on and picked up a photo of Clare and Rachel as little girls, putting it down again on a different table. Finally, she perched on a chair in the dining room, where a couple of open books and a map were in front of her on the table.

'I've organised the DNA tests,' she said. 'A package will arrive with you in the next week or so, they'll send you cheek swabs and you just follow the instructions and send them back to the company.'

'That's fine, Kate,' said Walter. 'I'll do just as it says.'

Behind him, the girls looked at each other and suppressed a giggle. This was the first time they'd spoken and already their father was calling her Kate. Sele threw a look at them and his meaning was clear. *Just shut up and listen.*

'The half-sibling tests can't be conclusive, apparently, because of our different mothers' genes,'

Kate said. 'But my uncle Jim, Dad's brother, has agreed to be tested and that will give us a definite yes or no. I should get the results after about ten days, and as soon as they arrive I'll call you.'

She fingered the map in front of her as Walter assured her that all the arrangements were perfect with him.

'I am confident,' he said. 'It will be yes.'

'I think so too.' Kate bent closer to her map. 'Walter, I'm looking at a map here – but Ocean View doesn't seem to be marked, at any rate I can't see it,' she said. 'What's the nearest place I should be looking for?'

'Kommetjie,' said Walter. 'Look on the west coast, south of Chapman's Peak. If you can find Fish Hoek it's more or less directly across the peninsula from there. Can you see that?'

'Oh yes! I have it!'

'We also have a book here, about Southern England. Mandisa bought it today in the bookshop at the mall. Sele has just found – what's the name of that place?' Walter asked Sele.

'POLESDEN LACEY,' shouted Sele, leaning across the girls and grabbing Mandisa's book. 'AND BOX HILL.'

'Oh yes, I heard that,' said Kate. 'Well, they're both quite close to here. Was that Sele? Can I say hello to everyone, Walter?'

Walter passed the phone to Sele.

'She wants to say hello to you,' he said.

Sele, caught off guard for a second, backed away.

'Go on!' Walter said, pushing the phone closer to him.

'Hello, ma'am,' said Sele. Then his confidence came bouncing back. 'I did Google Street Map in your village. It's very, very nice – I saw your house!'

Kate laughed. 'I wish I could do the same for Ocean View, but I'm afraid they haven't been round there yet. I guess I'll just have to wait. Maybe one day you'll come to England and see my street for yourself, would you like that Sele?'

'Man, that's...' Annie slapped Sele on the arm.

'Manners,' she hissed at him.

'That would be very nice, ma'am,' he finished, lamely.

He passed the phone to Mandisa, who, always more confident than her twin, was eager to speak to Kate.

'Do you ever go to London?' she asked Kate. 'I've been looking at the photos – it looks so nice. I'd love to see Harrods.' Elana tapped Mandisa's hand and mouthed the word "dogs".

'Ma'am, Elana wants to know if you have dogs,' she said, then to Elana, 'no, she doesn't.'

'What about horses?' Mandisa continued. 'We thought you might... oh, well, we just wondered... I'm going to give the phone to Mama now.'

As Mandisa abruptly came to the end of what she wanted to say and thrust the phone at her mother, Annie was momentarily unprepared to speak to Kate. There was a pause, then she spoke slowly and clearly, as if the distance between them might hamper conversation.

'It's nice that Walter can speak to you, Miss Hatchman,' she said. 'He is very happy that he found you.'

But there was no hint that Annie might also be happy with this new arrangement – her tone was flat, and guarded. Puzzled by the lack of enthusiasm in Annie's voice, Kate searched for something to say that might put her at her ease.

'And I'm happy too, Annie. But please call me Kate, and tell Sele and the girls that it's really not necessary to call me ma'am, Kate is just fine.'

But Annie had already handed the phone back to Walter.

'I'll call you each week, Walter. If this is a good evening for you then we'll stick to Tuesdays, at about the same time. Would that be OK?'

'That would be wonderful,' he said, beaming his widest smile, 'and Kate... send me a photo, will you do that?'

* * *

Kate slumped back in her chair and smiled. I did it, she thought. I spoke to my other family. She drew the map closer to her and placed her finger on the exact spot where Walter was.

He's right, she thought. It'll be a yes.

* * *

Walter replaced the receiver and leaned back. Then he looked around at his family, and nodded his head slowly.

'We'll get used to this,' he said, 'and it's going to be all right. The tests will come back positive.'

After the excitement of the telephone call Sele was irrepressible. Unable to sit still for five minutes, and getting louder all the time, Annie finally had enough and told him to go out and find his friends.

'Can I tell them?' he asked.

'NO!' everyone chorused.

'Let's wait a little longer, just until the tests come back,' said Walter.

'Then I'm going to the football pitch,' said Sele, his voice muffled as he rummaged under his bed for a football.

'That's a good idea,' his mother said, 'you need to run off some of this excitement, you silly boy.'

After he'd left the apartment Elana and Mandisa decided to call on one of their friends, just a short walk past the shops at the end of their road. They'd only just reached the junction with the main street when they saw Bheki Msonga and two of his gang just a little way ahead of them. He was walking away from them, and if they'd turned back immediately and disappeared around the next corner he would probably never have known they were nearby. Unfortunately, Elana chose that moment to twist her ankle on the uneven surface of the sidewalk, and she let out a sudden loud yell.

The boys looked round, picked the twins out of the people wandering about, and stood staring at them. Elana, bent double and rubbing her ankle, failed to notice that Bheki had turned and was now walking towards them, while his friends hung back and watched. But Mandisa noticed, and tensed.

Bheki strolled straight up to her, his hands thrust deep into the pockets of his jeans.

'Uyanda says you don't want to come to my party,' he said. He was smiling at Mandisa, whilst at the same time ignoring Elana completely.

'That's not what I told her,' said Mandisa, quietly. 'I'm busy.'

'OK. Tell me when you're not busy and we'll have a party of our own. Just the two of us – nice, hey?'

Mandisa looked down at the ground. Elana sat down right where she was on the sidewalk and examined her ankle more closely. Bheki jerked a thumb towards her, but didn't take his eyes off Mandisa.

'If your sister wants to come I can bring a friend or two for her.'

'She doesn't want to come.'

'Then it'll have to be just me and you.' He moved close enough for Mandisa to smell the alcohol on his breath. There was something else too, the sickly sweet smell of dagga, familiar enough in Ocean View where it was the drug of choice. She took a step backwards, but he reached out and caught hold of her hand.

'Hey, Mandisa, what's the problem? You scared of me or something? I like you, you know. We could have some fun together.'

Mandisa pulled her hand away.

'I don't think so,' she said.

'You know, you're wrong there. And I'm gonna prove that to you one day.'

From further down the road Bheki's friends called something to him, and he turned his head and yelled back. A couple of passers-by took a casual look at the unfolding scene but walked on without comment. Nearby a car door banged and Mandisa jumped, then Elana struggled to her feet and stood with her hand on her sister's shoulder. Looking Bheki straight in the eyes, Mandisa wound her arm around Elana's waist, helping to take her weight.

'Come Elana, let's go home. There's nothing for us here,' she said.

As they turned and walked away, Bheki put his hands back in his pockets and stood for a moment, just watching. Then he called after them.

'One day, Mandisa. Believe it.'

* * *

Kate couldn't settle to anything after speaking to Walter. She tried watching the television but gave up, checked her emails, made coffee, looked again at the map of Cape Town. Nothing occupied her for more than a few minutes. In the end she phoned Nina.

'I spoke to them!' she said. 'Walter and the family – I actually spoke to them all!'

'And how did that go?' Nina replied in a distracted way – she'd been interrupted in looking through a contact sheet of transparencies when the phone rang.

'It was great! They all sound really nice – except for Annie, couldn't figure her out at all, she was a bit odd. Maybe she's just shy.'

'Maybe she's just jealous,' said Nina. 'Strange position for a woman to find herself in.'

Kate thought about this for a moment. It hadn't occurred to her that Annie might see her sudden appearance on the scene in anything other than a positive light.

'I'll have to think of a way to make her feel more a part of all this, then. I certainly don't want there to be any bad feeling. Anyway, the kids sounded great. They wanted to know if I kept dogs and horses! Nina, I need to ask you a favour.'

'Ask away.' Nina leant back in her chair, abandoning the contacts as she realised she wasn't going to dislodge Kate easily.

'Walter wants a photo of me. You know I always look ghastly in photos and I don't think I have anything that's less than three or four years old anyway. Could you pop up here sometime and take a few pics of me? I don't want to scare him off...'

'Now you know I don't really do portraits, but sure, let's look at our diaries and come up with a date.'

Kate was thankful. It was suddenly important to her that Walter had a good likeness of her, something he could keep safe until they met in person. She hadn't mentioned that likelihood to him yet, in case it didn't actually come off, but as she reached for her diary it struck her that this was as good a chance as any to pin Nina down on possible travel dates.

'And maybe we could get Jeremy here too, then I could send Walter pictures of all of us.'

'OK, so I'll need to bring a tripod, then I can set up the timer and get us all together in one shot.'

They tossed some dates about, finally coming up with a shortlist of three, which Kate said she would put to Jeremy later that evening.

'And I meant it about all of us going together to Cape Town. You are still up for it, aren't you?' Kate asked.

There was a pause. Nina had looked at air fares since Kate first suggested it, then looked at her bank balance and discovered that the two weren't going to sit together very happily.

'I'd love to Kate, it's just that I'm not sure I could afford it...'

'I'm paying for all of us, that was always my intention. If you can come, and you want to, then please don't worry about the cost. It's really the least I can do, for the pleasure of getting both sides of my family together.'

CHAPTER 8

NOVEMBER 2010: ENGLAND

Rachel dropped the children off at the Little Starlets Nursery, and hailed a taxi. Different day, different hotel – it was Jason's theory that people got caught out by routine. That, and bits of paper.

'Never write anything down. You have to keep it all up here,' he said, tapping his head, 'where it can't be found.'

Since Clare's revelation that she'd been spotted in the St Martin's Hotel Rachel was uneasy about her meetings with Jason. She started to imagine people she knew popping out from behind potted palms or suddenly appearing in lift doors just as they were closing. Excitement and anticipation were slowly being replaced by a jittery dread of being wrong-footed. At the start she'd wished fervently for a more normal relationship with Jason – but as time went on it seemed that, contrary to outward appearances, there was little about Jason's life that was normal.

He was already in the bar when she arrived. As she walked towards him he reached out for her hand, kissed her and ordered her a drink.

'I need to pick the children up at five,' she said, as a glass of wine appeared in front of her. She hadn't eaten since breakfast, and knew from experience that it was a bad idea for her to drink in the middle of the day. But then so many things she was doing these days were a bad idea. Meeting Jason had been a turning point in her life, but she was smart enough to realise that Jason himself was probably her worst ever idea.

He made a theatrical show of checking his watch, although he knew perfectly well what it would tell him.

'Then we shouldn't waste too much time in the bar,' he whispered, picking up both glasses and leading her towards the lift.

The room was beautiful. Sumptuous and elegant in tones of grey and honey, with a view across London that any tourist would kill for. Rachel glanced out of the window towards the London Eye rising above the skyline, and stared at it until she could detect the slight movement of the wheel turning. These days, gorgeous rooms in expensive London hotels no longer held the same fascination for her. She was starting to feel the same about Jason.

Behind her, she heard him set the drinks down.

'Rachel?'

She turned back into the room and he wrapped his arms around her.

'You OK babe?' he asked, pulling back to look at her face.

'Yeah, I'm just tired, those kids are very demanding sometimes. Sorry, I'll liven up a bit in a moment.'

Jason was the tidiest person she'd ever known at undressing. His jacket, shirt and trousers went onto hangers, he folded his tie and even his socks were neatly placed one on top of the other with the heels facing the same way. Rachel was usually the complete opposite, which made him laugh. Today though, she found herself mirroring him, lining up her shoes and draping her jacket over the back of a chair.

'You're really not yourself, today are you?' he said jokingly. 'Here, let me help.'

So she sat on the edge of the embroidered grey silk bedspread, and gave in.

* * *

The letter from the clinic arrived in the post on a day when Kate was working up in Birmingham, so it wasn't until late that evening that she found it. She ripped the envelope open and sat down in the living room to read the results.

Half-sibling test: inconclusive. This was what she'd expected. There was a whole page of information about the markers used to compare their samples but it was the bottom line that interested her, and there was no real surprise there.

She placed the first result sheet face down on a lamp table, next to a framed photograph of her parents, and read the second one.

Uncle test: positive.

Positive! She leaned back in her chair and smiled broadly.

No doubts now, this was the confirmation she and Walter had both been hoping for. Kate wanted to phone him immediately, but it was after ten in England, and she couldn't imagine that Walter and Annie stayed up past midnight. A phone call in the middle of the night wouldn't be welcome, especially to Annie, so it would have to wait until the next day. She wondered if Nina would still be up, and toyed with the idea of calling her, but halfway through dialling her number she decided against it. Late night phone calls invariably mean bad news, she thought, and Nina would immediately think something had happened to one of the girls. Jeremy would probably be at a gig, so it was no good trying him. There was nothing for it, the news was Kate's alone until the following day, and the inevitable result was a restless night, laced throughout with strange dreams of Cape Town.

At one point in the darkest depths of the night she dreamt that she was being lowered over a sheer drop on Table Mountain to abseil down, and as she looked up Walter and a woman she somehow knew was Annie, were letting the rope out above her. Very early in the morning she drifted off briefly and found herself, Jim and Sue all running around the streets of a shanty town. She knew they were searching for Walter's apartment but nobody they asked knew him, and Kate was getting panicky. She woke up in a sweat and threw the duvet back till she cooled down.

By six the next morning, Kate had given up her struggle with sleep and was already in the kitchen making coffee. She assumed – correctly as it happened – that Walter would already be on his way to work, which meant that she had to wait another twelve hours before she could call him. It didn't seem fair that she should tell somebody else before him, and there was no chance whatsoever of her being able to concentrate on work until she had, so she did something the old Kate would never have contemplated – she emailed her secretary to say she was taking the day off. That done, she fetched the *Rough Guide to Cape Town* from the dining room, and settled down at the breakfast bar with it propped up against the toaster.

Well this is it, she thought – first day of the rest of our lives.

* * *

Before long Kate had made a plan. She would call Walter first with the news, and tell him about their proposed visit to Cape Town. Next she'd call Nina, and firm up some travel dates with her, then repeat the process with Jeremy. After that she'd go on the Internet to book flights and hotel rooms, before calling Walter back to tell him the itinerary. Somewhere amongst all of this she should also ring Jim and Sue, to let them know the outcome of the tests, and she would ask Nina to tell Janet and the girls. It didn't cross her mind to let David know, which in theory she could do via his daughters in America, and although she felt she should get in touch with Bobby she wasn't sure how to go about this. As far as she knew there hadn't been any regular contact between him and the rest of the family for years, so sitting down to write him a letter would certainly not be an easy thing to do.

Kate was puzzled and a little hurt by Janet's reaction, as reported back from Nina. She could only hope that once the truth was undeniable Janet would in some way come to terms with it. She had clearly misjudged the loyalty Janet felt towards her parents, although curiously Jim had viewed things in an entirely different light. From the start he and Sue had been totally supportive of Kate and she was profoundly grateful for that. She hoped that the good relationship she'd always had with Janet wouldn't be damaged by this, but if it was then she already knew she wouldn't hesitate to put Walter before her aunt.

The day dragged on. Kate thought again about writing to Bobby, but although she made several attempts at it she wasn't able to pitch the tone quite right.

The trouble, she thought, is that I have never really known Uncle Bobby. He has always just been the odd one, the uncle who sometimes turned up to family occasions but mostly didn't.

In the end she gave up and decided to go back to it when she was in a calmer frame of mind. It couldn't matter to him if he knew now or later – or bearing in mind what Bobby was like – if he knew at all.

By lunchtime the walls were closing in on her, and Kate grabbed her bag and went out for a walk round the village, where she smiled a huge, happy smile at pretty well everyone she met.

* * *

The taxi driver had instructions to head across the river to an address in Lambeth, before taking Rachel back to the nursery in Knightsbridge. As he said goodbye to her, Jason paid the cabbie the fare plus waiting time, and gave him a generous tip on top of that.

Rachel knew exactly where they were going. This wasn't the first time she'd been to the anonymous employment agency not far from Waterloo Station, with its racks of postcards in the window advertising jobs for care workers and cleaners. No matter what time of day she went there, the office was never open and she was obliged to ring the bell for the flat above. Once, while waiting in the street, she'd looked up and seen the frightened face of a young black woman peering down at her from behind the raised corner of a grubby net curtain. When Rachel caught her eye the girl dropped the curtain, becoming no more than a grainy image standing behind the windowpane. She'd wondered at the time if the girl would end up working for Jason in one of his many care homes scattered across the country.

Rachel had guessed long ago the reason why she was sent there, with a tightly packed jiffy bag and instructions to hand it to the man now answering the side door to her. Like the office, he was completely anonymous. She didn't know his name, and he would have been difficult to pick out in a crowd. He could have been mid-forties or he could have been much older, he had grey hair and glasses, and wore a grey suit that had seen better days over a dark pullover. There was absolutely nothing distinctive about the man. I could walk past him in the street, Rachel thought, and not even recognise him. Which she supposed was the point.

There was no need to say anything, since he was expecting her. She held out the package and he took it, nodded to her, and closed the door again. Not a word was exchanged.

Rachel got back in the waiting taxi, and the driver pulled away. Suddenly remembering the black girl, she turned to look out of the back window, but on that day there was nobody behind the net curtains in the room above the agency.

Months ago, when Jason had first asked her to take a package over to Lambeth, Rachel had asked him what it was all about.

'Just staffing arrangements,' he'd said. 'The government's crippling businesses in this country – you have to do what you can to ease the situation. The tax system doesn't work in anybody's favour, including the girls we employ.'

'But they're legal, aren't they?' she'd asked, straight out.

'They didn't come over in container lorries hidden under boxes of fruit, if that's what you mean. They want to work, we want to employ them. This just oils the wheels a bit, cuts through the bureaucracy.'

Rachel was no fool, and she realised what was going on. But love makes fools of even the most streetwise. Rachel was never that, and Jason knew it.

Now, heading back over Westminster Bridge, the growing realisation that she couldn't carry on doing this any longer suddenly jumped up and smacked her in the face. Getting out of it would be the problem, and right then Rachel didn't have the answer to that one, but she was sensible enough to know that there must be a way and someone else would find it if she couldn't.

The taxi dropped her back at the nursery gates, in plenty of time to collect her young charges. She could have rung the bell and gone in early, but instead she took her mobile phone from her bag, flipped it open, and punched in a number.

'Clare?... Yes it's me....Listen, can we meet up one evening? I know, I'm sorry... I need... I... oh Clare, I just need to talk to you.'

* * *

'Walter? It's Kate. The uncle test was positive, so it's official now!'

There was a silence from Walter, then Kate thought she heard a cough. Faintly, in the background there was the sound of the television. Then someone switched it off and there was no sound at all.

'Walter? Walter are you still there?'

'I'm still here Kate,' he said, huskily. 'I'm afraid I am just a bit emotional. It's wonderful news, I can't tell you how happy it has made me to hear this from you. Very, very happy.'

Kate smiled. She felt a bit emotional herself, but never expected him to be quite as choked as he obviously was. I suppose, she thought, if you don't know about your background then you don't know who you really are. This has obviously been a bigger journey for Walter than for me.

'I'm coming to see you,' she said, 'at the end of the month, and my cousins are coming with me.'

Walter was overwhelmed, and said so.

'All the way from England! I can't believe you would do this...'

'Well I am doing it! I'll call you back, probably tomorrow, when I've got more details,' she said. 'I'm so much looking forward to meeting you all,' Kate added.

* * *

Everything seemed to be working out just fine. Jim and Sue had taken the news well, and seemed almost as excited about it as she was. Kate had managed to speak to both Nina and Jeremy, and incredibly, all three of them were able to clear their diaries for the same dates. Booking flights was probably made easier by Kate insisting they travel business class, and that only left hotel reservations.

On her evenings spent touring Cape Town online, Kate had discovered the V&A Waterfront, and never one to settle for second best, this was where she started looking for accommodation. She soon discovered that late November in Cape Town was a popular time for tourists and was disappointed with her first two choices, but on the third attempt she made a booking at the Commodore Hotel.

They would have nine days in Cape Town – enough time on a first visit to get to know her new family, leaving plenty of time for the three of them to have some fun looking around too. Kate felt as excited as a teenager taking her first solo holiday without mum and dad. She would buy small gifts for them all, and since she didn't want to overdo this and embarrass anyone it was important to get it right. Nina would help, she thought. Nina was good at things like that. And what to pack? Kate spent the rest of the evening going through her wardrobe, with Ladysmith Black Mambaso as an accompaniment.

Meanwhile, as Kate swanned about her house, Nina was left with the task of telling her mother and daughters the good news. The girls, she knew, would be easy. Clare would just say 'cool' and Rachel would probably want to know how Kate & Walter had taken the news, but they'd both be supportive and interested. So Nina left the easy options till later. First, she called Janet, a much tougher nut to crack. In truth she was a bit peeved that Kate hadn't done it herself, but Kate was in a whirlwind of excitement and holiday plans, and that left no room for a delicate conversation with her aunt.

Predictably, Janet was not thrilled by the news that the DNA results brought.

'I find that very hard to believe, Nina,' she said. 'How accurate are these tests? Presumably Kate paid quite a bit to have them done – how do we know they don't just tell people what they want to hear?'

Nina sighed.

'Because they don't know what she wanted to hear, that's why. They're completely impartial; it's a scientific procedure Mum. I know you're not happy about this, but Walter's here to stay now and you'll just have to come to terms with that.' Nina was aware of the edge in her voice but couldn't stop it creeping in.

'Jim and Sue are perfectly fine with it. Why can't you just be pleased for Kate's sake?'

'Because Kate doesn't realise what she's stirring up.'

Nina was losing her patience, but there was one more hurdle to get over.

'Anyway, we're going to see them; me, Kate and Jeremy.'

'WHAT?' Janet's voice rose several decibels. 'Don't you listen to the news these days? A woman just got shot there, Nina, an innocent tourist on her honeymoon – murdered! And these are the sort of people you're dealing with – you must be mad, all of you!'

There was no talking to her in this mood, Nina realised.

'That's completely out of order Mum, and you know it. I'll talk to you about it some other time, if you can be reasonable,' she snapped, and put the phone down.

It took her half an hour and most of a bar of chocolate to calm down, pacing through the flat and finally settling down on the living room sofa. Nina had never known her mother take such a dogmatic view over anything before, and quite why this particular situation had got her so rattled she couldn't understand. It was a relief to speak next to Clare, the queen of cool.

'Well that's really wonderful for Kate,' Clare said. 'She must be thrilled.'

'She is completely bowled over by it,' said Nina, 'unlike your grandmother, who seems to hold the view that every South African is a murderer and rapist.'

'Yeah, well that'll be a generation thing, Mum. She needs time to get used to the idea, that's all.'

Nina hoped she was right but a feeling in her gut was telling her Janet's compliance would only be achieved at the end of a long war of attrition.

'I should phone Rachel now, just wanted to let you both know.'

'Actually Mum, Rachel's here, but... erm... we're just on the point of going out, so I'll pass the news on to her, shall I?'

* * *

It was the first time for many months that Clare had seen her sister. Since that day in Brighton, back in August, she'd phoned many times and tried to patch up the gaping hole in their relationship, but Rachel was having none of it. In the end Clare gave up, and an empty space opened up in her life, in the place which Rachel had occupied since the day she was born.

Her phone call, out of the blue, was both welcome and worrying. Rachel wanted to talk, and that could only mean one thing, or so Clare thought. She wasn't prepared for the one thing it really did mean.

'Rachel, this is people trafficking, not – what did he call it? – "staffing arrangements"? It's exploitation of vulnerable women and young girls.'

Rachel looked down at the pile of damp tissues in her lap. The story had come out of her a bit at a time, and Clare had been patient and solicitous. She'd hugged her, given her coffee, probed gently and listened without comment – but now she couldn't keep quiet any longer.

'I expect some of them do end up working in care homes,' Clare said, 'and maybe they're treated OK and get paid fairly. Maybe Jason is one of the better employers,' she added, throwing in a concession she didn't have much faith in for Rachel's sake. 'But most aren't that lucky. And you know what happens to a lot of these girls?'

'They end up in brothels or cannabis farms – yes, I know,' said Rachel, 'I've seen the programmes on TV too. I just never thought I'd find myself caught up in it.'

Clare's mind was running on overdrive. Rachel's involvement, even at such a low level, made her vulnerable. Simply ending her relationship with Jason wasn't the smartest way to deal with the problem – even supposing she'd do that, and Clare wasn't convinced she would. Refusing to run any more errands for him would indicate that she'd figured out exactly what he was up to, and that put her in an exposed position. Clare had no idea what Jason was like, or how much – if anything – he felt for Rachel. An anonymous note to his wife would push him into ending the relationship, which might work, although it would make it impossible for Rachel to stay in her job, given that the two families were such good friends. A tip-off to the police? That seemed like a dangerous move, and why wouldn't Jason implicate her as well if he was going down? If a twenty-pound police sledgehammer slammed through his front door early one morning it wouldn't take him long to come up with a short list of people who might have grassed on him, and Rachel's name would be at the top of it.

'You know what really did it for me?' Rachel said, cutting in on Clare's thoughts. 'It was thinking about the black girl I saw up at the window that day. It suddenly struck me that she could be one of Walter's daughters, and that was just too close to home.'

'We'll work it out, Rach,' said Clare, pulled back to her sitting room and her sister's anxious face. 'The answer's out there, we just need to find it.'

And then the phone had rung, and it was Nina. Clare looked across at Rachel, all puffy eyes and smeared mascara, and knew she couldn't let her talk to her mum in that state.

'We're just on the point of going out,' she lied, 'so I'll pass the news on to her, shall I?'

Clare put the phone down and wondered where this was going to end. She'd never lied to her mother in her life, until this thing with Rachel had come up. Now she seemed to be doing it more and more, and at the very time when she could have used her mother's common sense and advice instead of trying to deal with the situation on her own. I am completely out of my depth with this, she thought.

'The DNA tests are back,' she told Rachel, 'and the results were positive. Walter is officially related to us.'

Rachel nodded.

'What does that make him... second cousin to us?'

'Something like that,' said Clare.

'Well I just hope his girls are settled in decent jobs,' she said.

CHAPTER 9

NOVEMBER 2010: OCEAN VIEW

With less than a week to go before his English relations arrived in Cape Town, Walter was starting to feel nervous about the prospect of getting the two families together. He knew instinctively that he and Kate would get along just fine, and her cousins sounded like nice, decent people. He knew that the children would be shy at first, overwhelmed with the reality of meeting their new aunt, and then their natural curiosity and friendliness would take over. Sele might need reining in if he got over-excited but that was inevitable when you had an exuberant puppy dog for a son, and Walter would rather have his children behaving naturally and being themselves than let Kate see a false version of them.

But there was also Annie to consider, and Walter was concerned about her.

From the moment the initial arrangements were made, she'd clammed up on him. She refused to discuss any aspect of the visit, and used any means she could to avoid commenting on anything the children had to say about it. Elana had even asked Walter one evening why her mother was behaving so strangely.

'She's a little nervous about meeting your aunt,' he said. 'She's worried that she won't find the right things to say.'

He could see that Elana wasn't convinced by this, and in the end he realised there was nothing else for it.

He would have to confront Annie, and try to talk her round.

The opportunity came one evening when all the children were out somewhere. Annie had cleared the table and washed up the dishes and Walter was reading the Cape Argus. As she came back into the living room, he put the paper down.

'Annie, I think we need to talk about Kate's visit,' he said.

Annie stood facing him, unsmiling, eyebrows raised. Behind her, taped to the door of the wall unit were the pictures Kate had sent over; one of her on her own and one of the three cousins. Nina had been careful to avoid too much background, knowing instinctively that every square inch of the pictures would be examined and every detail commented upon. Kate had money and her beautiful home reflected this, and Nina was very aware that they mustn't come over as the rich relations dropping in for a charity visit. And for someone who never took portraits she'd made a good job of these two, getting the mood just right.

'What is there to talk about?' Annie said, defiantly. 'I don't have anything to say on the subject.'

'It's very important to me that this visit goes well Annie, you know that, and I need your help. Why are you so set against it?'

'You know why. I don't want this woman's money. We've always managed everything ourselves, and we will again now.'

'This woman,' said Walter, a little louder, 'is my sister. Her family are my family – our family. There has been no mention of money, not from her and definitely not from me, so why are you so concerned?'

Annie turned to walk into the bedroom, and Walter stood up.

'I've never before asked you to do anything for me,' he said, raising his voice, 'but I'm asking you for something now – no, I'm telling you. You behave correctly with Kate, and you smile and be friendly with them all while they're here. I don't think that's too much to expect. Annie, do you hear me?'

But Annie's response was simply to close the bedroom door. Walter slumped back into his chair, unable to figure out where to go from there. A few minutes later the bedroom door opened again, and Annie came back and faced Walter.

'You don't have to worry,' she said, 'I know my manners. But I will not be treated like a charity, and I will not stand by and watch you throwing your pride away trying to get money out of her.'

'I admit that was my intention at the start,' he said, 'but now I just want to meet my family so I can find out who I am and where I come from. You've always known that, and I never have, and I don't have the words to tell you how important this is to me. That's all.'

Annie softened. She and Walter had never had a real row about anything. There were people living in their block who argued all the time, sometimes windows got smashed and the missiles they'd used would end up on the ground outside surrounded by broken glass. In certain apartments voices raised in anger were common, minor injuries not unusual. But the Maketa household was quiet and sober and the family lived in harmony. Both Walter and Annie were shaken by the unaccustomed dissent between them.

'I will do as you say,' Annie said, finally. 'But they are not my family, and I cannot pretend we're friends if we're not.'

'Please try for my sake, and for the children – they are really excited about meeting their aunt and I don't want to spoil it for them. And you never know, you might actually like them, Annie.'

'And if she offers you money, then what will you do?'

'Then you and I will talk about it. But if her intention is good it would be impolite to refuse, especially where the children are concerned.'

'I see.' Annie's mouth tightened again but she made no other comment, and Walter picked the paper up and said no more, thinking he might be pushing his luck to go any further. But although he turned the pages and made a show of finding things of interest, he wasn't actually reading a word.

* * *

Elana got up the following morning, then went straight back to bed. The only one in her family to be plagued by migraine headaches, she had a bad one that day and couldn't go to work. It was impossible to figure out why they came when they did; she thought about the food she'd eaten the previous day, but could find nothing that might have triggered it. When she was at school Elana had found exams very stressful, and this was often blamed for an attack, but she wasn't under any stress now and there was no apparent reason why the migraines continued. And yet every so often another one reared up, and Elana was forced to spend the day in bed, with the curtains pulled tightly closed.

And so on that morning Mandisa went off to catch the workers' taxi alone, promising that she would stop off at the shoe shop where Elana worked and explain to her manager why she was absent from work.

Squashed into a clapped-out VW minivan with another twelve passengers wasn't the best start to the day, but it was the cheapest and most convenient way of getting to work. The air inside the Volksie bus smelt of exhaust fumes, sweat and stale cigarettes, and Mandisa tried not to breathe too much of it in before she was able to slide open the little window next to her. She knew everyone on the bus, many of them she'd been at school with including Uyanda, the girl who'd caught her reading her Southern England book that day at the mall.

'Where's your sister?' she asked Mandisa, turning around from the front seats to shout her enquiry back over the noise of the engine.

'Sick, she gets migraine headaches.'

'Too bad. So she won't be working at all today?'

'No, she has to stay in bed.'

As everyone piled off the bus at the shopping mall, Mandisa passed Uyanda, who had her cellphone clamped to her ear. She looked up and saw Mandisa.

'You tell Elana I'm sorry for her headache, OK?'

Mandisa nodded and followed the rest of the passengers as they made their way across the empty car park in front of the mall. Other workers joined them, as more Volksies arrived and disgorged their passengers, and the procession straggled their way towards another day's work.

Mandisa really liked her job. She worked in a store selling things for the home – nice, decorative things of the sort that her mother wouldn't buy even if she had the money. But Mandisa loved them. Cushions, candles and bedlinen in beautiful jewel-like colours sat on the shelves alongside china, glasses and table linen intended for sophisticated dinner parties. These were things destined for a world that Mandisa could only imagine, but she enjoyed setting out the table and bed displays and she was popular with customers because she was enthusiastic and helpful. When the new season's range arrived from the store's central warehouse it was always Mandisa who volunteered to unpack everything, because she couldn't wait to see the latest colours and designs.

And now that Kate Hatchman had appeared on her horizon, the alternative world which Mandisa sold to her customers six days a week had suddenly moved a lot closer to her own reality. She liked to think that Kate would come into her store while she was on holiday and buy something to take back to Surrey, so that she could tell people her aunt had this or that in her own house in England. Mandisa knew that would be a unique selling point where she worked. She imagined Kate saying to her friends, 'I bought this in the store where my niece works. They had some lovely things there – if only I could have brought more home with me.'

On late night shopping days the girls seldom got home before half past seven. Sometimes it was later, if they were asked to stay for stocktaking, or on a day when the security and evacuation procedures were tested. But on this occasion Mandisa was in luck; traffic was lighter than usual and the Volksie dropped them off at Ocean View before seven o'clock.

She had just started down the road towards home when a familiar figure stepped out from an alleyway, and blocked her path.

'Hey, Mandisa, on your own today?'

Bheki Msonga was a nice looking boy and in different circumstances she might even have fallen for him. But his reputation kept most girls away and it certainly made him unattractive to Mandisa, whose sights were set a good deal higher.

She stopped in her tracks, unsure of how to get past him.

'Sorry to hear about your sister,' he said.

Then she knew. Uyanda, with her cellphone and her spiteful tongue, had told him Elana wasn't with her that day.

She stepped into the road to walk past him, but he moved out to block her again.

'Please let me pass,' she said. 'I need to get home.'

Bheki smiled and held out his hand. 'A few minutes won't matter. We could take a walk.'

He reached out and took her arm, and when she tried to shake him off she only succeeded in making him grip her tighter. She looked around, but the other passengers on the Volksie bus had all disappeared and the street was empty.

'No harm in walkin', is there? I thought we could be friends, you know, real close? But you gotta do better than this, girl.'

'Let me *go*!' she cried, twisting her arm, but that only made it hurt and Bheki held on even harder.

'Why you making this so difficult? Hey? Loosen up baby.'

Tugging on her arm as she struggled to hold back, Bheki walked Mandisa up an alleyway until they reached the back of a shop, where there was a doorway. Turning her round till her back was up against the corrugated iron of the padlocked door, he manoeuvred till he'd squashed her flat against it.

'Don't fight me, Mandisa, you know I like you,' he said, his face inches from hers, 'and I really don't want to hurt you.'

Mandisa was terrified. She tried to shout, but then he pushed his mouth hard onto hers, banging her head back onto the doorway. The clank of corrugated iron echoed around them, but the shop was closed and nobody was there to hear it. She struggled to move aside, but Bheki was too strong for her and he had her pinned back. He tasted of liquor and cigarettes, and it made her want to throw up. Forcing his tongue into her mouth, he slid a hand down onto her breast and pressed it flat against her. She struggled enough to get her arms free and pushed against him with both hands as hard as she could. His response was to grab her hair and pull on it.

'Don't make me mad at you,' he said, 'just be nice,' and before she could shout out his mouth was on hers again. That was when she bit into his lip, and he yelped out in pain.

Holding her against the door with the weight of his body, he grabbed both arms, pulled them up above her head then caught her wrists in one hand and gripped them tight. Powerless now to do anything, Mandisa thought she might faint. She was aware of his free hand pushing under her skirt and up her leg. She felt him tug at her knickers and push his chest harder against her, and she knew she'd done everything she could and now it was all over.

Then there was a voice, sounding so close it almost seemed to be coming from inside her head.

'Well, well. Bheki Msonga.'

Bheki froze. Slowly, he lifted his head. Slowly, he released his grip on Mandisa's wrists. And then he looked over his shoulder.

Mandisa opened her eyes. Standing behind Bheki was a man she'd never seen before, with his hands deep in the pockets of his denim jacket, and a smile on his face. Mandisa turned her head and looked beyond him, to where a long silver car was parked across the end of the alleyway. The light was just starting to fade, but even though she couldn't see them clearly it was apparent that two faces were peering out from the open car windows, looking towards them.

'Time we talked, Bheki,' the man said.

He didn't look threatening, but it was obvious that they weren't friends. Bheki moved back from Mandisa, turned to the newcomer, and gave a short laugh.

'Your timing's not good, man,' he said, wiping a hand across his mouth where Mandisa had succeeded in making his lip bleed.

The stranger glanced at Mandisa, who stood rooted to the spot, her mouth open gulping in air and her eyes wide with fear.

'You better go, girl,' he said, with a flick of his head.

And she did. She ran, stumbled as she picked up her bag where she'd dropped it, and ran again, out of the alley and along the street towards home without looking back, until she was breathless and had a stitch in her side.

Stopping to get her breath back, she realised she couldn't walk into the apartment like that. Her clothes needed straightening, her hair was all over the place and she knew she would look as frightened as she felt. She would certainly be questioned, and if she told them what had happened there would be all sorts of consequences. Her father would march her off to the police, Bheki would deny everything, and it would be her word against his. There were no witnesses unless you counted the man who'd intervened and from the look of him he was hardly likely to come forward. And then, when it all died down, she would still have to walk around Ocean View and she'd be forever looking over her shoulder. Better by far to say nothing to anybody.

Mandisa looked around, saw the Divine Ministries Church, and headed towards it. She'd never been there before, but at that moment it didn't matter – the door opened as she pushed at it and thankfully she was alone inside.

Mandisa's wrists hurt and her mouth tasted foul. She knew she'd want to have a bath as soon as she could and scrub all traces of Bheki away. In the church she was at least able to tidy her clothes, and brush her hair. Her hands were trembling but she managed to put some lipstick on. Then she sat for many minutes waiting for her breathing to slow down.

She would say there was a security alarm drill at the mall, and that's why she was late home. She checked her watch and was surprised to see how little time had elapsed since she'd left the safety of the Volksie and the other passengers. When she felt calm enough to face them at home, she slipped quietly from the church, looked about her in case Bheki was around, then hurried the short distance home.

Mandisa opened the door on a silent apartment. There was no sign of her parents or Sele, and in the bedroom she shared with Elana the curtains were still drawn closed. Her sister's weary voice floated softly out of her bed.

'Hi Mandisa.'

'Hi Elana. How're you feeling?'

She sat on the edge of the bed and leaned across. Elana looked up at her from under the bedclothes.

'OK. Don't put the light on though.'

'Where is everyone?'

'Dad and Mama went to see Grandmama. Don't know where Sele is, just out. What time is it?'

'Nearly eight.'

'Oh, you're late. What was it tonight? Fire drill?'

Mandisa didn't reply.

'Is something wrong Mandi?'

'Listen Elana, if I tell you, you must swear to keep it to yourself because if anyone hears what happened tonight, things will get very bad for me.'

Elana propped herself up on her elbows and whispered a single word.

'Bheki?'

* * *

Later, safe and warm in her own bed, Mandisa battled with the impossible notion of trying to get to sleep. Every time she closed her eyes she saw Bheki's face up close, his eyes blazing with something she didn't recognise and his mouth set in a hard smile. Every time she turned over she felt the bruises that were coming out on her wrists.

Once, in the darkness of their room, Elana called across to her softly.

'Mandi, it won't happen again. He wouldn't risk it a second time.'

'He might if I were on my own. We must never be out alone now, either of us. If we aren't together then we must find someone else to walk with. Do you understand?'

'I won't leave you. It'll be OK.'

But in spite of her sister's assurances, Mandisa lay awake most of the night. At some time, as the blackness outside their window was starting to turn to grey, she drifted off into the uneasy sleep of exhaustion and her dreams took her away from Ocean View and into the imagined landscape of Surrey, and safety.

CHAPTER 10

NOVEMBER 2010: CAPE TOWN

Kate was wide awake as their plane started its descent into Cape Town. All three of them had slept reasonably well in the comfort of business class, thrown back their duvets, had breakfast and walked about, then settled down again to wait out the last hour till they landed. Jeremy was taking the opportunity of a last little snooze, Nina was reading her book and yawning, but Kate was leaning towards the window and staring out, waiting for her first glimpse of land, and Africa.

Finally the seat belt lights lit up and before long she was rewarded by a view of the shoreline, turquoise sea and lines of white foamy wavelets, as the plane made its approach to Cape Town from the south, flying in over the beaches of False Bay. Soon details started to appear on the landscape; houses and swimming pools, cars and trucks – then finally the wheels touched down and the runway was whizzing past the windows. More than eleven hours after taking off from Heathrow, they landed.

'I can't believe we're really here!' Kate said as the plane taxied past the airport buildings. No stranger to foreign travel, she'd been abroad a lot – mostly for business because holidays hadn't featured much on her horizon – and yet no trip had ever made her feel quite like this. Her excitement was infectious, and for all three of them it started to feel like a real adventure.

When they got outside the terminal buildings the African sun was a real treat after the cold and grey weather they'd left behind. Nina had been the best organised, with sunglasses and sandals at the ready in her cabin bag, and layers that she could peel off and stuff straight into her case. Jeremy and Kate, regretting now that they hadn't followed Nina's advice, could only jettison their jackets and were stuck in the remainder of their UK winter outfits for the journey to the Waterfront.

By the time they reached their hire car Nina had her camera round her neck, ready for action. At the sound of her voice, Jeremy and Kate looked up from loading the bags into the boot, and straight into her lens.

Click. The first photo.

'Hope that's not the most interesting thing you find to photograph while we're here,' Jeremy called to her, but it wouldn't be long before Nina found plenty more to interest her and the camera shutter started clicking in earnest.

Back in England she'd had some ideas about possible magazine articles, and suggested them to a friendly editor, who expressed an interest in looking at what she came up with. Nina was well aware of the many contrasts on the Cape. Wealth versus poverty was naturally a part of that but everything she'd read about the Mother City confirmed it as the meeting place of Africa and Europe, and Nina was eager to explore this strangely successful marriage of diverse cultures.

She loaded her luggage last while Jeremy started figuring out where the indicators and air-con were and Kate spread the map out on her lap.

'Looks like I'm in the back then?'

They were both too busy working out how to get to the Waterfront to take her up on this, so she clicked herself in, wound down the window, and waited – camera on stand-by – for something interesting en route. Disappointingly, according to Kate, it seemed that the journey would be all motorway. Nina sighed, and put the lens cap back on.

But driving away from the airport they passed the extreme perimeter of a shanty town, looking at first glance like an enormous rubbish tip until the eye started to make sense of it. Mile upon mile of shacks stretched away from the motorway. Corrugated roofs and broken down wooden structures, some leaning dangerously over to one side, were – unlikely as it seemed – home to somebody. Strung out between the shacks were lines of washing, bright patches of colour that broke up the background texture. Viewed from the motorway there was no discernible organisation, though it was reasonable to assume that roads of some kind existed through the jumble of salvaged wreckage that made up the township.

'You're sure Walter doesn't live somewhere like this?' Jeremy asked Kate.

'No, they've got an apartment. I don't suppose it's luxurious, but I get the impression it's OK. I can't believe people exist in these corrugated huts – surely they must have access to water or electricity supplies, the basic essentials?'

'There are wires stretched across, I suppose that's the electricity supply,' said Nina, peering beyond the perimeter fence. 'And standpipes, presumably.'

A graffiti covered wall took the place of the perimeter fence alongside the road, and shacks gave way to low-grade single-storey housing, until the landscape gradually became industrial units and factories. Billboards lined the motorway, advertising companies and products unknown to them, things which they supposed the shack dwellers would never have any use for. The shanty town lingered in their minds long after they'd driven past.

'This trip is obviously going to be an eye-opener in a lot of ways,' Kate replied.

For all of them that glimpse of the Cape Flats had been a sobering sight, a shocking confirmation of the huge gulf between rich and poor in the country. For Kate, it also signalled the gulf between her and Walter. She was sure his living conditions were nothing like the shacks they had just passed, but there was no getting away from the fact that their lives were poles apart in many different ways.

I can't right the social injustices that led to that awful place, she thought, but I can help one family here, my family. That much I can do.

Ahead of them a fluffy white cloud had settled along the top of Table Mountain, thinning in places to a gauzy covering. Just hours away from meeting her brother for the first time, Kate gazed at the mountain and realised how close they now were.

'Can't believe this is all happening,' she said quietly.

With a junction coming up Jeremy brought her attention back to the map.

'Directions, Kate?'

'Oh... M5 heading north,' she said. 'Look, it's signposted – V&A Waterfront. It's OK. We're fine.'

* * *

On his break at the garage, Walter checked his watch for the umpteenth time that morning as one of the boys handed him a mug of rooibos tea.

'You got a train to catch, man?'

Walter smiled.

'My sister just arrived here for a visit. She should be on her way from the airport right now,' he added, tapping his watch.

'She staying with you?' another mechanic asked him.

'We don't have the room,' Walter replied. 'She's going to a hotel and I'll be seeing her tomorrow.'

'Didn't know you had a sister.'

Neither did I, Walter thought, but now I do, and not only a sister but cousins, aunts and uncles too. In fact, a whole new family.

* * *

The hotel was plush. Kate and Nina had balconies overlooking the Waterfront and Table Mountain. Jeremy, across the corridor, looked out towards the new Greenpoint Stadium and the sea beyond. On a sparkling morning, with a turquoise ocean and brilliant blue sky, Cape Town was showing them its best and brightest face.

'Kate, this is wonderful! I hate to think how much it's costing you.' Nina said, on a visit from her own room next door. Kate was still unpacking, hanging clothes in the wardrobe and stowing away bags and shoes.

'I don't *want* you to think about it, it's my treat, all of it. I couldn't have done this without you two,' she said. 'And anyway, who else would I want to share it with? It will just be lovely to have both halves of my family together.'

I hope it lives up to your expectations, Nina thought. Please don't let Walter be a disappointment, she added silently.

Kate had arranged to meet Walter's family the following day, knowing that on a Sunday none of them would have to arrange to take time off work. She had figured out that a neutral meeting place would be best for a first meeting, and this was where all those evenings spent researching the area paid off.

'The Waterfront seems like a good place to meet – so we'll see you at the Nelson Mandela Gateway, around eleven in the morning,' she'd said on their last phone call before leaving England. 'Is that OK?'

Walter scribbled this on a piece of paper, with the telephone receiver tucked under his chin, although he really didn't need a reminder of the arrangement. It wasn't something he was likely to forget. He didn't tell Kate that he had no idea how to find the Nelson Mandela Gateway.

Sele was the only one of the family who'd ever been to the V&A Waterfront. He went once on a school trip, although he couldn't remember much about it and had no idea where or what the Nelson Mandela Gateway was.

'Sounds like the entrance,' he said, uncertainly.

None of the others had ever considered going there. Built as an unashamed tourist attraction, the V&A was thought to have nothing to offer most of the locals, and it was generally assumed that the shops were exclusive and the restaurants expensive. But since Walter didn't have a better alternative to offer Kate, the arrangement stood as planned.

The twins went along the mall to the book shop, and talked to an assistant there that they knew. Taking a book down from the shelf, she flicked through it and found exactly what they were looking for.

'Here,' she said pointing at a photo, 'this is it.'

The girls peered closer. The picture showed a building with 'Nelson Mandela Gateway' across the top, and at the front steps running across the width of the building. Elana skimmed through the text.

'The boats to Robben Island go from there,' she said.

'So she means to meet us on the steps, or in the building?' Mandisa wondered aloud.

'On the steps I suppose,' said Elana. 'Two families standing around just waiting – I guess we'll know each other,' she added. 'They don't have our photos but we should be able to recognise them.'

The information went back to Ocean View. Walter consulted his road map, although he'd driven past signs for the V&A Waterfront hundreds of times before. Everyone except Sele thought about what they would wear – privately or in consultation. They were as ready as they'd ever be – and nervous as hell.

***

With the rest of the day to themselves, Kate, Nina and Jeremy explored the Waterfront. They listened to street musicians, bought souvenirs and postcards and ate lunch in the sun, they found the Nelson Mandela Gateway and while they were there they booked a trip to Robben Island for later in the week. Nina took the first of hundreds of photos.

'Once we've met them maybe we could all go over there,' Kate said, indicating a restaurant close by. 'They look as if they could handle a group of eight.'

As the time got closer, so Kate became more nervous. Not normally a person to be fazed by meeting anyone new (she'd done it in her job a million times) she suddenly felt that she wouldn't be able to think of anything to say to Walter. It was all very well on the phone – if it got sticky the call could be ended at any time for any reason – 'Sorry Walter, someone at my front door, got to go' – but there'd be no walking away from the real thing. What if they all dried up after ten minutes? Kate was in Cape Town for nine days, and would have to see Walter more than once in that time, how would she manage that if they really, truly, had nothing more to say to each other?

Don't be silly, she told herself. He'll want to talk about his mother plus there's the rest of the family in England, that'll take some time, and of course he'll want to know about Dad. Kate had brought a photo album over for Walter, which Nina had put together for her. In addition to pictures of all the family, it also contained a family tree, which Kate had had drawn up by a professional and which included Walter, Annie and the children. She had gifts for everyone. This had been easy for the girls (perfume) and for Sele (Manchester United football shirt) but had caused a few headaches over Annie. Well aware that she must not overdo this, particularly with Annie, whose apparent hostility she was already concerned about, it had taken much discussion with Nina before she came up with a solution. Annie's gift of luxury hand treatment products looked modest, but was actually quite an expensive item in the company's range and Kate hoped it was something that she would find acceptable and useful.

She also had a special gift for Walter, in addition to the photo album, something she hadn't mentioned to either Nina or Jeremy. If things didn't go so well, she told herself, then she wouldn't give it to him and nobody would be any the wiser.

As they wandered around, Jeremy spotted a sign advertising "Jazz 8 Nites a Week", and headed off in the direction of the Green Dolphin restaurant. He found Kate and Nina twenty minutes later in a nearby shop.

'I booked us in for dinner tomorrow evening,' he said. 'Great place, there might even be a chance to sit in one night.'

'Did you book just us in – what about Walter and Co?' asked Nina.

'I don't imagine they'll stay around into the evening,' Kate replied, without really knowing why she said it.

'I thought of that,' said Jeremy, 'and if they do then we can change the reservation. They seemed pretty relaxed in there.'

He mentioned in passing that the pianist and singer were already there, working through some new arrangements. He failed to mention that he'd spoken to them both and that the singer was totally gorgeous.

In the way of musicians all over the world, communication between the two pianists had been instant and relaxed. In a matter of moments they were on first name terms and sharing a joke. Peter, an elderly man whom Jeremy rightly guessed to be of Cape Coloured origin had a strangely baffling BBC accent and was delighted to meet a fellow pianist from the UK, his adopted country.

'I lived there for many years, when I was younger,' he explained. 'Things were tough here and my parents sent me to England to live with some distant relatives. So I went to London when I was six years old, and stayed until I'd completed my musical education. After that I travelled around a bit and settled in Paris. I only came back to Cape Town after democracy.'

'Then you might know some of the people I've played with,' Jeremy said, and they bounced a few names backwards and forwards, finding that they did indeed have some contacts in common.

'And I played for Cleo Laine once in Paris,' said Peter. 'She was a fabulous singer to work with. But you know, we have our own jazz royalty in Cape Town too, and this is one of them,' he continued, as they were joined on stage by a tall black girl in jeans and a skimpy white shirt. She laughed a throaty laugh when she heard what Peter was saying, and then turned the spotlight of her smile onto Jeremy.

'This is Lebo, and she's just about the best jazz singer on the Cape, if not the whole country.'

Late thirties, Jeremy guessed, model-girl looks, with a stunning figure and long, black hair that shone like ebony – what wasn't to like? Jeremy shook Lebo's hand and held onto it just a little longer than was strictly necessary. She didn't seem to mind. In fact, as he reluctantly let go and her fingertips brushed across his palm there was a hint of something in her eyes that made him think his interest might not be entirely misplaced. A small shiver raced up his back.

The trip was suddenly looking a whole lot more interesting to Jeremy.

* * *

Back at the hotel Nina put a quick call through to Clare, just to make sure everything was OK back in England.

'I spoke to Grandma yesterday – she's fine,' Clare reassured her mother. 'She's a bit pissed off with you being in South Africa though – what's her problem?'

'I don't really know,' said Nina. 'This whole thing with Walter has pissed her off. She thinks Kate should let sleeping dogs lie.'

'Bit too late for that, the dogs are wide awake and barking now,' Clare said. 'Anyway, how's it going with Walter?'

'We haven't met him yet, tomorrow's the big day. Kate's getting jumpy about it but I'm sure it'll be fine.'

'Yeah, well good luck with that.'

'How's Rachel?'

'Oh, yeah, she's fine. I'll tell her you rang, no need for you to make two calls.'

The last thing Clare wanted at that moment was for her mother to speak to her sister. Since confiding in her, a dam seemed to have burst inside Rachel, and now it seemed that every time she spoke to Clare she was weepy. In the meantime, as they tried to work something out, she was still seeing Jason and trying to behave as if nothing had happened, although recently she'd invented some excuses not to see him. Clare knew this was a strain on her, but they hadn't quite got their heads around the problem yet, or how to deal with it.

Nina turned to look out of her open window at the glorious sunset, the sky streaked pink, orange and copper over the Waterfront. It hardly seemed credible that she was there, whilst her daughters were back in dreary November London.

'I wish you were here too,' Nina said to Clare. 'You'd love it. It's like... well, I know I'm in a foreign country of course, but there's so much around that makes me feel at home here. And there's no problem with the language, of course. This hotel is beautiful and the Waterfront is fantastic, you should see the shops!'

'It all sounds wonderful, I'm glad you're enjoying it Mum, you could do with a break. Rachel and I looked at travel sites on the internet the other evening and we thought Cape Town seemed like a pretty good place to be. Maybe I'll come with you next time – maybe we'll both come.'

'If there is a next time – I'll update you on that after tomorrow,' Nina said.

They had an early dinner at a seafood restaurant on the Waterfront, then on Jeremy's suggestion looked into the Green Dolphin for a drink. The break was just coming up and this gave him the chance to renew his acquaintance with the musicians and Lebo.

'Maybe you'd like to sit in on a couple of numbers?' Peter suggested.

'Yeah, that'd be great, if nobody minds,' Jeremy said.

'Well, we're about ready to go back on,' Peter added, looking at his watch. 'I'll introduce you... what do you want to play?'

Jeremy suggested something he was pretty sure they'd all know well and then once they'd got onstage there was a bit of a pause as they sorted out the logistics. Suddenly there was a gale of laughter from the musicians at something Jeremy had said.

'OK, man,' laughed the drummer, and then they were up and running.

And so although it hadn't been planned or rehearsed Jeremy was able to play a couple of numbers, winning the approval of both the audience and the band.

'I had no idea he was that good!' Kate said, feeling a little like a proud parent at the school nativity play. 'Just goes to show how long it is since I heard him play.'

Nina smiled. 'Oh, yes, he's certainly good. And so is that girl,' she added, indicating Lebo, who had poured herself into a skinny black dress, put dozens of thin gold bangles up each arm and balanced her shapely legs on a pair of killer heels.

Peter resumed his place at the piano, and there was some banter between him, Lebo and Jeremy before the session continued, which the punters at the front seemed to enjoy. Perched on a bar stool, and starting to feel really tired from the flight, Nina leaned rather precariously towards Kate.

'Is it my imagination,' she said, 'or does it look to you as if our Jem is making a play for the singer?'

'Well that's just typical of him,' Kate laughed. 'How smart is that, starting a relationship with a girl who lives several thousand miles away!'

'Talk about long distance lovers – it'll be the most expensive affair he's ever had,' said Nina. 'But it's almost a year since that Georgina moved out and I'm not aware of anyone serious since then.'

Jeremy re-joined them at the bar, and was forced to endure a grilling from both cousins, which he stood up to pretty robustly until he managed to steer the focus away from himself and back onto Walter's family.

'Who'd have thought any of this might happen a few short months ago?' Kate said. 'I didn't know anything much about South Africa – certainly hadn't imagined myself coming here, unless it was for business or on a safari holiday. It still doesn't seem quite real to me.'

They left Jeremy in the Green Dolphin and walked slowly back to the hotel. The evening was warm and still; the Waterfront in her evening dress of fairy lights with music drifting out of every restaurant.

'How do you feel about tomorrow, Kate? Nervous?'

Kate nodded. 'A bit,' she said, 'but excited too. God, if only Dad knew we were going to meet.'

'Do you think he'd approve?'

Kate hesitated for a moment.

'I've been thinking about this, and yes, I think he would approve,' she said. 'It seems that he really loved Grace, but let's face it, even if he hadn't already been married to Mum, it could never have worked. A white man and a black woman in 1950's South Africa – they were much too far ahead of their time.'

Nina slipped her arm through Kate's.

'But it's a different place now, and you and Walter can make it work for them.'

'I hope so, Nina. I really hope so.'

* * *

Walter's family were on the road long before they needed to be, because he was so worried about being late. He hadn't slept much the night before, and as a consequence, neither had Annie. After they'd both lain awake for some time, having tossed and turned most of the night, they got up early and sat drinking tea in the living room as the sun rose.

'This is a very big day for me,' Walter said, sipping from his mug of rooibos, 'and for Kate too.'

'I know it,' Annie replied, her hands cupped around her mug. She looked across to the photos of Kate and her cousins. 'But your worlds are so very different, I don't want you to be disappointed if this doesn't work out,' she said.

'We share the same father, that has to count for something, doesn't it?'

Annie shrugged. 'I don't know. Maybe the lives you've had are more important than the father you shared.'

At that moment Elana came into the living room.

'I couldn't sleep either,' she said smiling broadly, her face shiny and her hair tousled. 'I'm too excited to stay in bed.'

She crossed to the front window and opened it wide, letting the morning air into the apartment, and breathing deeply. Somewhere outside, a bird was singing.

'This will be a day we'll always remember,' Elana said, and looked back over her shoulder to her parents, 'won't it?'

By ten-thirty Walter had his family assembled on the steps of the Nelson Mandela Gateway. After walking through one of the malls to get there, the girls were wide-eyed and animated, comparing the V&A shopping experience with their own small-town mall. Sele, deprived of his music and headset for the day, looked across at the boats in the harbour with his hands sunk deep into the pockets of his jeans, and kicked languidly at the edge of the step.

'We got here too early,' Annie said.

'Better than being late,' said Walter, nervous and uncomfortable in a collar and tie which was already making him feel hot. He ran a finger around the neck of his shirt for the umpteenth time.

'We could have a walk around and come back a bit later,' Annie suggested. 'The children would enjoy it,' she added, leaving it open to discussion whether she would personally find this an enjoyable diversion.

Walter looked at his watch again. Twenty-five minutes to go.

'OK,' he said, 'but let's be back here in ten minutes, in case they're early.'

Annie sighed heavily, called to Sele and the twins, and they filed off the steps and towards the swing bridge that crossed the harbour.

* * *

Kate struggled to eat anything for breakfast, but she drank three cups of strong coffee, until she felt the caffeine hit her. Jeremy, on the other hand, was impossibly cheery as he worked his way through a massive cooked breakfast.

'Are you always like this first thing in the morning?' Kate asked him.

Jeremy just laughed and kept his attention on his eggs and bacon.

'What time did you get to bed?' asked Nina, realising as soon as she said it that she sounded like his mum.

'Oh... one-ish I suppose.' He buttered more toast and smiled across the table at her. 'Are you checking up on me, dear cousin?' he asked.

'I just have your welfare at heart, Jem. Burning the candle at both ends...' she said, leaving the sentence trailing off into mid air.

'Is a lot of fun,' Jeremy finished. 'You should try it sometime. Just ask if you need any tips.'

'Hmm. I should imagine advice of that nature from you could land me in a lot of trouble,' Nina replied.

Kate, unused to their banter early in the morning, stepped in between them with a grown-up observation.

'I couldn't get to sleep for ages,' she said. 'Too excited I suppose.'

'Yeah, me too,' said Jeremy, which earned him a slap on the arm from Nina.

'These last few hours really seem to be dragging,' said Kate, oblivious. 'I just want it to happen now.'

'It will soon, don't worry,' Nina said. 'Almost there, Kate.'

The swing bridge was open when they got down to the Waterfront, and there was a frustrating wait of several minutes till the incoming boat had cleared it and they were able to cross. There were plenty of people wandering about, and some Zulu dancers had attracted a crowd in front of the steps at the Nelson Mandela Gateway. A family with three small children stopped immediately in front of them, the children holding onto their parents' hands, mesmerised by the dancing and drumming. Jeremy turned to Nina.

'I'd quite like to stay here and watch this,' he said quietly.

'Me too, but we can't. Let's hope they'll be here another day. I'm envying those guys up at the front with their cameras.'

Just ahead of them, Kate was on red alert, scanning the crowds for a familiar face. All of a sudden she spotted Walter, and stopped dead in her tracks.

'That's him,' she said quietly.

'Then go,' said Nina. 'We're right behind you.'

Walter, also searching the faces milling around, looked across and suddenly saw Kate heading his way.

'That's her,' he said to Annie.

He hurried down the steps to meet her coming up, and for a moment they stood facing each other and smiling and neither knew what to do or say next.

'Kate,' he said softly. 'Kate.'

And then Walter opened his arms wide, and Kate walked into them.

CHAPTER 11

NOVEMBER 2010: LONDON AND CAPE TOWN

Before they went out for the evening Nina rang Clare.

'What's happened to Rachel's phone?' she asked. 'I tried her twice this afternoon and couldn't get through.'

'Oh... well it was OK earlier today when I rang her. She must have had it switched off for some reason.'

Clare knew that Rachel had been with Jason that afternoon, in fact she was on the point of calling her herself to find out if she was all right.

'Maybe she was in the cinema,' she added.

'What, all afternoon? I wouldn't have thought so,' said Nina, and on her end of the call Clare grimaced as she realised how stupid that must have sounded. There was a delay on the line this time, which was disconcerting and didn't encourage normal conversation since there was no natural flow. Clare decided the only thing was to move on swiftly.

'So, how did it go with Walter and his family?' she asked.

'It was emotional,' Nina said, 'very emotional for Kate and Walter.'

'Kate? You don't mean tears, surely?' Clare asked incredulously.

'Oh yes I do. We're seeing a different Kate these days,' said Nina. 'Softer. You know, this has done her good – she's a changed woman.'

There had been tears. Kate and Walter hugged, smiled and cried all at the same time and while this was going on there was a slightly awkward moment for the rest of the group, now merely onlookers at a very personal reunion scene. Jeremy broke the ice by stepping forward and shaking hands first with Annie, then Sele, and suddenly there was a jumble of hands, hellos and hugs as everyone got in on the act and reached out to each other.

'What do I call you?' Sele asked, flashing a brilliant smile at them. 'Aunt Nina and Uncle Jeremy?'

Annie looked sharply at him, but Nina stepped in smartly with her reply, which cut her admonitions off before she had a chance to get going.

'Just Nina,' she said. 'I can't really work out these relationships,' she added, in an aside to Annie. 'And he's just Jeremy.'

Throughout all of these exchanges Walter kept hold of Kate's hand.

'This is a wonderful day in my life,' he said.

'Mine too.'

'We thought maybe we could go across there for coffee?' said Nina. 'Then we can all sit down and have a chat.'

Since Kate seemed unable or unwilling to do so, Nina was taking charge of proceedings. Otherwise, she thought, we'll be standing on these steps for hours.

Kate had abandoned her bag of gifts on the ground the moment she spotted Walter, and had apparently forgotten it since, but Nina had picked it up and she now led the way to the restaurant. The staff obligingly moved tables to accommodate everyone, and Nina then made sure everyone was sitting where they wanted to be. The twins sat together, as she imagined they always did, Kate was next to Walter, of course, and Jeremy took a seat alongside Sele. Nina put herself on one side of Annie, with Sele on the other. By the time they were all settled and the waitress had taken their order Kate was back in the real world.

'Oh Nina, thanks for remembering that,' she said, indicating the bag. 'I brought over some little gifts for you all, nothing special but I just thought of all the birthdays and Christmases that we weren't able to mark, and... well, maybe I can start catching up on that now.'

Kate handed out the gifts she'd put so much thought into, keeping Walter's back till last.

'This is something a bit different,' she explained. 'We'll come to it in a minute.'

Sele ripped his parcel open and put the football shirt on immediately, which made everyone laugh, and the girls were excited about their perfumes, trying them out on each other. Annie opened her gift, and then put it straight back into the wrapping paper.

'Thank you, Kate,' she said. 'There was no need. You're very kind.'

'I didn't see it,' said Elana. 'Let me look.'

Annie passed it across to her daughter without comment and Nina jumped into the small silence with a few comments about how excited they were to be in Cape Town. The awkward moment passed, and little by little Annie found herself warming to Nina.

'I hope you like this, Walter,' said Kate. 'Nina helped me to put it together.'

Walter unwrapped the photo album, and opened it to the first page. He studied it for a few moments then turned it around for the rest of the family to see. Sele leaned across the table on his elbows, earning himself a warning slap on the hand from his mother.

'My family tree,' Walter explained, 'and we're all here – see?' he added, pointing his finger to the branch next to Kate, which his family occupied.

As he turned the pages the Hatchman family popped into view, four generations captured on a succession of Box Brownies through to digital. Some of the oldest ones, of the Hatchman grandparents, had been repaired and restored and all the photos were mounted and carefully labelled by Nina.

'We had to guess at the dates on some of these,' Kate explained. 'Our parents weren't very good at writing on the backs of photos. I think this one,' she turned back a page and indicated a photo of her parents, 'is probably just after Dad came home from South Africa.'

'So that's how he would have looked to my mother.'

Mandisa reached out to move the album a little closer.

'We should have it enlarged to see if you have any of his features,' she said.

Nina thought guiltily of the first time she'd seen Walter's photo, when Kate came down to Brighton for the weekend – and her sarcastic comment; *can't see any family resemblance*. Kate, however, showed no signs of remembering it.

'Why didn't we think of that?' she said to Nina. 'Good idea, Mandisa.'

Kate felt duty bound to point out David, since Walter was his half-brother too.

'Nothing like the rest of us, though,' she said cheerfully, 'so no contact there any more,' but in order to complete the family archive Kate had included photos of David's two ex-wives and daughters. The latest wife and new baby were recorded, but naturally without photos.

'I'll treasure this,' said Walter. 'We'll look at it more carefully later on, won't we Annie?' he continued.

'Best to put it away now,' she said, 'before someone spills their coffee on it.'

Far from the excitement of the family gathering at the V&A Waterfront, Rachel arrived at Clare's flat later that evening to the smell of garlic drifting out into the corridor.

'I made us pasta and garlic bread,' Clare said, at the front door. 'And there's a bottle of wine in the fridge.'

Clare's flatmate, an air stewardess, was seldom home and when she was there was frequently sleeping off jet-lag.

'She's in Chicago tonight, or maybe still en route, I can't remember the timings,' Clare explained. 'At any rate she's not here, so we've got the place to ourselves.'

Rachel slumped on the sofa without taking her coat off, and sighed deeply.

'I had to go home via Lambeth again today,' she said, leaning forward and then swishing her hair back from her forehead with both hands. 'There were two girls leaving the building just as I arrived. Poor things, they looked like frightened rabbits. They were huddled into thin coats and neither of them had gloves or scarves or anything – I almost went over to them to give them mine. They were just carrying a small bag each, the bloke there bundled them into a minicab and off they went, to God knows where or what.'

'Maybe theirs was a legit arrangement.'

'Yeah, and maybe not.'

Rachel sighed again, and started unbuttoning her coat.

'They looked so lost and... just totally vulnerable. I still can't understand why Jason's mixed up in something like this. He's got just about everything a man could want – why risk it all?'

'The usual reason I suppose – money.'

'Yeah, like he needs it. I was mad to get into this whole thing, Clare.'

'Don't beat yourself up about it too much – people do mad things for love. You weren't the first and you won't be the last.'

Rachel rummaged around in her bag for a tissue, and blew her nose.

'I thought he loved me, Clare. And it was all so... exciting, daring...so unlike anything I'd experienced before. Now it's just a mess, and every time I see him I have to keep up this pretence.'

'Well, not for much longer hopefully. At least now you see him for what he is.'

'And they're such good friends with my family, who can't have a clue about any of this because I'm sure they'd go ape-shit if they did.'

The family Rachel worked for were not short of influential friends, the sort that she imagined wouldn't think twice about freezing them out the minute the first mud was slung, just in case some of it stuck to them. Dinner parties at the Knightsbridge house were lavish, and on occasions Rachel had watched from the front window of her flat as taxis disgorged celebrities or politicians onto the driveway below. Both successful professionals, theirs was nonetheless old money, the house a family inheritance.

Mr. Wingate, or Stephen as he preferred her to call him, was a consultant psychiatrist with his own practice in Harley Street. Jessica Wingate was a TV producer for the BBC, and the driving force behind the marriage. They'd married somewhat later in life than their contemporaries and their three children had all been adopted in quick succession. Thanks to their previous and current nannies, there was no necessity for either of them to take more than a few days off work each time, an arrangement which suited them both perfectly. The children adored Rachel, and the Wingates were generous to her. It was a harmonious arrangement, and life ran smoothly in their household as a result. But Rachel knew they wouldn't hesitate to dispense with her services if they found out about her involvement with their friend and neighbour, and by extension his 'staffing arrangements'. The Wingates didn't do dirty linen, theirs or anybody else's, and nannies were not difficult to find when you could offer the benefits Rachel currently enjoyed.

Clare went into her tiny galley kitchen to serve the pasta, and Rachel trailed along behind her and loitered in the doorway.

'The only way out for me is to leave the Wingates,' she said. 'But I need to give them a reason – and apart from the truth I can't imagine what that would be, can you?'

Clare put a bowl of salad and a bottle of wine in Rachel's hands and she backed out of the kitchen doorway.

'I mean, I can hardly say I need more money because they pay me top rates as it is – and if I did they'd probably give me a rise anyway.'

Pasta bowls in hand, Clare breezed past Rachel to get to the table.

'I've got nothing at all to complain about,' Rachel said, following her sister. 'They give me plenty of time off, my accommodation is way better than most of the girls I know, and the children are just lovely.'

They sat down opposite each other and Clare poured the wine.

'Then it could only be some personal reason.'

'Like what?'

'Well, like maybe you have to go down to Brighton to live with Grandma because she's got Alzheimers and can't manage on her own any more. That sort of thing.'

Clare ground black pepper over her pasta, picked up a piece of garlic bread and bit into it.

'Actually, that's not such a dumb idea, if you think about it,' she mumbled through a mouthful of bread. 'It's perfectly feasible, and nobody would be able to check on it, including Jason. You don't even have the same surname so he'd never track her down.'

Rachel looked doubtful. 'Grandma would kill me if she knew,' she said.

Clare laughed.

'Yeah, you're right, she would. But luckily, she never would know. OK, it doesn't have to be that, there must be loads of family dilemmas we could dream up.'

Rachel picked over her salad, moving a tomato slice around the plate.

'OK, I take your point,' she said.

'The other thing is; the timing. The minute you hand in your notice Jason will hear of it. Then what? The potential threat to him increases the minute you up and go because then it's obvious you've got no reason not to nail him. So that's going to be tricky.'

Rachel sipped her wine.

'Actually, I had already thought of that. They go off to the States every year straight after Christmas to see her family – and this year they're going to be away for longer because someone they know has offered them a yacht to sail around the Bahamas for a couple of weeks.'

Clare raised her eyebrows.

'Yeah, I know. Like I say, no shortage of money. So they'll be out of the country for five weeks.'

'Perfect! You give in your notice as soon as they go and by the time they get back you've disappeared. No forwarding address. Get a new phone and email address and he'll never track you down. It'll work Rach, trust me.'

'Right. Just two things spoil this brilliant idea: I'll have nowhere to live, and no job to go to. How do I manage that?'

'We'll think of something,' said Clare, refilling their glasses.

'I don't want Mum to know the truth of this,' said Rachel.

'Then we'll find a way of dealing with it so that she doesn't need to know.'

That's the hardest part, Clare thought. There's a limit to how many lies I want to tell Mum, and before long I'll have reached it.

'She called before you got here, by the way. Mum I mean.'

'Oh, right. How's the trip going?'

'Good. They've met Walter's family. She said Kate got very emotional.'

'Kate? Goodness, that's a turn-up. Whatever next?'

* * *

While Clare and Rachel were washing up and finishing off the wine, Nina, Jeremy and Kate were getting settled in the Green Dolphin and studying the menus. The pianist, they noticed, was different from the previous evening. A young black musician had replaced Peter for the gig, and he was clearly eager to make an impression. Although the rest of the band introduced Jeremy to him before the show, with Lebo in particular recommending his talents highly, there was no offer to sit in that night.

'Are you disappointed?' Kate asked him.

'Not at all,' Jeremy replied. 'I'm on holiday, I'm allowed time away from the keyboard. Anyway, I may be playing here again another evening,' he added, 'or somewhere else across town that Lebo has in mind.'

Kate and Nina looked at each other.

'She's a long way from home, Jem,' said Nina.

'Just be careful,' said Kate.

Jeremy laughed.

'I'm always careful,' he said, 'in every respect, so you don't have to worry about history repeating itself.'

'That's not what I meant,' said Kate. 'We wouldn't want you to get attached to Lebo and then be unhappy because you're worlds apart, that's all. We do care, you know.'

Jeremy blew her a kiss across the table.

'Ah, thanks for your concern, Kate. You two have been looking after me since I was a little boy and I've always loved you for it,' he said with a smile. Then he turned his attention back to the menu. 'Now, what are we ordering?'

The music finished at midnight, and for the second night in a row Kate and Nina found themselves walking back to the hotel on their own.

'He's a grown man,' said Kate. 'He's got to make his own mistakes.'

'Mmm, like that ghastly Georgina. *She* was certainly a mistake.'

'Lebo seems nice.'

'She does, doesn't she?'

'We shouldn't worry about him.'

'No, you're right.'

They walked on in silence for a minute, night-time Waterfront tourists all around them, everyone out for a good time.

'I do, though.'

'What?'

'Worry about Jeremy.'

'Yeah, me too.'

CHAPTER 12

NOVEMBER 2010: CAPE TOWN

Walter had negotiated a few days off work. He had annual leave owing to him – the family never went on holiday, but they usually had extra time off over the Christmas and New Year period just to go to the beach or drive up into the Karoo with a picnic. This year he had managed to bring some of his leave forward so he could spend precious time with his new-found family.

'I'm taking you to Simon's Town,' he told Kate on the phone. 'It's where my mother met Ray, and where I lived as a boy.'

'Isn't there a naval museum there?' Kate asked, actually already knowing the answer but not wanting to sound too well informed, as if there was nothing left Walter could tell her.

'Yes, there's the South African Naval Museum, and also the Simon's Town Museum – we can look in both if you like. We might even find something out about the ship Ray was on. We took the children once, but I haven't been since.' Walter paused for the briefest moment, then rushed on before he lost his nerve.

'Shall I pick you up at the hotel tomorrow morning?' he asked.

Walter had acquired more than just a family; he had a new confidence to go with it. The old Walter wouldn't have dreamt of walking into a swanky hotel at the Waterfront – but this newer version of himself had a sister and cousins from England, and their self-possession was starting to rub off on him.

He made a point of including Nina and Jeremy in the invitation to Simon's Town, saying how much he would enjoy them all being there together.

'We don't want to be in the way tomorrow,' Nina said, as they planned their day over a late breakfast. 'We can easily find things to do on our own.'

But Kate wouldn't hear of it.

'No, you must come – at least tomorrow to Simon's Town. After that... well, we'll see what happens next.'

If she were honest with them and herself, Kate would have admitted that she wasn't completely sure how it would work out without them for a whole day. There was still the nagging thought at the back of her mind that she would run out of things to say to Walter, and she definitely didn't want either of them to feel uncomfortable. Once they'd spent a bit more time together she'd have a better idea of just how easy they would be with each other.

There was something else; Walter was bringing Annie along. It had been obvious to Kate that Annie wasn't comfortable in her company. On the other hand, she seemed to relate well to Nina, who Kate supposed was sufficiently far enough removed to present no threat at all to her, so with Nina along the Annie problem was diluted. Due to her decreased work schedule, Annie wasn't working tomorrow anyway but on the other days Walter had taken off, she would be. So this was a one-off one-day problem, because at the weekend the twins or Sele would also be around.

'Won't we need two cars?' Jeremy asked, and for a moment Nina thought he was going to say he would make things easier by not coming with them, but then he added, 'I don't mind driving as well.'

That'll be a tricky one to work out, Nina thought, as she mentally arranged and re-arranged the passengers.

'Well, he obviously gets all his family in their car, and we shouldn't take up any more room than they do,' Kate said. 'You'll just have to breathe in a bit.'

This settled, they brought their minds back to the current day's itinerary.

'There are so many things I want to see – where do we start?' Kate asked.

They tossed some ideas around and there was no shortage of attractions to start them off. Cape Point, Kirstenbosch gardens... the guidebook Kate had bought one wet and chilly day in Guildford lay open on the table, by now starting to look well-thumbed.

'I'd really like to see the District Six museum,' said Nina, 'but you don't have to come with me, I don't mind going alone...'

'We can't go home without doing some wine tasting,' said Kate, turning the book towards herself and flicking it on a few pages, 'so we should put that on the schedule. How on earth are we going to fit everything in?'

'We can't. We'll never be able to do everything, but all the guidebooks I've seen say you shouldn't plan a day for Table Mountain,' said Jeremy. 'When there's no cloud cover you just drop everything else, and go.'

Nina stood to look across the terrace towards the mountain.

'There's no cloud,' she announced.

'Then that's today sorted out,' said Jeremy, getting to his feet. 'See? This whole tourist business is easy when you know how.'

* * *

The mall was busy that day, and neither Mandisa nor Elana took a proper lunch break. Not only was it right at the height of the tourist season but quite soon the schools would break up and the shops were crowded with mothers doing their Christmas shopping before they had the added disadvantage of kids in tow. By the time the stores closed at five thirty, the girls felt as if they hadn't sat down all day.

In the warm fug of the Volksie bus Mandisa fell asleep, her head on Elana's shoulder. Elana was tired but not sleepy. That afternoon an ex-boyfriend had called her up and begged to see her again and Elana, having just got over the broken heart he'd left behind, now had to re-adjust her mindset. She had things to think about that kept her awake for the half hour journey back to Ocean View.

She looked out of the window without seeing much, until they arrived at the drop-off point. Mandisa stirred, lifted her head and yawned. Elana, gazing out of the window, saw him before her sister did.

Bheki Msonga, waiting, leaning against a wall with his arms folded and his legs crossed at the ankles.

Mandisa picked up her bag and waited for the people in front of them to get off the bus. Turning to Elana to say something she looked out of the window and suddenly tensed.

'Bheki,' she said softly.

'It's OK, Mandi, he won't try anything while we're together,' Elana whispered.

But it was soon apparent that whoever Bheki was waiting for, it wasn't Mandisa. He barely glanced at the Volksie as the passengers started climbing out. Uyanda, always up at the front because she knew all the drivers, was the first off.

'Hey, Bheki!' she called across to him.

He turned in her direction and seemed to take a few seconds before he registered who was calling him. He raised a hand briefly in greeting and then turned his face away again.

The twins peered out from the rear window.

'He knows we're always on Uyanda's taxi,' said Elana. 'He's not waiting for you, he's not even looking in this direction.'

'Journey's end!' the driver called. 'Come on you two, you got to get off here!'

Reluctantly, the girls stepped off the Volksie and although Bheki glanced at them he didn't move. They'd gone about ten metres towards home and thought they'd got away with it, when they heard running feet approaching from behind.

'Hey, girls, wait for me!' Bheki came up behind them and put a hand on Elana's shoulder. 'So, what's going on with you two? Let me walk you home, and you can tell me what you've been doing. I never get to see you these days, you know.'

Mandisa looked up at him but there was no trace of the Bheki that had tried to rape her that night. Instead he was smiling and friendly, turning on the charm. Elana shook her shoulder free.

'We don't need you for an escort,' she said. 'Why can't you just take no for an answer?'

Bheki laughed a little nervously.

'Oh, come on now, don't be mean to me – we can still be friends, can't we?'

In a somewhat awkward threesome, the girls trying to walk briskly ahead, Bheki jumping around beside or in front of them, they turned off the main road and into the street where the Maketa family lived. The moment they were round the corner he took off like a sprinter leaving the blocks, raced to the next junction and disappeared off to the right.

The twins stopped walking and looked at each other.

'What was all that about?' Elana wondered aloud.

Mandisa shook her head and frowned in confusion, then she turned to look back the way they'd come. There, on the main road, a long silver car came slowly into view and stopped at the end of their street, the same car Mandisa had seen that awful night, the car the stranger had arrived in.

The driver peered in their direction, then put the car into gear and drove on.

'I think Bheki's in big trouble,' Mandisa said.

* * *

Kate was very taken with Simon's Town, tucked invitingly along the shore between the mountains and the sea. The main road, lined with colonial buildings, was pretty and quaint, the shops a curious mix of the essential and the purely for tourists. Walter stopped his party in front of an estate agent's office.

'This was where my mother was working when she met Ray,' he said. 'It was a cake shop and café then, popular with the sailors.'

Behind her sunglasses, Kate was unreadable. But when she spoke her voice was soft.

'Gosh, it's taken a long time to close that circle,' she said.

'I suppose he came here on the day before his ship left port, to give her the letter I sent you.'

'Poor Dad. He must have been in such turmoil.'

'Well, I don't suppose they were the first couple to find themselves in that situation,' said Walter, 'or the last.'

They walked further along the main road.

'Can you show us where you lived?' asked Nina.

'I can point out roughly where it was,' he said. 'But there's no trace of my neighbourhood now. We were all moved out in 1967 and the community was re-housed.'

'At Ocean View?'

'Not at first. We went to Gugulethu – that's where Annie lived though we didn't meet then.'

'My mother's still there,' said Annie. 'She won't budge.'

'Simon's Town became a White Group Area, and all non-whites were forced to leave. Gugulethu was our first stop, then they created a township at Slangkop and later on it was named Ocean View.'

'Seeing it on the map... I wouldn't have thought you'd be able to see the sea from there,' Jeremy said.

'You can't, but calling it Ocean View was no mistake, the first residents gave it that name on purpose. You see when we were here,' Walter pointed up to the mountains above Simon's Town, 'we *did* have an ocean view. It was one of many things we lost.'

'I can't imagine what that must have been like, a whole neighbourhood moved out in one go. What about people who worked here? Could they still keep their jobs and travel in?' Kate asked.

'Some tried, although it was very difficult. When we first went to Ocean View there were no buses, schools, shops – nothing. It's all been added around us, a brick at a time.'

'Terrible to uproot all those people,' said Jeremy, 'and stupid too, perfect conditions to breed resentment.'

'I was only ten,' said Walter. 'At the time I didn't understand what it all meant.'

'It must have been very hard on your mother,' said Nina.

'Well, you have to realise that the whole community went at the same time, so she wasn't on her own. But

146

it *was* hard, on everyone, leaving the place we thought of as home. She was married by then and had two step-children, quite a lot older than me. I don't know what happened to them or where they are now.'

'Our children don't realise how lucky they are,' said Annie.

'Oh, I'm sure they do,' said Nina.

'Maybe. But the things we lived through are just history to them,' said Walter. 'Now we've been re-invented as the rainbow nation – and they're too young to appreciate what came before.'

'Surely they teach it to them at school?' asked Jeremy, as he and Walter lagged behind the others.

'Yes they do, but you had to live through those years to know what it was really like. It's hard for them to understand.'

'And things have changed a lot in that time?' Jeremy asked. 'For everyone?'

'Not everyone,' said Walter. 'You've seen the shacks out near the airport, nobody could say that the lives of those people have changed much. But we have democracy, and if you walk into a restaurant now you'll see black and white people eating there, and black and white people serving them. So some things have changed a lot for some people, but not everything for everyone. Maybe we expected too much too soon.'

'I guess your kids will be the ones who reap the benefits.'

'I hope so, although they might have to leave Cape Town to make full use of their opportunities – there's a black ceiling here that doesn't seem to exist in Johannesburg or Pretoria or other big cities. Annie doesn't want any of them to leave home but I disagree with her on that point. If their best career chances are away from Cape Town then that's exactly what they must do.'

They'd reached the end of the line of shops by then. Walter and Jeremy caught up with the others, stopped and turned to them.

'Now,' said Walter, 'where shall we eat?'

They had lunch on the quayside, overlooking the dockyard, where a couple of frigates and many more smaller vessels were berthed. Against the perfect blue of the sky and softly lapping waves the two naval ships managed to look both incongruous and perfectly at home, at the same time.

There was an awkward moment when the bill arrived. Walter reached into his jacket, but Kate put a hand on his arm.

'Please let this be my treat,' she said. 'There are three of us, anyway, to your two. It's not fair.'

'No,' he said firmly. 'Today we are your hosts and your guides.'

Nina held her breath, waiting for Kate to have an answer ready, or reach for her bag, and she willed her not to. The meal wasn't expensive by UK standards, and certainly not by Kate's, but they all knew without voicing it that it would be a huge bill for Walter.

Just let him do it, Nina thought. You can make it up to them some other time.

Kate's hand hovered over her bag, but then she reached a decision.

'Well, that's really kind of you Walter. Thank you both.'

'In that case the drinks are on me later,' said Jeremy.

Kate wanted to visit the naval museum in Simon's Town, and this was something Jeremy also expressed an interest in. Nina looked at Annie and sensed this might be the time for the group to split.

'Would you show me some more of the town?' she asked. 'Unless you want...?'

'No, no – I've been there before,' said Annie, rather too quickly and sounding relieved that she didn't have to go through it all a second time.

'We can all meet up again later,' said Nina, 'if that's OK with everyone?'

So they headed off in the opposite direction to the rest of the group.

'What do you want to see?' Annie asked.

'Oh, I don't know. Anything that would make a good photo,' Nina smiled, patting her camera. She'd been taking photos all the time, but it had occurred to her that Annie might be her passport to a more personal, insider's view of South Africa.

'Well, could you face climbing all these steps?' said Annie, indicating a narrow lane that led straight up the mountain side off the main road. 'There are good views of the dockyard from up there.'

It wasn't quite what Nina had in mind, but she was just glad that Annie seemed content to be in her company.

'Don't you work in Simon's Town, Annie?' Nina asked breathlessly as they plodded up the steps and reached the road on the first level. Annie nodded.

'You want to see the house? It's up on the next level.'

Nina looked up, standing for a moment to get her breath back.

'Do you walk up here every day for work? That must be why you're not out of breath and I am!'

'Before my lady cut back on my hours,' said Annie. 'But not every day now.'

'That must have been really hard on you,' said Nina as they crossed the road and carried on up another flight of steps. 'Can you make the hours up some other way? With another family?'

'I'm looking. But it's not easy to find work these days.'

'When did this happen?'

'Back in the winter. July, maybe August, I can't remember.'

Oh. When Kate first heard from Walter, Nina thought.

They reached the next level and Nina turned around.

'Wow! You were right about that view, it's beautiful!' she said, reaching for her camera. 'But let me take a picture of you, Annie...'

Annie waved her away, laughing. It was the first time Nina had seen her laugh, and it transformed her, lifting years from her face.

'Go on! Over there, with the sea behind you... stand in front of that bougainvillea...'

Nina took more photos when they reached the house where Annie worked. It was massive, cut into the mountainside and built on many levels to accommodate the steep incline. One of several houses in a similar style, there was clearly no shortage of money up there on the mountainside.

'And why did they cut your hours, Annie?'

'Their children are all away from home now and she doesn't need me every day. I can understand it, the house doesn't get dirty with just the two of them there.'

'Yes, but all the same...' Nina was thinking that with a property like that it would hardly place a strain on their resources to keep Annie coming every day. But she didn't feel she could say it.

'I mean, things still need doing don't they?' she added, as they started the walk back down. 'I live alone, but there's always stuff to do, ironing and sorting out cupboards.'

'I thought your daughters lived with you,' said Annie.

'No – they're both in London, independent young women now.'

'Don't you miss them? I'm sure I'd miss my children, I can't imagine living without them.'

'Yes, I miss them, but they have to go sometime and live their own lives. And it's not as if they're really far away, they can get to me by train in about an hour. They wouldn't have got the jobs they wanted if they'd stayed at home and in the end you just want the best for your kids, don't you?'

Annie was silent. Then as they were about to start on the next steps down – these steeper than the last – she turned to Nina.

'I don't want them to long for a life that's out of their reach. I don't want them to be disappointed in what they have.'

'Are they disappointed? They seem very sensible and well-adjusted to me, and anyway it's good to have ambitions and dreams.'

Annie sighed, and putting her hand on the railing, started down the steps.

'Mandisa hasn't put that book about England down since she bought it.'

Ah, thought Nina. So that's the problem.

They walked down the steps in unison, one on either side of the centre rail.

'Letting my girls go was just about the hardest thing I've ever done,' Nina said. 'I helped each of them pack their things up, and stayed cheerful and positive because they were excited about getting started on their future. And then after they'd gone I just sat down and howled. Rachel was the first, when she went off to college. I remember going into her bedroom and picking up the soft toys she'd never wanted to throw out, and thinking that my baby had gone forever.'

Annie nodded. 'I'd be like that too,' she said.

'But of course she hadn't gone for good. At the end of her first week she came home for the weekend, and after that it wasn't so bad. Then when Clare went as well I was completely alone for the first time in more than twenty years.'

'I can't imagine how that must have been.'

'Watching them leave the first time is the worst, but it gets easier. We don't talk every day, but it would be unusual for a week to go by without them phoning or emailing me.'

As she said this Nina realised that there had been times lately when she hadn't talked to Rachel in a while, and she briefly wondered again if there was something going on there that she didn't know about.

'Do you think Mandisa's got ambitions to travel?' she said after a few moments.

'Maybe,' Annie replied, 'but she couldn't afford it, and we can't help out with anything like that so it's never going to be a possibility. I don't want her getting any ideas in her head about going away when it can't be done. But of the three of them she's the most restless.'

She fell silent again until they reached the bottom of the steps and were back on the main road.

'And what if it were a possibility?' Nina asked gently, knowing – as Annie probably also did – that Kate would stump up the money in an instant if Mandisa wanted to visit her in England.

Annie shook her head, and kept her gaze low.

'I'm afraid of losing her,' she said quietly. 'I'm afraid if she went she wouldn't come back. And you see how she and Elana are? They're always together...'

'The twin syndrome, yes...'

'...and Mandisa is the stronger one. If she went Elana might follow her. We'd be a lot more than an hour away.'

When she turned around there were tears in her eyes. Nina hooked her arm through Annie's.

'They always know where home is, Annie. You wouldn't lose them.'

They walked along the main road towards the tearoom where they'd arranged to meet the others.

'Walter would encourage all of them to travel and see other places,' Annie continued. 'His world has opened up since he found Kate and he would like this for the children too. He's ambitious for them in that way.'

'Have you told him how you feel?'

'No. I'm sure he would say I was holding them back but I'm also ambitious for them, I just want them to have a future nearby. Of course if they went away he would miss them too but it's different for a mother,' said Annie.

Nina couldn't argue with that. At that moment they saw Walter, Kate and Jeremy at the far end of the road approaching the tearoom from the opposite direction, and Nina asked the question she wanted to before the chance was lost.

'Annie – would you take me to see your mother one day?'

Annie was astonished.

'In Gugulethu? Why do you want to go there?'

'I'd like to meet her and I want to see what a township is really like,' said Nina.

'There are township tours...'

'I know, but you only see what they want you to see.'

'Well... yes I suppose we could go one day but we'd need a car to get there – it's right across town.'

'That's OK, I could use our hire car on a day when the others didn't need it. Do you think your mother would mind talking to me? And let me take some photos while I was there?'

'I don't think she'd mind.'

'Well perhaps you'd ask her, because...'

'Hey – there are photos there! Photos of some of the crew...' Kate, rushing forward to meet them, couldn't contain her excitement. 'The crew of the Comus, taken here in Simon's Town!'

'And your father?' asked Annie as they reached Kate.

'Maybe, I can't be certain,' Kate replied, 'because the pictures aren't very distinct and quite honestly when they were in uniform the sailors all looked pretty much alike. But there was one at the back of a group – it might have been him.'

'What did you think?' Nina asked Jeremy as he and Walter joined the group.

'Hard to say,' he replied. 'But it's possible.'

They filed into the tearoom, Nina and Jeremy at the back of the others.

'Is she just seeing what she wants to see?' Nina whispered, tugging on his tee shirt to hold him back.

Jeremy shrugged. 'I don't know, there was certainly a resemblance... he reminded me more of Bobby but it could have been Uncle Ray.'

* * *

It was two days after the Simon's Town trip that Kate, Nina and Jeremy were booked on a 9am ferry to Robben Island. Too late to get another ticket on the same tour for Walter, they had to make a compromise arrangement.

'I will meet you at the terminal as you come back,' Walter said, as he dropped them off at their hotel, the four of them having spent that afternoon at Cape Point. 'Then we can go somewhere together for the rest of the day. Annie has to work until two, so I don't think you'll see her again tomorrow. And,' he added, 'she's naturally disappointed about that.'

Nina saw her chance and leapt in.

'If I take the hire car, I can pick Annie up from work – she said she'd take me to meet her mother one day. That would work, wouldn't it?'

'Well, yes – if that's what you'd like,' said Walter, clearly surprised that Nina should want to do this. 'But you might not want to risk taking your hire car right into her neighbourhood. I'll talk to Annie about this. She knows the buses from the city centre.'

Jeremy cleared his throat.

'I'll probably go straight back to the hotel, if that's OK with you. I'd like to catch up with some of the musicians I've met and that might be a good time...'

Kate raised her eyebrows.

'What?' said Jeremy in response. 'That's not a problem, is it?'

'Not at all,' said Kate, smiling. 'We're not joined at the hip.'

'Just remember what we've told you...' Nina teased.

And so the next day was planned out in three very different ways.

CHAPTER 13

NOVEMBER 2010: LONDON & CAPE TOWN

The whole day had been dreary and damp. In typical November fashion most of the southern part of the country woke to fog, which barely cleared from some places before midday. By three-thirty it was getting dark again.

'It hardly seems worth opening the curtains on days like this,' said Clare on the phone to her mother. 'The first thing I do when I get home is close them again. I'm glad I don't live in Finland, they get six months of this.'

'I'm really not looking forward to coming back to that,' said Nina. 'But if it's any consolation we had a bit of rain the other day.'

'Oh dear, poor you. That must have ruined your day.'

'I was visiting Annie's mum in Gugulethu. And Walter took Kate back to his flat in Ocean View.'

'Where was Jeremy while all this was going on?'

'In bed with a jazz singer.'

'Really? Well, why am I surprised, good for him. So tell me about Annie's mum.'

Nina smiled. 'She was lovely! And I think I got some good shots there.'

Annie's mother, Rose, had treated Nina like royalty, inviting some of her neighbours round so she could show her off. When she knew they were coming to visit her, Rose made a batch of spicy koeksisters, and then hosted a tea party for as many people as she could cram into her tiny shack, with the overflow standing around outside.

'Was it awful, her place?' asked Clare.

'No, it was spotlessly clean and everything shone. From the outside it looks like an old garden shed, but once you get inside it's rather cosy. Rose made pot after pot of rooibos tea and people brought their own cups! I kept trying to give up my seat to old ladies but they wouldn't hear of it.'

'Gosh, celebrity status at last, Mum.' Clare walked across to the central heating thermostat and tweaked it up a notch. 'How does Kate feel about coming home?'

'Mmm, good question.'

Nina was quiet for a second, considering. Kate and Walter had certainly become close, and Nina could imagine emotional goodbyes with him in particular but also the children. Kate had tried hard with Annie, but it was clear there was never going to be much of a bond there. It was an evening flight, and Walter had arranged to leave work an hour earlier so that the whole family could go to the airport. Nobody was looking forward to it.

'She'll miss Walter, that's for sure. I wouldn't be surprised if she came over again before too much longer.'

'And you?'

'Yeah, I'd love to come back sometime. But most of all now, I'm looking forward to seeing you and Rachel again – and Grandma of course. How has she been?'

Clare groaned. 'Hard work,' she said. 'Unaccountably cross a lot of the time.'

'Oh well, she'll get over it. Give her my love. I managed to get hold of Rachel earlier – she sounded very upbeat.'

'Yeah, we're all fine Mum. Absolutely fine.'

Rachel certainly was upbeat. And whilst Clare didn't like to see her sister unhappy, she also didn't like her sudden change from misery to joy. Or to be more accurate, she didn't like the reason for it.

Jason, sensing that he was losing his grip on Rachel, had attacked her with charm, and given it to her with both barrels. There had been dinner at a posh restaurant plus a delivery of flowers, red roses naturally. There had been a gift in a small jeweller's box, which turned out to contain earrings.

'I think I may have got it all wrong,' said Rachel.

'He's still married – you didn't get that wrong,' said Clare, turning the earrings over in her hand. 'Are these real diamonds?' she asked, holding one of them up for scrutiny.

Rachel ignored her. 'He's been so unhappy,' she said, 'and I haven't been any help lately. They're really having problems at home and he's talking about leaving her, making a fresh start.'

Yeah, right, thought Clare.

'So are you saying now you think that whole business over in Lambeth is all above board?' she said. 'Brown envelopes and all?'

'I think I got a bit carried away, maybe I just read too much into it. Seen too many films, I guess.' Rachel grimaced a tight little smile in an embarrassed sort of way.

Clare sighed.

'Well, they'll be off to the USA soon for the Christmas break. And then you'll have time to reflect on the whole thing and deal with it in whatever way you decide.'

'No, the trip's off. The American's are coming over here after all.'

Bugger, thought Clare. There goes my cleverly contrived get-out scenario.

But later on, after Rachel had gone home, Clare had a lightbulb moment and the tiny seed of an idea which came to her slowly blossomed into a plan.

* * *

They were all a bit quiet on the short journey to Cape Town International. There was an air of anti-climax affecting the occupants of both cars as they converged on the airport from the Waterfront and Kommetjie.

Kate hadn't had much to say all day and it was obvious that she wasn't looking forward to leaving Cape Town. Jeremy had already said his goodbyes to Lebo, that morning at the hotel. They hadn't made any plans to stay in touch, which he was already regretting. Replaying their last conversation in his head he couldn't believe how casual they'd both sounded.

'Next time I'm in town...'

'You'll know where to find me – or anyone at the Dolphin will tell you...'

'Or of course if you find yourself getting a call from Ronnie Scott's...'

'You'd better be there!'

'I'll be up the front, cheering.'

But when it came to it, although nothing more was said, neither had wanted to let go of the other.

In the passenger seat of the car Kate slipped a hand into her jacket pocket, and closed her fingers around a small bundle of tissue paper, the gift she'd left till now to give to Walter.

As they set off for the airport from the opposite direction, the Maketa family were equally subdued. A silence settled over them, the mood affecting even Sele.

'I'm sure we'll see them all again before too long,' said Walter after they'd been going for some time. His voice sounded more cheerful than he felt.

'It's been fun, hasn't it?' said Elana.

'More fun saying hello than goodbye,' Sele replied, gazing out of the window at surfers riding the waves rolling up onto Muizenberg beach. Sele had never surfed, although it was something he felt he would be good at and really wanted to have a go. He leaned forward to get a better look.

'I like them all so much,' Mandisa said softly, pushing Sele back in his seat as he was blocking her light. 'I wish I was going with them.'

Annie turned in the front seat to face her daughter.

'Don't start wishing for something you can't have,' she said. 'You've already got a lot to be thankful for.'

'I know Mama. But it's nice to have a dream, for horrible days.'

'You don't have horrible days,' said Annie.

Elana glanced at Mandisa, but neither replied.

They arrived at the airport as Kate, Nina and Jeremy were checking in. With plenty of time in hand they found somewhere for a coffee and began moving tables together.

'Like the first time,' said Sele.

Everyone made a determined effort to stay cheerful, and an outsider would have seen them as a jolly crowd, a family seeing off some friends. And then their flight was called and suddenly it was time to go. In the midst of all the hugs Kate edged Walter to one side, took the tissue paper bundle from her pocket and pressed it into his hand.

'This was Dad's, he wore it all the time. I think he'd like to know you had it.'

Walter unrolled the tissue to reveal a gold signet ring. He opened his mouth to speak, but something caught in his throat and no words came out.

'It was a bit scratched but I had it polished and it's come up quite well.'

Walter slipped the ring onto his finger, put his arms around Kate and hugged her to him.

Standing back a little, Jeremy glanced at Nina.

'Kate,' he said softly, 'we have to go now.'

'Yes,' said Walter, coughing slightly and loosening his hold on Kate. 'Yes, come on you three, don't keep the pilot waiting. Come on,' he said again, wiping a tear from Kate's cheek with his finger, 'and be sure to call me as usual on Tuesday evening, same time. I'll be waiting.'

Kate nodded, smiling as best she could, trying to compose herself. There were more handshakes, hugs, waves – and then they were at the departures entrance. Turning around she blew a kiss to Walter, and Ray's ring caught the light as he waved back at her one last time.

* * *

Leaving the Tube at Lambeth North, Clare came up into unfamiliar streets, and headed south. It wasn't difficult to find the road she wanted and she walked slowly, trying not to look conspicuous and keeping her eyes on the shops and offices she passed. It wasn't a long road and the agency was near the start, looking exactly as Rachel had described it. There were the advertising postcards in the window, and at the side was the door to the flat above. Clare had no doubt she was in the right place, but she walked to the end of the road anyway, just to be sure, and came back on the opposite side.

There was no name over the window of the job agency, but the empty shop next door had a number above the door, and she made a mental note of it. Opposite, was a café, empty at that time of day except for two men sitting across from each other at a table in the corner, both reading the sports pages of tabloid newspapers.

Not wanting an all day breakfast or pie and chips, Clare ordered a coffee. The woman behind the counter was friendly and wanted to chat as she went about the task of making Clare's drink.

'Haven't seen you round here before,' she said. 'Looking for accommodation? We get a few students over this way because it's cheaper than central, but I expect you already know that.'

'Mmm... well, can you suggest any letting agencies?' said Clare as she cupped her hands round the mug of coffee that was passed over the counter to her.

'You could do worse than looking in here,' the woman said, handing Clare a free local newspaper. 'What're you studying, love?'

'Oh... erm... law,' said Clare. 'Thanks for the paper,' she added, tucking it under her arm as she carried her mug across to a PVC covered table in the window. The glass was a bit steamed up, but from her seat she could see directly across to the office door, and the door to the side of it. There was no sign that anyone was in the building.

The coffee was surprisingly good. She made a show of looking through the small ads section of the paper, all the while keeping an eye on the building opposite. But by the time she'd drunk her coffee there'd been no activity at all, and Clare was beginning to lose faith in her grand plan.

Because she couldn't stay there much longer without it looking odd, she re-folded the paper and rummaged in her bag for her purse. Just as she found it and lifted her head again, a car pulled up opposite and a middle-aged man got out. Leaving the engine running, he rang the bell to the side door. As if he'd been waiting, the grey man of Rachel's description opened the door almost immediately, something appeared to change hands between the two, the door closed again, and the man got back in his car and drove away.

Clare leaned back, her heart pumping, and mouthed a silent 'YES!' It was all the proof she needed. She scooped up her curls, squashed them into a woolly hat, then gathered up her bag and scarf and headed for the counter.

'Lovely coffee, thank you,' she said as she handed over her money.

'Well I hope you find what you want,' the woman replied, indicating the newspaper sticking out of Clare's bag.

'I think I already have,' said Clare, buttoning up her coat.

It had started to rain and since she didn't have an umbrella she ran most of the way back to the Underground station, but just as she got there and was about to dive through to the ticket barriers she spotted a phone booth on the opposite corner. Dodging both the traffic and the puddles she dashed across the road and in the shelter of the booth pulled a notepad from her bag.

And then Clare called Crimestoppers.

CHAPTER 14

CHRISTMAS EVE 2010: OCEAN VIEW & LONDON

Across the Cape, December had been characterised by a strong, warm wind that whipped the sand up, keeping people off the beaches at the weekends and sending them up into the Karoo instead. And then suddenly, a few days before Christmas, the wind dropped and left a string of perfect, hot summer days in its wake.

In Ocean View, fairy lights and decorations had been up for weeks in shops and houses. In Walter's apartment the Maketa family were banned from doing so until the last week before Christmas.

'This Christmas creep gets worse every year,' he said. 'I really don't see why we need to start celebrating so early.'

Behind his back, Annie rolled her eyes at Mandisa and Elana. But none of them questioned his decision and so the decorations stayed in their box until even Walter couldn't hold out any longer. The girls hung tinsel and baubles in the living room – mostly the Christmas decorations of their childhood because there had never been enough money to replace them, although Mandisa had bought a few special pieces from her shop. These were reserved to pin around the pictures of their English family, and Nelson Mandela. Sele scoffed at these festive adornments, but helped anyway with the high bits that they couldn't reach. Walter struggled with the fairy lights for most of the evening, patiently working his way along the length and replacing part of the cable that had worn, but in the end he managed to get them working. There was no Christmas tree to put the lights on so they fixed them up around the window.

In the early hours of Christmas Eve morning there was a commotion in the silent, dark streets of Ocean View. The Maketa family, and most of the residents of their part of Ocean View, were roused by the wail of police sirens as several vehicles rushed past the apartment at high speed, the sound pitch modulating down as they sped away across the township. Mandisa saw the flashing blue lights from behind closed eyelids, and pulled the sheet up over her head. Sele, who slept the sleep of the dead, was the only one who wasn't disturbed.

'I wonder what was going on last night,' Elana said, as she and Mandisa were getting ready to leave for their last, and busiest, day at work.

'Another robbery or a fight I expect,' said Annie, making up lunch boxes for the girls. Sele, rubbing sleep from his eyes, shuffled into the living room and sat at the table.

'There were a lot of them if that's all it was,' said Mandisa, checking in her bag for keys and purse.

'What?' said Sele. 'What did I miss?'

'We don't know yet,' said Annie. 'There were police cars, maybe an ambulance too, it was difficult to tell from the sirens.'

'I could tell,' he replied. 'The sound is different.'

'It's a pity you weren't awake then,' said Elana. 'Now we'll never know.'

'Yes we will, I'll find out later. Someone always knows what happened.'

Sele was right, someone always did, and news travelled fast in close communities such as Ocean

View, especially news like this. He got a version of the truth from his friends, and Mandisa and Elana heard something similar in a discussion on the Volksie bus. At the garage, Walter listened to three different accounts, shaking his head in disapproval at what he heard. Annie, on one of her non-working days, heard nothing at all and forgot about it until that evening when the whole family was gathered around the dinner table.

Although the details differed, they were all in agreement about the basic facts. Several people were involved, one person had been killed, and guns were the weapon of choice.

'It might be on the local news,' said Walter, not at all confident because events like this were not infrequent in Cape townships although rare in Ocean View, which was seldom mentioned on television. But to his surprise there was a feature on the early evening news.

The murdered man was not local to Ocean View but he was known to the police as a gang leader dabbling in drugs and prostitution. He had been shot at point blank range, through the window of his car. Unusually, the police issued the names of three men they wanted to interview in connection with the killing.

And one of them was Bheki Msonga.

* * *

In a freezing cold London, Jason managed to get away from his American family for a couple of hours on the afternoon of Christmas Eve, and Rachel quickly changed her plans so that she could see him.

'They're driving me nuts,' he said, 'an invasion of five big, noisy New Yorkers who want to hang out with me the whole time. I gave them the slip today by saying I was having a late lunch with my accountant.'

They were sitting together in a packed wine bar in Covent Garden, holding hands across the table.

'How much longer?' asked Rachel.

'Oh, still another two weeks to go. I can't wait for them to go home so life can get back to normal. So *we* can get back to normal,' he said, stroking the back of her hand.

'Rachel,' he added, 'I don't like to ask you as I know you're getting ready to go away for Christmas, but you couldn't just stop off on your way home, could you?'

Jason pulled a jiffy envelope from his pocket and slid it across the table to her. 'It'll only delay you by a few minutes, and I can't get there myself with the Yanks following me around all the time.'

Rachel hesitated, for little more than a heartbeat.

'Sure', she said. 'No problem.'

* * *

Rachel's taxi driver swung his cab round the corner, and hit the brake immediately. A section of pavement at the top end of the road was cordoned off with black and yellow incident tape and there were two police cars and a forensic vehicle lined up along the pavement. As they edged their way past, Rachel could see a uniformed officer at the front of the agency, standing with his back to the splintered door leading to the flat above. His eyes followed the cab.

'Looks like somebody's in trouble,' the taxi driver said. 'What number was it you wanted, love?'

Rachel twisted in her seat, looking back at the scene through the rear window. Her heart was pumping. Then she took a deep breath and pulled herself together.

'Oh... it's right down the other end of the road,' she said, lamely.

When Rachel got home almost an hour later she rushed in and picked up the phone to call Clare. Then before she'd finished dialling she changed her mind, grabbed a woolly hat and scarf and the weekend bag she'd already packed for the Christmas break, and went straight out again.

It was rush hour and the Tube was packed, carrying groups of partying office workers and last-minute shoppers, but Rachel hardly noticed them as she made the journey to Clare's flat on auto-pilot.

Clare was surprised to see her much earlier than they'd arranged, and saw immediately from the look on her face that something had happened.

'I was so wrong,' Rachel blurted out as soon as she opened the door. 'Whatever this is all about the police are on to it now. I am such a *fool*!'

'Oh my God!' said Clare, wide-eyed, as Rachel pulled off her woolly hat and started breathlessly relating her account, leading the way into Clare's lounge as she did so.

'You were *there*!'

'Well, yes,' said Rachel, surprised by the reaction she was getting. 'I wasn't expecting to go but then I never am.'

Clare paced up and down, while Rachel watched her. It was the first time she remembered seeing her sister quite so agitated, and it was unsettling.

'Had this particular taxi driver taken you there before?'

'Don't know – I shouldn't think so. Is it important?'

Clare shrugged. 'It could be. I'm just trying to think of everything, that's all. Did he know the exact address you were heading for?'

'No.' Rachel frowned. 'He just knew the road name. I'm certain of that because it wasn't till we got there that he asked me for the number. I couldn't just tell him to drive on because that would have looked a bit funny and this policeman had already clocked the taxi and was looking at us... so I told him to go right to the far end of the road. I knocked on a complete stranger's door and made a big show of pretending I was looking for someone, then got back in the taxi and we drove off.'

'Who did you say you wanted? Not a real person? Not someone you know?'

'I'm not that stupid,' said Rachel. 'No, I made up a name. God, it was awful – I didn't know what else to do... it all seemed a bit like a scene from a film, and I was in a panic... '

Clare sat down on the sofa.

'And where did he bring you back to?'

Rachel, lost in her own thoughts of the afternoon's drama, was momentarily confused and looked at Clare with a frown.

'The taxi driver,' said Clare. 'Did he take you right back to Knightsbridge? To the house?'

Rachel shook her head. 'No, not to the house, I asked him to drop me up by the Tube station because I needed to top up my phone. Then I walked the rest of the way.'

'Well, that's good. So he won't know where you live.'

'Clare – you're spooking me! This is so unlike you, why are you so jittery?'

'Because,' said Clare, 'because *you* could also be in trouble if the police can trace this back to you. That's if we're right about what's going on there, and it looks like we are.'

'They won't trace anything back to me because they won't even find me, I'm totally anonymous. I kept my cool and made myself look a complete idiot at a stranger's door. And then we drove away; end of.'

'Where's the package, the money?'

Rachel pulled a small jiffy envelope out of her handbag. 'Here,' she said. 'I didn't know what to do with it. I thought I could leave it with you.'

Clare took the envelope from Rachel's outstretched hand and turned it over and over, handling it carefully as though it might explode.

'I don't know what to do with it either,' she said, finally. 'I suppose the logical thing would be to give it back to Jason, then you're out of it.'

Rachel sat on the arm of the sofa and dropped her head.

'I don't want to see him again,' she said quietly. 'I can't bear to. The police don't go battering people's doors in over nothing, and it's obvious Jason's a part of whatever they're going after. He's lied to me, over and over again and I was stupid enough to be taken in. How many second chances does a person deserve?'

She rubbed the heel of her hands across her eyes, then lifted her head. Clare reached across and took her hand.

'What if he calls you? What if he asks for it back?' she asked gently.

Rachel tossed her hair out of her eyes and sniffed loudly.

'If I have to speak to him I'll say I was there at the same time as the police and saw what was going on. And I was scared of having the jiffy bag on me so I threw it into the Thames.'

Clare smiled. 'Yeah, that'll do it,' she said. 'But I think *you* should call *him* and say all that, not wait for him to contact you. Get in first so he won't think it was you that tipped them off.'

Rachel shook her head. 'I can't,' she said. 'The way he's used me is unforgivable. I never want to speak to him again.'

'I know, Rach, but listen to me. If you wait, it starts to look as if you knew something about it. He won't know you were there when the raid was going on unless you tell him – for all he knows you left him at Covent Garden and went straight back home with the dosh, or straight to the police. If they come looking for him and he thinks you're less than completely innocent he might try to implicate you.'

'How would the police make the connection to him? I don't suppose there'll be a paper trail.'

'The Grey Man might talk,' said Clare.

'Yeah, he might. But Jason can't have been the only one dealing through him. And they'll never trace the girls, I expect they just get swallowed up. They won't check all the care homes in the country, rounding them up.'

'We don't know that. Make the phone call, get yourself in the clear first. But do it now, or it'll be too late. A couple of hours have already gone by – he'll wonder why it took you so long.'

Rachel considered this, and sighed. Then she took her mobile out of her bag.

'Right, how does this sound? I've just spent two hours walking about London in a panic, wondering what to do,' she said. 'Then I chucked the jiffy bag in the Thames and got the tube to Victoria. He knows I'm going down to Mum's for Christmas.'

Clare nodded. 'OK,' she said. 'Do it now. I'll make us some coffee.'

From the kitchen Clare heard Rachel talking urgently, pacing up and down as she did so. It seemed she was doing a good deal more of the talking than Jason.

'How dare you put me in this position,' Rachel said, her voice rising, 'how *could* you?' Then there was a pause and after another moment, Rachel said flatly, 'Victoria Station.'

Clare held her breath, jumping as the kettle at her side switched itself off.

'And why would you care? You've just *used* me!' Rachel yelled into her phone. 'I can't do this any more Jason. Just piss off and get out of my life!'

Then there was the sound of her phone hitting the wall.

Clare came back into the room with two mugs of coffee, sat back down on the sofa and looked up at Rachel, who was standing with her hands covering her face.

'You OK?' she asked. Rachel nodded and ran her hands through her hair, then picked her phone up from where it lay on the floor and switched it off.

'He's in a panic,' she said, sitting down next to Clare.

'Oh, good,' said Clare. 'Now, shall we have a look and see how much is in here?' she added, picking the jiffy bag up from the coffee table. 'Unless you really were thinking of chucking it into the river.'

She removed a flat bundle of fifty pound notes, and counted them out carefully as Rachel looked on.

'Eighteen hundred pounds,' she said, placing the last note on top. They both stared at the pile of notes, surprisingly small for what seemed like such a large sum.

'What'll we do with it?' Rachel asked eventually.

'Well,' said Clare, 'to start with I'm going to pay it into my savings account, and then we can think about what happens next.'

Rachel nodded, miserably.

'Maybe we can turn it around, make something good out of it,' she said quietly.

'Yeah, perhaps we can.'

They drank their coffee in silence.

'Come on,' said Clare. 'Let's make a move. We've got to get down to Brighton for a jolly Christmas.'

'I don't feel very jolly,' said Rachel.

Clare put her arms around her sister and felt her stifle a sob.

'It'll be fine, you'll see. It's over now.'

* * *

Mandisa watched each news bulletin throughout the evening, but there were no further details and the last one of the day omitted the report completely. One more township death in violent circumstances – it had ceased to be newsworthy.

As Christmas morning dawned, Mandisa lay awake in the room she shared with Elana and listened to her sister breathing softly as she slept. But Mandisa hadn't been able to sleep.

Bheki was out there somewhere, on the run. She had no idea where he would go, or who might offer him refuge – if indeed anyone would. But she had a feeling that he wouldn't leave Ocean View unless he absolutely had to. Like her, it was the only place he knew and if he felt safe anywhere, it would be here.

Mandisa turned to face the window and saw the sky growing lighter behind the curtains. And although there was no logic to it, something told her they were not finished yet, and she would see him again.

CHAPTER 15

JANUARY 2011: CAPE TOWN AND MOSCOW

January 7th, 2011. Walter was working late and Sele was out with his friends, kicking a football about. As she stood in front of the television doing the ironing, Annie could hear Elana and Mandisa in their bedroom, giggling over something.

On the television, Jacob Zuma was talking, amongst other things, about unemployment. In Polokwane for the ANC's 99th anniversary celebrations he gazed into Annie's living room and told her, 'We still have unacceptably high levels of poverty and inequality.'

As if we didn't know, thought Annie. In spite of all her efforts, she had so far failed to find another job, and the Maketa budget was being stretched thinner and thinner. Annie smoothed her iron across sheets and table linen and tried to think, as she had so many times before, of a way forward. Walter was putting in all the overtime the garage could give him, but it didn't amount to much. The girls had increased their contributions to the weekly purse and Annie had stopped going to Shoprite in favour of cheaper supermarkets. And yet, as hard as they tried, they were still slipping further behind.

'It is only through all our people working together that we will create a better life for all...' said Mr Zuma. Annie stared at his shiny round face, his complacent piggy eyes behind rimless spectacles, and she put her iron down to fold a pillowcase.

No, she thought. That's not good enough. You can make as many pies in the sky as you like, but it won't help us because we need something to happen *now*.

And she came back, reluctantly, to the only credible solution. They would have to ask Kate for help, and as much as Annie kicked against the idea she knew they would not be refused.

* * *

January 18th, 2011. It was Tuesday evening, and Walter was waiting for Kate's regular call to come through. He and Annie had discussed their worsening financial situation and to his amazement, Annie had suggested doing the very thing she had been so much against not that long ago.

'If Kate could just let us have some money – a small loan...'

'A loan? How would we pay her back?'

'Well, I know it would not be for a while, but when Sele's working...'

Walter stared at her. '*When*?' he said, incredulously. 'Don't you mean '*if*'? I don't think we can rely on Sele getting any kind of job in the near future.'

Annie shut up. This was an argument she was not going to win, and she knew the best way to tackle the problem was to let Walter turn it over in his mind and then come round in his own time. After all, she reasoned, it had been his idea to ask Kate for money in the first place, and another week or so wouldn't make much difference.

When Kate phoned she and Walter chatted about this and that.

'I miss you all!' she said. 'I must see if I can get over again before too much longer, but I've got a few work trips coming up soon – I'm off to Russia next week and then Poland the week after.'

'I envy you the chance to travel,' Walter said.

'Then come and visit me!'

'Wouldn't that be something?' Walter replied, knowing it was highly unlikely. Annie would never entertain the idea, even if they could get the money together, which was impossible. Kate would probably pay for them all anyway, but that would just give Annie another reason not to go. It wasn't going to happen.

'It's always interesting to see other countries but the actual travelling bit soon loses its glamour – if it ever had any,' said Kate. 'And for me it's mostly just one hotel to another. They're all very much the same.'

After about half an hour the call ended with Kate's usual promise to ring him again the following week, and Walter said goodbye without mentioning anything about money.

***

January 23rd, 2011. Nelson Mandela, a frail 92 year old, was admitted to hospital in Johannesburg for 'routine tests', and an adoring nation went into panic mode. Churches were fuller than usual as people from all walks of life added their prayers that Madiba would be spared, and children in schools across the country pasted 'get well soon' messages on their windows. Annie took Mandela's photo off the shelf unit and propped it up behind a small vase of flowers.

That evening SABC television news showed police controlling traffic around Milpark hospital in Johannesburg, and checking for journalists trying to sneak through in visitor's cars.

The ANC called for calm.

The nation, collectively, held its breath.

* * *

January 24th, 2011. Kate was en route to Moscow with one of her assistants, Judy, for a trade fair. It was just an overnight stopover, and then the following week they would be doing the same in Warsaw.

She wasn't fond of flying, finding it essentially boring. Judy did some work to fill in the three and a half hours, then watched a film. Kate glanced through some paperwork and then turned her mind to something that interested her much more.

Since returning from Cape Town she'd been toying with the idea of buying a property there. If (as she hoped) she was to be making more frequent trips to South Africa to see Walter it made sense for her to have her own place, and when she wasn't there maybe Jeremy, or Nina and her girls could use it too. She liked the thought of Clare and Rachel getting to know their South African cousins and imagined them becoming friends with Mandisa and Elana. So the more she thought about it, the more attractive the idea was.

Kate had started viewing properties online in areas that interested her and pretty soon saw that Simon's Town was winning hands down, for a lot of reasons. Firstly, there was the emotional connection – it was where Ray had met Grace while his ship was in port. Secondly, it was a very attractive little town and had everything she could possibly want. And thirdly, although it was close to Walter and Annie at Ocean View, it wasn't too close. Kate was aware that she should keep some distance between them and not be forever barging into their lives.

In the immediate Simon's Town area there were several 'lock up and go' houses that seemed to fit the bill and fell within her price range, so she had contacted the relevant agents and started the ball rolling. Kate hadn't mentioned the idea to Nina or Jeremy yet, although she knew they'd think it a sensible thing to do. She didn't want to say anything about it to Walter until there was something more definite, but when she told him on the phone the previous week that she was going to 'try to get over again before too much longer', it was house hunting that was on her mind. There were a couple of options coming up soon when clearing her diary for four or five days wouldn't be too much of a problem.

The prospect of this enterprise was one that filled her with a nice glow, her own little part of the place she was already thinking of as her adopted country.

Mandisa can help me to furnish and equip it from her store, she thought, imagining the fun it would be for the two of them to choose cushions, china and table linen together. They would all be able to come over to her sometimes for a barbecue or sundowners. It would be a real home from home.

And so, with all this going through her head, time passed. The flight was uneventful and the landing at Domodedovo airport just a little bumpy.

Several other flights came in at about the same time and the baggage reclaim areas were packed. Neither Kate nor Judy had luggage in the hold, but there were two large bags of advertising material and samples to be collected. Judy found a trolley and they jostled alongside the rest of the passengers until their bags appeared and they were able to haul them off the carousel.

In the crush of people and trolleys they became separated and Judy found herself way behind as Kate reached the end of the customs hall and kept going with the tide of travellers. She glanced back and waved, then moved on into the arrivals hall, knowing that Judy would catch her up there.

And then without warning Kate stepped straight into a blinding white flash of light and the ground disappeared from beneath her. For a fraction of a second, she felt totally confused – what was going on? A thunderous, echoing boom filled her head, and people, suitcases and bits of debris rushed past her.

The world narrowed down to a pinprick, and then it was gone.

CHAPTER 16

JANUARY & FEBRUARY 2011: ENGLAND & OCEAN VIEW.

Just after 2pm on the afternoon of January 24th, the phone rang in Nina's flat. Jeremy had heard on the radio about the Moscow bombing.

'I can't remember when she was flying, can you?' he asked. His voice carried the unnatural lightness of someone who still hoped to hear good news, but was already playing out the alternative scenario.

'No, I don't think she told me her schedule,' said Nina. 'I'm going to ring her office.'

'They've been giving out a number for relatives...' Jeremy's voice trailed off.

'I'll call the office first then get back to you,' said Nina. 'If she's sitting there at her desk there'll be no point in us ringing the emergency number.'

But Kate was not at her desk. The people in her office were already in shock, still clinging to the increasingly faint hope that Judy and Kate had not been caught up in the bombing. Calls to both their mobiles had failed. It was too soon for anyone on the ground to have the information they needed, although Kate's PA, Sophie, was trying to contact the embassy.

'We'll call you back when we have some news.'

Nina picked up her mobile. 'Ring the emergency number,' she said to Jeremy. 'I need to keep my landline free.'

Twenty minutes passed.

The emergency number was unable to give out names although it could confirm that a UK flight had landed shortly before the explosion and it was reasonable to assume that some passengers had got as far as the arrivals hall. The situation at the airport was chaotic.

Nina paced up and down, her landline in one hand, her mobile in the other. Time dragged on slowly – minutes that felt like hours.

Eventually, the landline phone rang, and Nina jumped. It was Sophie.

'Judy's just phoned,' she said. 'She's got some cuts from flying debris but she's basically OK. She was still in the customs hall, but Kate was ahead of her. She would have been in arrivals when the bomb was detonated.' There was a pause. 'We don't know any more than that. We're still hoping...'

Nina clicked the phone off and set it down on a side table. She sat on the edge of her sofa, closed her eyes and pressed her hands to her mouth.

Kate. Please, not Kate.

Her mobile rang.

'Still no names,' said Jeremy.

'Judy called the office. Kate was in arrivals,' said Nina. 'She was right there when it happened...'

'I'm coming straight down to you,' said Jeremy. 'I'll get there as soon as I can and I'll try the number again on my way. Nina,' he added, 'we don't know yet. Try to hold it together.'

Nina nodded, wordlessly, and clicked the phone off.

Jeremy arrived, with no further news. They sat together on her sofa and held hands. They tried the emergency number again but couldn't get through.

Minutes passed; fifteen, twenty, thirty. And finally, Nina's phone rang, and it was Sophie again.

'I'm so sorry,' she said, crying into the phone. 'So very sorry...'

Nina put the handset down and turned to Jeremy.

'We lost Kate,' she said. And then they sat in each other's arms for a long time, and when the numbness subsided, they both cried.

* * *

Later, they started making calls to the family, splitting them up between them. Jeremy phoned his parents and at the same time Nina called Janet. Their shock at the news was palpable and hung in the space between them.

'Jeremy's still talking to Jim and Sue,' said Nina, 'and I must call Clare and Rachel next.'

'Don't worry about Bobby, leave him to me,' said Janet.

'He was on Jeremy's list...'

'No, I'll call him. It'll be better coming from me, Jeremy hardly knows him.'

'Well, if you're sure...'

'I'm sure. I'll ring Bobby,' Janet insisted.

Nina spoke to Clare, who was too shocked to say anything for several moments, but when she could speak said that she would break the news to Rachel.

And that only left one person in the immediate family, the most difficult call of all to make.

Annie answered the phone on the second ring and was genuinely pleased to hear that the caller was Nina.

'Annie, I'm calling with bad news. Please fetch Walter to the phone – and then stay with him,' said Nina.

There was no easy way to tell Walter that Kate had died, but she tried to do it as gently as possible. Walter didn't say a word or make a sound, just listened to what she told him. Nina began to wonder if the line had been cut, then she heard Annie's voice in the background, soothing, and there was a scuffling noise as she took the receiver from Walter's hand.

'How?' was all she said, and Nina explained.

'I'll call you again tomorrow evening, Annie.'

'Tuesday – she would have been phoning him tomorrow.'

Nina sighed. 'Yes, I know. Look after each other tonight.'

Annie took Kate's picture down from the wall unit, moved Nelson Mandela along a bit, and left both of them propped up behind the flowers. Tomorrow, she thought, I'll get some fresh flowers.

Sele came home first, and listened to Annie's quiet account with a mixture of disbelief and horror, then dealt with it in his own way by disappearing into his bedroom and changing into the Manchester United shirt Kate had brought over from England for him. When he came back into the living room Annie took one look and hugged him for long minutes until he gently prised her away and went to sit next to his father. Walter was unreachable, silently locked into his grief at losing Kate and the shock of hearing that it had happened in such a sudden and violent way.

When Mandisa and Elana heard the news from their mother they clung to each other, and as tears started to run down Mandisa's face it was Elana who suggested their local church.

'I think it would be the right thing to do,' she said, softly.

'The right place to be,' Mandisa added, her voice catching.

'You two go, if that's what you want to do,' said Annie. 'We'll stay here. Sele, do you want to join the girls?' But Sele just shook his head.

The church of St. Clare of Assisi was not the nearest to home, but it was where Walter and Annie had married and all the children had been christened. They were not a family of regular churchgoers, but of all the many churches in Ocean View this was the one they felt they most belonged to. So it was natural for Mandisa and Elana to walk the few streets to St. Clare's, without discussion as to where they were heading.

The doors were open and some of the lamps lit, but there was no sign of the pastor or any of the churchwardens. They sat holding hands, alone in the building, in silent contemplation. After several minutes, Mandisa was the first to speak.

'I hoped I could go to see her in Surrey,' she said. 'It was my dream.'

'Nina and Jeremy are still there, you could go to see them one day.'

'But it wouldn't be the same. Kate was our aunt.'

'I can't believe she's gone,' said Elana, 'and we knew her for such a short time.'

'Too short. It was a horrible way to die.'

'Poor Dad. I think he is really suffering, he'll miss her so much.'

'We'll all miss her. Poor Kate.'

After about fifteen minutes Elana turned to Mandisa. 'Shall we go home now?'

'You go, I think I'll stay a little longer.'

So Elana slipped quietly from St. Clare's, and walked home alone.

A door to one side of the chancel opened softly, and Mandisa was aware of someone walking through into the church. She looked across, expecting to see the pastor, but as the figure came closer and moved into the light she saw with a shock that it was Bheki Msonga.

Mandisa let out a startled cry and leapt up from her seat, wondering if she could get back to the main door before he did. But Bheki made no attempt to move forward and block her way, just stood a few feet away from her.

'I heard you and Elana talking,' he said. 'I'm sorry for your loss.'

'What are you doing here? The police are looking for you – they say you shot a man,' Mandisa said.

Bheki sat down on the nearest seat and put his head in his hands.

'Lots of people are looking for me, not only the police. But where would I go Mandi?'

'Khayelitsha? You could disappear in there and they'd never find you.'

Bheki shook his head. 'It's not as easy as that. I can't just disappear. If the police don't find me there are other people who will, wherever I go. I don't know what to do.'

Mandisa edged out into the aisle.

'I can't tell you what to do. And why should I care what happens to you anyway?' she said.

Bheki turned in his seat and looked up at her.

'You shouldn't care,' he said. 'You're right to hate me.'

In a sudden flash Mandisa realised she didn't hate him as he supposed, nor was she afraid of Bheki any longer. She could walk to the door and he would just sit there and watch her go. As she looked down at him she saw that he was defeated, and there was no fight left in him. And all she felt for him at that moment was pity, for a wasted life that could have turned out so much better.

'Have you been here all the time?' she asked.

Bheki nodded. 'Mostly.'

'I can't help you,' she said.

'I know that.'

'Get as far away as you can.'

Mandisa picked up her bag and walked to the church door. When she looked back Bheki hadn't moved.

And then she did something she couldn't explain to herself then or at any time afterwards. She went to the nearest late night store, bought packs of sandwiches and bottled water, and took them back to St. Clare's. She stepped inside and waited for her eyes to adjust to the low light level. There was no sign of Bheki, so she walked down the centre aisle and placed the bag of food on one of the front seats, took a hundred rand note from her purse and tucked it into the plastic carrier. Then she left the church, and walked slowly home.

* * *

Nelson Mandela was improving. His respiratory infection had started to clear up, and President Zuma urged South Africans to let him grow old with dignity.

'We should give the family and the medical team the space to look after him, on our behalf, in privacy,' he said.

The nation heaved a sigh of relief. Mandela had been spared.

In Ocean View, Annie taped his picture back onto the wall unit and moved Kate's into centre position.

186

The vase of flowers had been joined by a candle, which Annie kept lit from first thing in the morning until she went to bed.

Walter took two days off work. Without consulting him, Annie had spoken to the garage owner, who was not insensitive to her request for some time away from work. Of course he would not get paid for the days he stayed at home, but Annie could not bear to send him out under such a great weight of grief. They would just have to manage on a little less for one week.

True to her word, Nina phoned the Maketas each evening and spoke to everyone, letting them each express whatever they needed to. The distance between them seemed very great on those first evenings, their conversations subdued and emotionally charged. There were frequent tears, on both sides of the call.

'Will they bring her home?' asked Annie, a question she knew Walter wanted to ask but couldn't bear to.

'Yes, but we don't yet know when this will happen. The Foreign Office has been helping us make the arrangements,' Nina replied. 'Because it wasn't a simple case of a death abroad there are government agencies involved that wouldn't normally be. The important thing is that we'll be able to hold her funeral here.'

'You'll let us know...?'

'Yes of course, as soon as there's something definite.'

On the third evening, with Walter preparing himself emotionally for a return to work the next day, plus the inevitable questions this would bring from his colleagues, the Maketa family settled down together to watch the late evening news.

Much was being made of President Mandela's continued recovery, whilst other apparently less important reports came later in the bulletin and covered financial issues, unemployment and ministerial scandals. Then, tucked in right at the end and coming just before the sports round-up, was a piece from the nearby township of Mitchell's Plain.

'Police are describing this gangland killing as retribution,' the commentary ran, over filmed footage of the bleak outer edges of the township. The camera panned over a scrubby area of trampled grass with a line of trees spaced out along the length of it.

'The victim had been tied to a tree, before being repeatedly slashed and stabbed and then set on fire. The dead man is believed to be Bheki Msonga, wanted by police in connection with the shooting of...'

The rest was lost to Mandisa as she leapt to her feet and rushed from the room, before being violently and repeatedly sick.

* * *

Kate's office staff had been very helpful, but the legal team her company used hadn't handled anything personal for her, so in the days since she died nobody had been able to make contact with the solicitor holding Kate's will. A copy and the rest of the paperwork would be somewhere in her house, it was just a question of locating it.

Her cleaning lady, alerted by Kate's PA, who'd often had occasion to phone her on Kate's behalf in the past, had agreed to be there to hand over the keys to Nina and Jeremy. She didn't linger once she'd unlocked, just stayed long enough to switch off the alarm and tell them the code.

'I didn't know her very well,' she said, 'because she was usually at work when I was here. But it's terrible that an innocent person like her got caught up in this. It came as such a shock when Sophie phoned to tell me about it.'

'Yes I'm sure, it was a huge shock to all of us, too. You never expect that events in the news will affect you personally, do you?' said Jeremy.

He closed the front door behind her and then stood in the hallway with Nina for a few moments. There was a silence about the house that felt unnatural. It wasn't just the silence of a house that had been empty all day, waiting for its owner to put a key in the lock, this ran deeper. Nina shivered. The chill wasn't only due to the lack of central heating, somehow Kate's house seemed to be frozen mutely in time.

'I feel like an intruder,' said Nina.

'Well let's just do what we absolutely have to do today.'

'I've only been here a few times – where do we start looking?'

'She must have a desk or something.'

Jeremy opened the doors leading off the hallway, and little by little they started moving through the house. They kept their coats on, trying to look past the small personal items that surrounded them, trying not to think about Kate.

There was a vase of flowers in the living room, the water almost dried up and dead petals scattered on the table and carpet. Nina made a mental note to clear them up before leaving and looked around the room, hoping for an unlocked bureau and a quick resolution to the problem. There wasn't one. She swooped on a small side table with a drawer, but when she opened it found only a pack of cards, some pens and a notepad.

Where was Kate's office? She sometimes worked from home, so at the very least there had to be a room set up with drawer space and a computer. Nina couldn't remember the lay-out of the house. She wandered from the living room into the dining room and stared out of the French windows at the garden. Kate had gardeners, that much she knew for certain. They would have to be contacted and paid up to date – and asked to continue for the time being.

So many things to think of and nobody else to do it but us, she thought, with a sigh.

Sophie had been Kate's PA for many years and could possibly help with contacts, as she had with the cleaner, although she hadn't known the name of her personal solicitors. But Kate was used to being efficient and organised and would surely have had a file of household information. Things would certainly become much easier once they found it.

Adjoining the main lounge was a smaller sitting room with bookshelves and hifi, but nowhere there to store files. So Nina went into the kitchen, where Jeremy was emptying the contents of the fridge into the rubbish bin.

'We can't leave this stuff here. Take a quick look in the cupboards Nina, in case there are opened packets that we need to chuck out.'

There were plenty of cupboards to check, but with nothing much in most of them it didn't take long. Nina thought of her own kitchen, where the cupboards were packed tightly with an untidy assortment of half-used packets and jars.

'Kate wasn't much of a cook as far as I knew,' said Nina. 'She probably only kept the bare essentials here because she was away such a lot or out on business lunches.' Half a packet of biscuits joined the rubbish, then a near-empty jar of olives.

'I'm going to look upstairs,' she said.

It wasn't easy to be in Kate's bedroom right at that moment, and Nina stood in the doorway for a moment, holding back before she could steel herself to step into the room. It all felt so personal; earrings lying on her dressing table amongst bottles of perfume and cosmetics, a tote bag on the floor beside it, slippers next to the bed. Just as if she'd be walking back in at any minute.

It took considerable effort for Nina to open the wardrobes in hopes of finding a briefcase, or a personal organiser. Kate's perfume rushed out to greet her. Nina stepped backwards and sat on the edge of the bed, staring at the rails of clothes, many of them familiar. Don't crack up now, she told herself. We have to do this.

She heard Jeremy coming up the stairs and forced herself off the bed. When he found her she was peering in the bottom of the wardrobes, but there were only shoes and handbags there.

'You OK?'

'Just about. Take a look in the other rooms, Jem. I'll finish up in here.'

The room next door, and the first one he tried, held a filing cabinet and desk.

'OK, this is her office.'

By the time she got to the door he already had the top drawer open, and was flicking through the files.

'It's all business stuff in here,' he said, closing the drawer and opening the next one down.

'And in here.'

But it was the bottom drawer that held Kate's personal files. Immaculately tidy and well-organised as they'd expected all along, it seemed everything they needed was there. Each hanging file was clearly labelled: 'Home', 'Pension', 'Car', 'Bank' and at the back of the drawer, 'Legal'.

Jeremy sat down at her desk and they started going through it together. A large brown envelope marked up 'Copy Will' was at the front, with recent correspondence from the solicitor paper-clipped to it.

'It looks as if she only just changed her will,' said Nina. 'Look at the date on this letter, December 15th.'

'Walter?'

'Probably. I'm really glad.'

'Me too.'

There was another file, unlabelled and still on Kate's desk where she'd left it before setting off for Moscow. Jeremy flipped it open and took out the contents, mostly print-outs from the computer. A photo of himself and Kate, loading bags into a hire car at Cape Town airport, slid out from between the papers and landed face up on the desk.

'Look at this,' he said, showing Nina one of the pages. 'She was going to buy a house in Simon's Town.'

And that was the moment that Nina broke down.

＊

There wasn't much of Kate to repatriate, but her incomplete body was flown home some days later in a simple wooden casket, and Nina and Jeremy were at the airport to meet her. Janet had wanted to go with them, but Nina persuaded her against it, knowing that for all her superficial strength it would be too much for her. A Foreign Office official was present to help with the paperwork, and a hearse stood waiting to carry Kate back to Surrey.

'This feels totally unreal,' said Jeremy, as they climbed into his car in order to follow the hearse.

'If only it were.'

'Yeah, if only.' Jeremy clicked his seatbelt on. 'Come on, let's see her into the care of the undertakers, and drop these papers off at the solicitors. Then I think we could do with a drink.'

CHAPTER 17

FEBRUARY 2011: SURREY

Rachel was running late. She'd underestimated the length of time it would take her to drive to Guildford, and now she was only just leaving the outskirts of the town with fifteen minutes to spare.

'Come on!' she yelled at the car in front, slow to pull away from traffic lights.

Rachel hadn't been to Kate's village for years and although she had the SatNav to rely on for getting her there it wouldn't help her in the tricky business of finding a parking space. Clare had talked her through parking arrangements the night before: double yellow lines through the village centre, nothing right at the church, best to try a side street. Trouble was, it seemed the world and his wife had turned up, already cramming the side streets with their own cars.

As she drove towards the church for the second time she could see that the hearse had arrived and Kate's coffin was already being lifted out of it. Rachel glanced across as she drove past, at the same time darting her eyes towards the streets running off the main road. Every single one was nose to tail, as far as she could see.

'Shit. Mum will kill me,' she muttered.

Then she spotted the pub at the end of the road, and a Range Rover that was just leaving the car park to the side. Ignoring the 'patrons only' sign – this was an emergency after all – she swung in and parked, grabbed her bag from the back seat and raced back to the church.

It was so full that there were people standing outside. Rachel manoeuvred her way past them with an apologetic 'Please excuse me, I'm family,' which seemed to do the trick. She stood for a few moments just inside the doors, getting her eyes used to the dim interior, then scanning the pews for a space. There was one, ten or so rows from the front and it was on the aisle – actually only half a space but she reckoned she could shoe-horn herself into it and maybe the other people would budge up a bit when she pulled the 'family' line again. At the front she could see her mother, grandma and Clare, and then Jeremy with Sue and Jim next to him. Kate's coffin was already in place on the bier, with the minister standing at the head of it.

Rachel glanced around the church but it was full of Kate's work colleagues and she didn't know anyone. Then she stopped at a face in profile that did look familiar. Sitting right at the back – was that Uncle Bobby? It was many years since she'd seen him but there was a family likeness which reminded her of Jim. Her mind flicked back to Sunday lunch in Brighton last August. That was the last time they'd all been together and the day she and Clare had gone to the beach and everything had started unravelling. So much had happened since.

Rachel gulped. Can't start thinking about all that now, she thought, as she tip-toed as quietly as possible down the aisle to the empty half-space, and squeezed in.

'Sorry,' she whispered. 'I'm family. Had trouble parking.'

The line of people next to her shuffled along until there was just enough room to get herself in more comfortably. Rachel glanced behind to where the man who looked like Bobby was sitting, hoping for a better sightline from her new position, but she couldn't pick him out from all the other people. Maybe his head was bowed.

Then the service started and Rachel forgot about him.

* * *

They held the wake in the church hall, a typically high-ceilinged room with trestle tables and plastic chairs. Nina had left all the reception arrangements to Clare, who booked the hall and then arranged for florists and caterers she'd worked with before and trusted.

'That church hall *is* a bit gloomy,' she'd said, 'but it's the only place round there that's big enough to get so many people in. And we don't want to be driving off somewhere else, do we?'

But on the day the sun put in a welcome appearance and streamed through the high windows, bringing with it a hint of spring and cheerfulness and lighting up big vases of flowers which Clare had placed carefully around the otherwise featureless space.

The room started to fill up, a steady trickle of grey and black clad mourners, filing in, quietly accepting drinks and then gradually being absorbed by the growing mass of people. After a while individuals started to become apparent, there was movement across the room, hand-shakes and conversations in subdued tones. Waitresses with trays of canapés appeared, moving efficiently between the clusters of people, and little by little the atmosphere gradually softened, tensions started to lift and everyone relaxed. Several people moved to the sides of the hall and sat together in groups.

Nina and Jeremy worked their way around the room, meeting people from Kate's professional life, most of whom they'd never even heard about before. The woman who'd founded the company jointly with Kate and retired just over a year ago, had flown in from Crete specially for the funeral. The other company directors and their wives were there, plus the rest of the office staff, executives from advertising agencies, company solicitors, designers, magazine editors, accountants – it was a bewildering experience, and impossible for them as outsiders to figure out who everyone was. They were helped in this by the ever-loyal Sophie, making introductions and generally easing the whole operation, in much the same way as she'd done for Kate over so many years as her PA.

The rest of the family stayed together, with Jim moving chairs and organising them all round a table. Clare went briefly to the kitchen to check that everything was running as planned, and it was then that Rachel remembered Bobby. She stood up and looked around.

'I think Uncle Bobby was in the church,' she said to Janet, 'but I don't see him here.'

'Oh... he did say he would try to make it,' said Janet.

'Well he might have popped over to say hello,' said Jim, also getting to his feet and scanning the room. 'We only see him once in a blue moon as it is – you'd think he'd stay for a chat.'

'Would you?' said Sue. 'I wouldn't – not unless he's changed since the last time I met him.'

'Maybe it wasn't him. I just got a glimpse of someone, right at the back of the church, and at the time I thought it looked like Uncle Bobby.'

'Did he know the details?' Jim asked Janet.

'Well, yes. I rang him last week. But you know Bobby,' said Janet, 'not the most reliable of people.'

Sue laughed. 'You can say that again.'

After an hour or so the first guests started to drift away, which set off a gradual chain reaction and it wasn't much longer before there were only family, Sophie and a few neighbours left.

And then suddenly it was all over and Nina sat down for the first time since leaving the church.

'Did you eat anything?' Clare asked her.

'Not really, I picked up a couple of canapés but that's all. Jem and I were too busy working the room. It was good that so many people turned out for someone they really only had a business connection with. Thank goodness for Sophie, she was a star.'

'And the caterers did a great job, Clare, well done,' said Rachel. She looked across the empty hall. 'What are we going to do with these flowers?'

'I'll have to get the vases back to the florists tomorrow but we can all take some flowers home with us, I brought plastic bags with me. There wasn't any food left – sorry Mum, you could probably do with something.'

Jeremy checked his watch. 'There's a pub along the road – they'll be serving food by now.'

'And I expect we could all do with another drink,' Jim said, then caught the look of disapproval on Sue's face and added, 'or a coffee would be nice.'

'I left my car in their car park so I probably owe them some business,' said Rachel. 'Wouldn't it be funny if we got down there and found Uncle Bobby already propping up the bar!'

'Rachel thought he was in the church,' Sue explained to Nina and Jeremy, 'but there was no sign of him here. It's possible, because Janet had told him the where and when, but you know what Bobby's like.'

'I might have been mistaken,' said Rachel, 'in fact I probably was – I mean, how likely would he be to come all this way?'

'I'd like to think he'd make the effort,' said Jim. 'After all, Kate was his niece as well as ours.'

Janet got to her feet abruptly and started gathering up her coat and bag. 'Right, let's get going then,' she said. 'Clare's got things to finish off here and while she's doing that the rest of us can walk along the road to the pub.'

***

Rachel stayed behind to give Clare a hand, and took the opportunity to update her on Jason's movements.

'He keeps calling me but I just let it go to answerphone.'

'And does he leave messages?'

'Yeah, but nothing that makes me think he doubts me. Just "I miss you" sort of stuff. They haven't been round to my family – at least not while I've been there so we haven't come face to face yet.'

'Thank goodness for that,' said Clare, checking the fridge and extracting a few stray bits that had been forgotten about. 'How long can that go on for, though?'

Rachel held a carrier bag open for Clare to throw the things into.

'Well, their nanny's looking for another job now because according to her they're planning to go to America.'

'What for? Holiday or permanently?'

'Permanently I presume. She's been given two month's notice although they've told her she might not have to work it all if they can get everything sorted sooner. I suppose he'll get in OK because the wife's a US citizen.'

'So, two months max and you're in the clear.'

'Yeah. I'm thinking of moving on as well. Maybe I need more of a challenge than I get with the Wingates.'

'Don't rush into something if it's just a knee-jerk reaction to the Jason business. Have you said anything to Mum about finding another job?'

'Not likely! And definitely not while she's got all Kate's stuff to handle. It's going to take ages to sort out her affairs, I should think.'

Clare started wrapping flowers into plastic bags. 'I suppose so, what with the business and everything. Now, if we can just deal with the rest of the flowers and get everything across the road to my car we're done here.'

'I wonder if that *was* Uncle Bobby in the church?' said Rachel, carrying the last vase into the kitchen.

Clare emptied the water down the sink, then put the vase on the worktop.

'I doubt it – surely he would have spoken to one of us at least, even Uncle Bobby isn't that odd. And I notice nobody's mentioned David, the other family member who didn't show. Of course he might not even know about Kate, I'm not sure that anyone has a contact address or anything for him.'

'But there was quite a bit about the bombing on television and the British victims were named, so even if he didn't see it someone would surely have told him. It's not a common name.'

'I guess so.' Clare took a last look around the church hall. 'Well, I think that's everything, let's go down the road and join the oldies.'

* * *

Over the course of many phone calls and a couple of personal visits to the office Nina had built up a good relationship with Tim Garvey, the solicitor handling

Kate's will. There were many unusual aspects to her case and it made a change from the usual run-of-the-mill probate work he undertook, so when an unexpected twist landed in his lap he was on the phone to Nina in pretty short order. It was less than a week after the funeral and his call certainly came as a surprise to her.

'Did Ms Hatchman have a brother?' he asked, 'And I don't mean Mr Maketa.'

Nina's heart sunk. This could only mean trouble.

'Yes, David, estranged from the whole family. Why do you ask?'

'Because he's been on the phone to me. He's expecting to be a beneficiary but as you and I both know, he's going to be disappointed in that.'

When Jeremy and Nina had last been to see Tim Garvey he'd run through the contents of Kate's will.

'Her shares in the company are to be evenly split between her PA Sophie Isherwood, and each of you two. There are five legacies of...' he'd rustled the paperwork looking for the figure he wanted, 'five thousand pounds to each of your daughters, Mrs Redford, and to each of the three Maketa children. The residue of the estate – which I think we can assume will be a considerable sum – will be split in three equal shares, between yourselves and Mr Maketa.'

There had been no mention of David – until now, when he'd popped up out of the blue.

Nina was so unsettled by Tim's call that after she'd put the phone down she went straight round to Janet's flat.

'*David*?' said Janet, as surprised as Nina had been. 'How on earth would he know where to find her solicitor? He'd had no contact with Kate for years.'

'The solicitors have to put a notice in the local paper before starting the legal work and presumably David did at least know roughly where she lived. She'd been in that house for quite a few years and living in the same area long before that. I think she kept in touch with his daughters occasionally so maybe they pointed him in the right direction.'

Janet made coffee and carried it through to the living room. 'I take it he wants a share of the spoils?'

'I think that's safe to assume. The solicitor said it could delay things considerably and, as he put it, "become rather messy."' Nina stirred sugar into her coffee. 'I don't mind for myself and I know Jem won't either, but I have a feeling Walter and Annie could use their share of the money sooner rather than later – if they end up getting anything at all now that David's stuck his oar in.'

'Yes, I guessed she'd have included him. I said at the start Nina, it does no good raking up the past.' Janet snapped a chocolate digestive in half and jabbed the air with one of the pieces. 'Now look what's going to happen, recriminations that might go on for years, *in public*, and... oh, I just wish she'd left well alone,' she finished, before biting furiously onto the biscuit.

'Mum, what's done is done. Walter is one of the beneficiaries because that's what Kate wanted. But since David is her full brother he has a better claim – and if it has to go to court then of course the whole Walter story will come out and I'm guessing that David will do his darnedest to discredit him and see that he doesn't get anything from Kate's estate.'

'Poor Isobel and Ray will be turning in their graves,' said Janet.

'If Kate had just stated in her will that she didn't want David to have anything it would have been all right. Unfortunately, she didn't mention his name at all and in the eyes of the court that could have been a clerical error or an oversight on her part.'

'An oversight? What does that mean, that he'd just slipped her mind? How ridiculous!'

'Yes it is, but I'm just telling you what Tim Garvey told me. David could pursue that line and because he's her closest living relative that might give him the power to overturn her will.' Nina sighed. 'If only her death hadn't been so... public... he might never have known a thing until it was too late.'

Janet sat back and folded her arms across her chest.

'This is not what Kate would have wanted,' she said, her mouth drawn into a tight line of disapproval, 'the family squabbling over her money for all the world to see. And whether any of us agree with it or not, Kate's wishes are not going to be served if David has his way.'

'Even if Walter had never contacted Kate we'd still have been in this position – according to Tim Garvey she didn't include David in her previous will either,' said Nina, in an attempt to shift Janet's focus away from Walter. 'He didn't even know David existed or he would have advised her differently.'

'Yes, but then we wouldn't have to cover...'

'Anyway there's nothing we can do about it, Mum,' said Nina, reaching across to take a biscuit. 'The solicitor just told David that all the beneficiaries would be hearing from him in about a week. He didn't say whether he was one of them or not, so we won't hear any more until David realises the letter he's waiting for hasn't arrived.'

Janet's reaction to the news took Nina by surprise. She'd half-expected her mother to take the line that in doing Walter out of his share, David was only getting what was his by rights. Redressing the balance, keeping it in the family – the *real* family, that is. On her walk back home Nina tried to see it from Janet's angle.

Maybe Mum thinks he'll try to go after the whole lot, she thought. She would have realised from the start that Jem and I are named in Kate's will and she wouldn't want us to lose out to him. And it's important to her that Isobel and Ray aren't tarnished by this – the last thing Mum wants is for the Walter story to emerge in public.

And so it started to add up to Nina.

Meanwhile, Janet stood at her living room window, gazing out at the sea, mulling things over and wondering how it had all gone so wrong after so many years. She sighed deeply and pulled herself back to the moment. There was, she thought, reaching for her phone, only one thing for it.

At the other end of the line the call was picked up on the fourth ring.

'We need to talk,' said Janet.

CHAPTER 18

MARCH 2011: OCEAN VIEW

When Mandisa was called into her manager's tiny office at the back of the stockroom she couldn't imagine what she'd done wrong. True, she'd been a bit distracted lately – first there was Kate's death and then, as if that wasn't bad enough, the business with Bheki had jolted right through her. But she was a diligent worker and she didn't think she'd let any of this get in the way of her work.

'Don't look so worried Mandisa, I'm not going to discipline you for anything,' her manager said, 'quite the opposite, in fact.' She shuffled a few papers around on her hopelessly untidy desk.

'Somewhere here... ah yes, this is it,' she said, extracting a single sheet from the tangle of paperwork. 'Last month Head Office sent round a circular asking if we had any members of staff we thought suitable for management training. I put your name forward, and it seems that you've been accepted to go on a course.'

Mandisa's mouth fell open. 'Me?'

'Of course you! You're very good with customers and popular with the other girls. I think you could do well and I'd like you to have the opportunity to prove yourself. You'll have to work hard – but I don't think you mind that, do you?

'No ma'am. I enjoy the work.'

'Can you drive?'

Mandisa shook her head.

'Then you should think about having some lessons, you don't know where you might end up – we have stores all over the Western Cape so you'll need to be flexible about where you work. But that's some way ahead. First you have to pass a four-day training course, and after that you'll come back here, and gradually take on a little bit more responsibility. How do you feel about that?'

Mandisa considered how she felt. She loved her job. She loved the shop and the products and dealing with the customers. She was excited by the idea of having more responsibility – but never in a million years had she expected to be singled out for promotion. She smiled her widest smile.

'It's a great opportunity, thank you for giving me this chance.'

Together they went through the arrangements for the course.

'Now, is there anything else you want to ask me?'

There was, but Mandisa was reluctant to bring it up.

'Well,' she said, 'I was just wondering if...'

'Yes?'

'Erm, ma'am, will this mean I earn more money?'

* * *

On the Volksie bus that evening Mandisa and Elana sat together as usual, but in a whispering huddle that had Uyanda at the front of the bus puzzled and curious.

'Four days in Port Elizabeth, and I don't have to pay for anything!'

'You mean, there's a hotel and transport and everything?'

'Yes, I'll show you the information pack when we get home. Elana, I'm so excited!'

From her seat next to the driver Uyanda turned around again, in time to see the Maketa girls with their heads together, giggling. It was infuriating, but she was too far away to hear what was going on above the noise of the Volksie's engine. She hung back when everyone got off at Ocean View and called across to them, but Mandisa and Elana ignored her completely and headed off towards home arm-in-arm and at a fast pace.

It was high time the Maketa family had something to celebrate, and they did so in fine form when Mandisa burst in breathlessly with her news. Walter pulled out a bottle of wine from the back of a cupboard – it was left over from the Hatchman's visit before Christmas, but nobody wanted to put a dampener on the occasion by mentioning that so the unusual appearance of alcohol in the apartment passed without comment. From somewhere in the depths of his tiny, chaotic bedroom Sele found a map of the Garden Route and worked out roughly how far it was to Port Elizabeth – further certainly than any of them had travelled before.

'About seven hundred kilometres! Man, that's a long drive!' he said, clearly impressed.

'There'll be eight of us travelling together from different stores around Cape Town, and people will be going there from other areas too.'

'Well done Mandi,' said Walter proudly, raising his glass. 'You're a credit to your mother and me, and you deserve a chance to show what you can do.'

'I'll be getting a little more money each week too, so I can help a bit more here with the housekeeping.'

Annie and Walter looked at each other.

'Just enjoy the extra money,' said Annie. 'We can manage.'

* * *

A Volksie bus was due to pick Mandisa up at six o'clock in the morning for the journey to Port Elizabeth, but even though she had got everything ready the night before she was up far earlier than necessary. In the small flat, where every sound travelled through the thinnest of walls, this meant that everyone else – except Sele, who could sleep through anything – was also awake early. Nobody in the Maketa family had ever needed a suitcase before, so Mandisa had bought herself one in the mall. It was a red and white striped cabin bag, big enough to take everything she would need for this trip and small enough to store under her bed.

'One day,' she'd said to Elana the night before, 'this suitcase is going to fly to England.'

Now, it stood by the door to the apartment, and it seemed to Annie that it symbolised the one thing she'd dreaded – except that on that morning she didn't have any negative feelings. She was so proud of her daughter that her overwhelming feeling was one of happiness that she was making a success of her life. OK, Mandisa would only be away for five days in total this time, and that was easy to bear, but Annie knew this was just the start of it and she realised suddenly that Nina had been right that day in Simon's Town when she'd said *'you just want the best for your kids'*. Annie's growing ambitions for them all, sparked by Mandisa's sudden elevation to management trainee, had overcome her own reluctance to let them go out into the world.

'They always know where home is,' Nina had said. Annie stood next to Walter and Elana at the front of their apartment block, waving Mandisa off in the Volksie bus, and hoped some of her neighbours were up early enough to see her daughter taking her first steps away from home and into the wider world. If not, she'd certainly be telling them about it at the first

opportunity. When the bus reached the end of the road, Mandisa turned and waved from the back window. Walter took hold of Annie's hand and squeezed it, and when she looked up at him she was amazed to find that the only tears that morning were his.

* * *

There were five girls and three boys in the Cape Town group that travelled together to Port Elizabeth. The seven hour journey was long enough for them to find out about each other, and by the time they arrived and met up with about another twenty trainees from other parts of the province friendships had been formed.

Their accommodation was basic but clean. Mandisa was sharing a room with two other girls, Naledi from the Tokai branch and Jewel from Claremont, and they hardly had time to drop their suitcases before setting off to the head office training centre for the first session.

It soon became apparent that Jewel was the high-flyer of the entire group, and that there were one or two other trainees who didn't seem very likely to make the grade at all. Mandisa evaluated the group as a whole, and felt she was somewhere in the middle, but as the course progressed she proved herself as the queen of role-play.

'My husband was very angry when he saw the poor quality of this,' she said, in her role as the complaining customer. 'Look, you can push your finger right through it quite easily! What has happened to the excellent reputation this store used to have? I demand my money back!'

And when it was her turn to placate an irate shopper she was calm and controlled. 'Ma'am, let's sit down together and see how we can best resolve the problem to your satisfaction. We certainly don't want to lose you as a customer and I do understand your disappointment.'

Mandisa blossomed. Her confidence grew visibly and she was having fun, enjoying the challenge and the company of the rest of the group. As the course came to an end she realised how much she'd moved on in such a short space of time.

On the last day they finished early, and with an hour to spare before the Volksie bus picked them up for the journey home, Mandisa went with several other girls to the shopping mall. They rushed around from one shop to another, each looking for some special little thing to take back with them. Mandisa didn't want anything for herself, but she was determined to find something nice for Elana.

Jewel stopped to buy a hair ornament, took ages over choosing, ended up buying the most expensive one she'd looked at, then left the shop wearing it. Naledi found a big, chunky necklace in a basket of reductions, then rummaged around a bit more and discovered a ring to go with it. Mandisa spotted another shop across the mall and dashed over in search of a scarf for Elana – and there were reductions there too, so she bought one for Annie as well.

Rushing back out of the shop to show the other girls she suddenly came to a standstill, and the smile fell from her face. There, coming towards her, was a familiar figure.

For a moment Mandisa thought she was going to faint but she just stumbled and then recovered her balance. He hadn't seen her, looking ahead confidently, over the heads of shoppers in the mall towards the exit. Somewhere in the background she could hear one of the girls calling to her but she was physically unable to turn to the sound, her eyes glued upon – what? A look-alike? A ghost?

And then from a couple of metres away he saw her, and it seemed to her that his eyes registered something. In no more than a heartbeat he'd drawn level with Mandisa. There was the smallest smile on his lips, and without changing his stride or looking directly at her he walked straight past.

'Mandisa – come *on*! We're going to miss the pick-up if we don't go now!'

She turned around to look behind, searching amongst the people in the mall. But there was no sign of him.

Jewel grabbed her hand and pulled her back into the moment.

'Come *on*! What's got into you?'

'Nothing – I just thought I saw someone I knew...'

Mandisa let herself be rushed along by Jewel, and all the time her head was in turmoil. How could it be him? He was killed... wasn't he?

* * *

The journey home wasn't as much fun as it had been on the way to Port Elizabeth. Most of the group fell asleep for at least some of the time, but Mandisa couldn't. She was wide awake with her head buzzing all the way on the long journey back to Cape Town. It couldn't have been Bheki, that was ridiculous. It wasn't as if she'd heard the news second hand, she'd seen the TV report herself... the police had said it was a retribution killing... they'd said that the body was Bheki's... Then as she went back over the news report in her mind she started to wonder, did they say it *was* him, or did they just say they *believed* it was him? Had he staged the whole thing? Or just taken advantage of somebody else's mistake? Had she really just seen Bheki in Port Elizabeth, a dead man walking... or simply someone who looked like him?

She was one of the last drop-offs, at Ocean View, and all she wanted to do by then was to get back home and sleep.

But Annie had other ideas. The evening meal had been delayed so they could all eat together.

'I'm starving!' Sele had complained over an hour before Mandisa arrived home.

'You'll just have to wait a little longer,' his mother replied, from the steamy kitchen. 'Tonight nobody eats until Mandisa gets here. Drink something, your stomach will fill up that way.'

When she opened the door to the apartment and wheeled the red and white striped suitcase in, Mandisa took one look at her beaming family and burst into tears.

'Oh, Mandi, didn't you get on very well? It doesn't matter...' Annie put her arms around her daughter while Elana and Walter made sympathetic noises.

Mandisa wiped her eyes and gulped.

'No, I loved the course, it was really great,' she said. 'I'm just so tired, we worked very hard. And I'm so pleased to see you all again.'

They all gave her a hug, Elana took the suitcase off to their bedroom and much to Sele's relief Annie went directly to the kitchen and then served Mandisa's favourite meal of bobotie.

Over dinner, she talked almost non-stop about the course and the other trainees she'd met. Gradually, the shock of running into the Bheki look-alike receded and by the following day she could only wonder that she'd made such an issue of a stupid mistake.

Mandisa slotted straight back into her work routine, and the appraisal that came back from the course leaders was very complimentary.

'They put you in the top five,' said her manager, waving the report in front of Mandisa. 'Very good indeed – I knew I'd chosen you well. Now you're on the next level, lots to learn here and then another course later in the year. If there's a suitable assistant manager's vacancy somewhere before then you might get moved on sooner.'

A week or so later a letter arrived at the Maketa apartment, addressed to Mandisa. Annie handed it to her when she came home from work one evening while she was taking off her coat and slipping out of her shoes. She took a look at the envelope but didn't recognise the handwriting, and the postmark was smudged beyond reading.

'Could be from Jewel, she had something she wanted to send me,' she said, taking coat, shoes, bag and letter into the bedroom. She sat on the bed and tore open the envelope.

But it wasn't from Jewel and there was no letter inside.

Just a hundred rand note, which fell out onto Mandisa's lap.

CHAPTER 19

APRIL 2011: LONDON

The front doorbell rang at around 3pm.

Rachel was in the house alone, the Wingates having taken their children out to an Easter egg hunt at a National Trust house somewhere in Kent – a rare midweek family excursion and an opportunity for Rachel to have a day on her own. She'd spent the morning shopping in the West End – London was knee-deep in Royal wedding frenzy, with flags and bunting everywhere and an atmosphere that was joyful and celebratory. In the centre of the city it was hard not to get caught up in the excitement and by the time Rachel got home from the shops she was in a happy, carefree mood.

She ran down the stairs from her flat to answer the door then pulled herself up suddenly, pausing just for a moment on the bottom step. What if it were Jason? She knew from their nanny that tomorrow they were flying to the USA, and that the house was chaotic. Jason and his wife had called on the Wingates a couple of nights ago to say their goodbyes, and when she saw them walk up the front drive Rachel had kept herself tucked away upstairs to avoid coming face to face with him. But what if he'd come especially to see her? She'd steadfastly refused to return his phone calls, and finally they'd stopped. She thought he'd got the message, but maybe not...

She hesitated. The doorbell rang again, and as she peered at the stained glass panel in the door she saw with relief that whoever was on the other side was considerably taller than Jason. But still... Rachel put the chain on and then opened the door the few inches it would allow.

The first thing she saw was a police warrant card, pushed forward into the gap between the door and the door frame.

'Mrs Wingate? I'm Detective Sergeant Phillips. I wonder if I might come in for a moment? Nothing to worry about...'

An electric shock ran right through Rachel's body. She opened her mouth to speak, but for a moment nothing came out.

'Mrs Wingate?'

Rachel gulped. 'I'm not Mrs Wingate, I'm just their nanny.'

'Ah. Any idea when she might be back home?'

'Oh... well, not really. 5-ish?'

He passed a business card through the gap.

'Perhaps you'd be kind enough to ask her to phone me on this number – any time will do, whenever she can.'

Rachel took the card.

'Yes, yes of course.'

'Don't look so worried,' he added with a smile, 'nobody's in any trouble. But I would appreciate a call from Mrs Wingate.'

She closed the door and moved to the staircase, sitting on the bottom step to wait for her heart to stop racing. Through the glass of the front door she could see that the police officer was still standing there. Then he stepped back, and stayed there for a moment as though surveying the upper floors of the building. After what seemed like hours he turned, and she heard his footsteps going down the front steps.

Rachel closed her eyes and let out a sigh. Her hands were shaking.

I can't do this any more, she thought, as she placed the card on the hall table. I need to get right away from here.

And then she remembered someone mentioning a magazine article they'd read recently and an idea came to her, tentatively at first, but it was a good enough idea to send her back upstairs to her computer for a little research.

Later that evening, with the idea starting to solidify into a plan, Rachel called Clare. Even her uber-cool big sister was taken aback by the audacity of it.

'Africa?' she said, astonished.

* * *

Janet didn't like London. She'd never liked living there, and had not grown any fonder of it after she and Terry moved to Brighton. Ordinarily she would avoid a trip to the city, but this time it was strictly necessary.

She'd managed to negotiate the Tube across town from Victoria – and was surprised to find that even down in the Underground the stations were awash with red, white and blue. Plus of course there were the inevitable tourists swarming around in silly Union Jack hats, waving flags and pictures of Kate and Will. In her current mood this had all combined to irritate Janet, who'd looked around disapprovingly at these expressions of celebration and felt even more of an alien.

At the heart of all this fuss are two families looking forward to a happy event, she'd thought, while mine gets ready to tear itself apart. And even though the alternative scenario wouldn't be the end of the world it would certainly be dishonest, and contrary to Kate's wishes. Janet couldn't imagine how she would live with herself, knowing she could have put it all right – or at the very least, tried to do so.

Now, feeling slightly more comfortable after her arrival in suburbia, and with a cup of tea in her hand, Janet came straight to the point.

'I understand your reluctance Bobby, but we can't let this go on any longer,' she said. 'You've simply got to tell them the whole story – because if you don't then I will.'

1958

CHAPTER 20

AUGUST 1958: LONDON

They sat together in Isobel's freshly painted sitting room, not far from Ladbroke Grove tube station, two young mothers with plenty to chat about. Out in the hallway three-month-old Nina snoozed in her Silver Cross pram, snuffling occasionally in her sleep.

'She's such a good baby,' said Isobel. 'Unlike David, he was born grumpy!'

'We're very lucky with her, most of the time she goes right through the night.'

Janet picked up a copy of Woman's Own magazine from the coffee table and fanned herself with it.

'Goodness, it's close today,' she said. 'I hope there's not going to be another thunderstorm – at least not before I get home.'

'After all the rain we've had this summer it doesn't look as if the Bank Holiday will be much better. Still, it's a day off work I suppose.'

'Not for you and me! But Terry will be glad to have a break – I suppose we might take a picnic to the park or something if it's fine. Have you heard from Ray lately?'

Ray's ship was patrolling Icelandic waters, deployed to protect the fishing rights of UK trawlers in the so-called Cod War.

'Yes, he says it's cold and boring – a bit of a change for him after all the hot, sunny tours he's had. He's home on leave in about six weeks.'

'Well he'll see a change in David, that's for sure.'

As if on cue, a wail from upstairs signalled the end of David's nap.

'I'll just get him up, Janet. There's a jug of lemonade in the kitchen, I made it this morning. Help yourself,' said Isobel, heading for the staircase and the penetrating sound of David exercising his lungs as he pulled himself up onto wobbly legs and rattled the sides of his cot.

Janet went along the passage and into the kitchen. Isobel had evidently been busy; gone were the old cream painted walls and brown glossed woodwork that were the common currency of post-war kitchen design. Instead there was wallpaper in a checker-board design and woodwork painted a light cream, with tangerine and white gingham curtains at the window and back door. The kitchen dresser, which Janet remembered as pale blue, had been painted a sunny tangerine to match the new decor. Not only would Ray be seeing a change in his son, he might wonder if he hadn't walked into the wrong house too.

Isobel appeared in the doorway with David balanced on her hip, rubbing his little fists into his eyes.

'This looks very modern Issy, it must have taken you a while to do all this work,' said Janet, admiringly. 'I thought you weren't staying in this house?'

'I'd like to move further out of London. It's not so bad round here, this is quite a nice road, but over at Notting Dale there are so many blacks now – you hear of fights all the time these days. I don't want David to grow up with all that going on around him.'

Janet nodded sympathetically. 'These immigrants are getting to be a real problem,' she said.

'There's a family of blacks in one of the houses across the road – actually I think it might be two families, there seem to be lots of people coming and going and several children,' said Isobel, adding, 'I've never spoken to any of them, of course.'

'No, probably best that way. What does Ray think about moving?'

'He's never here so it doesn't bother him, but he's only got another year in the Navy and then, who knows where we'll end up?'

'Well, you've made a really good job of this kitchen, anyway.'

'Bobby did most of it,' said Isobel, bouncing David on her hip. 'He painted the sitting room too.'

'Yes I noticed that had had a coat of paint. He's recovered, then?'

Bobby, invalided out of the Navy after a second bad bout of pneumonia, was lodging at Ray and Isobel's house till he was fully fit.

'More or less. He's working odd days in the local greengrocer's, just temporary till he gets something better, and he's out a lot of the time.'

Janet held her hands out to David, who covered his face and shrunk back into his mother's side.

'I couldn't understand why he didn't just go back to his mum and dad's,' she said. 'Rose would have liked having him home again I expect.'

'Well, he never really got on with Frank. I think that was what took him into the Navy in the first place, just to get away from home. Once all his brothers had left it got a bit too much for him.'

David started wriggling and kicking in his mother's arms.

'Down,' he demanded, until she put him down on the kitchen lino.

'He's getting too big now for me to carry around,' Isobel said, as they watched him waddle off into the hall.

'Baby, baby, baby,' he chanted, head wagging from side to side.

'Maybe Bobby could get a job as a decorator,' said Janet, looking round the kitchen. 'He seems to have a talent for it.'

'He was talking about that, it's certainly something he enjoys. In the meantime I don't have any objections to him practising here!'

'Tell him to come round our place if he gets bored – Terry's hopeless...'

Suddenly Nina started crying and they looked out at the pram in time to see David pulling at the wheels and shaking it backwards and forwards.

'David, *no*!' Isobel shouted at him, which startled him so that he overbalanced, fell onto his bottom with a thud and then he started crying as well. By the time both babies were pacified rain was coming down in big, fat drops and Janet looked out at the grey skies dolefully.

'If this keeps up I'll be soaked by the time I get home, I've got a half hour walk.'

'Stay and have tea, it might have left off by then. Bobby'll be home soon, if necessary he can pop round to the phone box later and then Terry will come and pick you up.'

Terry was generally considered to be the high-flyer of the family. He and Janet had a phone, a car, a television – and aspirations. Terry's job as branch manager of a national chain of newsagent and stationery shops presented opportunities to move away, and he and Janet had their sights set on Brighton, her home town. In time, all four brothers would leave London and spread out, but for now they stayed in the city where they'd grown up. The slight exception was Jim, living closer to his fiancée, in a bedsit just south of the river – which to the rest of the family was a foreign country.

As it turned out the rain that day was short-lived, no more than a summer shower, and Janet arrived home before Terry got in from work.

'Bobby seems to have got his feet under the table,' she said to him that evening. 'When Ray comes home he'll feel like a stranger in his own house.'

'It was Ray's idea in the first place,' said Terry. 'Anyway, it won't be for long I don't suppose. How many lads of twenty-one would want to live with their older brother and sister-in-law? He'll be up and off again soon I expect.'

* * *

One evening the following week Bobby came home with a parcel tucked under his arm.

'This is the latest thing,' he told Isobel. 'Handy for parties.'

'We're not having a party,' she said.

'OK, well it's small enough to take to someone else's party.'

He unwrapped the brown paper, with Isobel looking on, intrigued. Inside was a red and cream leatherette-covered box with a grille at the front and suitcase clips at the sides, which he flipped open to reveal a record player.

'The Dansette Junior,' he said proudly. 'They're all the rage now.'

'Bobby, we've got nothing to play on it.'

'Oh yes we have.'

Bobby carefully extracted two seven-inch vinyl records from the brown paper and held one up for inspection.

'Only released today Issy – I bet we're the first house in the street to get it!'

Isobel peered at the label.

'"Move It",' she read, 'Cliff Richard and The Drifters – I've heard of him, there was something on the wireless recently. Don't have it up too loud,' she warned as Bobby plugged the Dansette in and took the record out of its purple and white paper case. 'I don't want David waking up, it took me ages to get him to sleep.'

But Bobby was too busy getting the record player set up to take any notice. Seconds later, Cliff Richard's voice burst out into the living room. Bobby grinned at Isobel.

'Great isn't it? British rock 'n roll arrives in Cornwall Crescent, thanks to Bobby Hatchman! Move over Elvis...'

Isobel laughed.

'You're daft – but you might be right about the music...'

The record finished and Bobby started moving the furniture back to the wall.

'Now what are you doing?' Isobel asked.

'C'mon Issy, I'll teach you how to rock 'n roll,' he said, pushing the settee further along and blocking the doorway.

'You must be joking! I'm too old for all that!'

'At twenty five? No you're not, come on!'

He put the record on again, and grabbed Isobel's hands, pushing and whirling her around till she fell in a dizzy, giggling heap onto the settee.

'I'll never get the hang of this!' she said, breathlessly, as 'Move It' came to an end, and Bobby lifted it carefully off the spindle. Then he took the other record out of its paper case, put it on the turntable and lowered the needle onto it.

'You must know this one,' he said, waiting for Isobel to recognise the tune.

'Oh yes, this is Dean Martin.'

Bobby took hold of her hand and pulled her to her feet. 'It's a bit slower, give you a chance to get your breath back.'

'Why? You don't think I'm going to have another go at that jiving, do you?'

Bobby put his arm round Isobel's waist and slow-danced her to 'Volare'.

'Yep, till you get it right.'

'Anyway,' she said, 'how did you get enough money for a record player?'

'I had a bit of luck on the horses,' said Bobby, and when she looked questioningly at him, he winked and smiled, and spun her round again. 'Next time I back a winner I'm going to get a television set.'

Isobel shook her head, but she laughed too.

By nine thirty she was doing pretty well at the jive, but then the neighbours banged on the wall and David woke up, and that was the end of that for the night.

* * *

About five o'clock the following evening, with David in his high chair – failing to eat his tea but enjoying mashing it up with his hands – and Isobel chopping the supper vegetables and meat for herself and Bobby, the first of many police cars raced along Ladbroke Grove. Its clanging bell faded as it sped away, but Isobel barely registered it. Nothing unusual in that, after all.

'Come on sweetie, just a little more.' She picked the spoon up from where he'd abandoned it on the tray, and scooped a little food onto it. When he saw it coming his way, David clamped his lips firmly closed and turned his head away.

'Ooh, lovely,' said Isobel, making yum-yum noises of encouragement. David hesitated and turned towards the spoon again. Isobel moved forward. David moved back. One gooey hand came up over his face and the other pushed the spoon away.

'NO!' he said. 'Don't like.'

Isobel sighed, and reached for a flannel to clean him up.

'You win,' she said. 'I suppose this means you aren't hungry, does it?'

She cleared the bowl and spoon away, reached into the biscuit barrel and held a Rich Tea out to him. Fearing a trick, David looked up at her suspiciously for a moment before deciding it was worth the risk, grabbing the biscuit and jamming it into his mouth.

Isobel ruffled his hair and turned back to the casserole she was preparing. Another police bell, quickly followed by a second, sounded on the main road. When the third one came along she noticed it, and when the next car followed immediately afterwards she noticed two other things; it seemed to be travelling extremely fast, and it stopped not long after passing close to the end of Cornwall Crescent.

Isobel wiped her hands on a cloth, and moved to the front of the house. As she opened her front door and looked up the road, a voice from behind made her jump.

'Oh, Mr Howard, you startled me. I wonder what's going on?'

Her elderly neighbour was also at his front door, and further down the road a huddle of people had gathered at someone's gate, all looking in the same direction.

'Put your wireless on, Mrs Hatchman. There's trouble down at Notting Hill – gangs of those Teddy Boys are taking on the blacks,' he said, adding 'and I'd advise you to stay indoors till this is over.'

Alarmed, Isobel nodded her thanks and glanced across at the house opposite before going back in the house. She wanted to put the chain on the door but realised if she did so Bobby wouldn't get in when he came home. And thinking this prompted her to look at her watch. He was usually there by that time.

Back in the kitchen, David was finishing off his Rich Tea. He looked up at Isobel and she lifted him out of the high chair.

'Come on you, bath time.'

'David go bath Mummy.'

By the time David's bath was over and he was tucked up in his cot, Bobby still hadn't turned up and Isobel was starting to get worried. Last time Ray was home on leave he'd bought her a transistor radio, so she listened to this in the kitchen, cooking the evening meal at the same time.

The news wasn't good. Riots were breaking out all over the Notting Hill area, white youths targeting black families. There were reports of bottles and stones being thrown and fires breaking out in many places. Police were being drafted in from all over London.

Isobel checked her watch again. It was almost seven o'clock and still there was no sign of Bobby. She turned the oven down and tried not to get too worked up. She had no idea who Bobby's friends were, or what he did when he went out in the evenings. Where did he spend his time? She thought of his lame explanation of how he'd afforded the record player, and the wink he'd given her when they were dancing. He could be mixed up with anyone for all she knew. He could be in all sorts of trouble.

At nine o'clock she turned the oven off. She wasn't hungry any more and the food had dried up in the casserole dish in any case. Each news bulletin on the radio said the same as the last – the police were making arrests; there were many injuries, some looting and damage to property. Cafés frequented largely by blacks had been the subject of vicious attacks, many left burning and seriously damaged, their terrified owners nursing injuries. All evening the clanging bells of emergency vehicles continued; some she supposed were ambulances and fire engines. At one point, when she looked out of the front room window in hopes of seeing Bobby coming up the road, a gang of Teddy Boys ran past the house at great speed, heading away from Ladbroke Grove. Isobel shrank back from the window and stood in the darkened room, shaking.

At a quarter to ten she heard a sound at the front door and froze in fright.

'Issy – it's me.'

Isobel ran along the hallway and into Bobby's arms.

'I've been so frightened,' she cried into his neck. 'I didn't know what had happened to you, the news has been awful all evening and there were Teddy Boys running past the house earlier on. You're not hurt, are you?'

'I'm fine,' said Bobby, stroking her hair. 'I'm fine. I couldn't get home, the police have sealed the whole area off. The Tube stations are closed and there are no buses running through Notting Hill. It's like a battleground out there. There are police stopping and questioning people at every junction. I got pulled into a police station just because I happened to be in the wrong place when a fire bomb was thrown through a shop window.'

Isobel loosened her grip on Bobby and stepped back. 'What were you doing over there in the first place?' she asked.

'I heard of a firm looking for a painting and decorating apprentice, thought I'd give it a try. In the end I never even got to see them. You haven't got a pot of tea on the go by any chance have you?'

They sat together in the kitchen drinking tea, and sharing a packet of cigarettes. Bobby told Isobel about some of the things he'd witnessed that evening.

'... and there was this black man with his head cut, he was bleeding really badly and I stopped to help him, then some white blokes started shouting and swearing at me – I didn't want to walk away but things were starting to get nasty. I hope he was OK after I left him.'

Isobel frowned and shook her head. 'I think white people just feel their homes and streets are being taken over by the blacks. And some of the stories you hear about the way they carry on...'

'...are just stories, Issy.'

'But they say black people eat cat food, that they don't even know how to use a toilet. Well that's what I've heard people say, anyway.'

'Yes, ignorant people, frightened people – people who've never even spoken to a black person. How do they know what goes on in their homes?'

'How do you?'

'I don't, but I don't make stories up either.' Bobby poured them both another cup of tea. 'We saw this all the time in South Africa. We came off the ship that first time ashore after hearing all these stories about how the ignorant blacks needed to be held down and kept in their place. But they were really nice to us, friendly and kind – much kinder than many of the snooty whites who just looked down on us because we were only ordinary ratings. The whites over there still treat the blacks as slaves – in their own country.'

Isobel frowned. 'Ray never said any of this to me when he got home from Africa.'

No, Bobby thought, he wouldn't.

'He would probably be saying it now if he were here. People are people, Issy, it doesn't matter if they're black or white, what matters is if they're good or bad. That's something I learned from the time I spent in Africa.'

Isobel sighed and got up from the table. 'There's a bottle of sherry in the sideboard left over from Christmas,' she said. 'I think we could both do with a glass now, don't you?'

The sound of emergency vehicles continued into the night, and every so often there was shouting in the street – alarmingly close on one occasion, almost as if there were people standing in the front garden.

Bobby and Isobel sat together in the kitchen, talking quietly, until the sky began to lighten and the distant noises associated with the rioting subsided. Isobel cleared the cups, glasses and ashtray off the table and rinsed them at the sink.

'I expect this has put you off the idea of staying round here,' she said, hoping it hadn't. 'You should look for an apprenticeship somewhere else, if that's what you want to do.'

Bobby stood up and pushed his chair in.

'No,' he said. 'I think I'll stay.'

* * *

The atmosphere in the streets around Notting Hill was tense the next day. Isobel needed milk and bread, but Bobby wouldn't let her go out.

'I'll go,' he said. 'I'm not having you and David leave the house till this is all under control. I'll give Janet a call while I'm out too, just so they know we're OK.'

So David, sitting ready in his pushchair with his favourite teddy bear grasped tightly in his hands, had to be unstrapped and taken out again. This didn't please him at all, and the sound of his wails followed Bobby along the road to the corner shop.

Isobel took David, the bear and some other toys into the tiny back yard. At least he'll get some fresh air, she thought, although the surroundings were less than perfect. A washing line, the dustbin and the coal-hole in the corner were all the yard had to offer, and until then Isobel had never thought of it as a place to sit, not even on a nice sunny day. But without making the trip to the park, this was the best she could do at the moment. She put an old rug down on the concrete, sat David down on it, and played with him until Bobby came back from the shop.

'Janet asked if we wanted to go over and stay with them. I told her we'd be fine, I think the worst is over now,' he said.

'Let's hope so.'

Isobel was glad Bobby had resisted the idea of staying at Janet and Terry's. It was a kind thought, but she knew it would be an awful crush fitting everyone in there, and David would be out of sorts away from his normal routine at home. A difficult child at the best of times, he was quite likely to throw a tantrum in unfamiliar surroundings – and even easy-going Terry would surely find that irritating.

'I'm going along to the greengrocer's, in case there's anything I can do to help them there,' said Bobby. 'I could probably make a few deliveries.'

'Don't go anywhere near the trouble spots, will you?'

'No, I'll be fine, don't worry. Just stay at home, Issy, and I'll see you later.'

There was plenty she could do, the insides of the windows could all do with a clean for a start, and when David was having his nap that would keep her busy. In the meantime he was happy enough, surrounded by his favourite toys, and getting her undivided attention.

Isobel looked round at the drab yard as if she'd never seen it before, which in a way she never had, because she only went out there to hang out washing, empty the bin or fill the coal scuttle. Everyone she knew had yards similar to this, some had made a narrow flower border down one side but most hadn't bothered. In the magazines she bought there were sometimes pictures of pretty gardens at the back of houses in places she'd never heard of before – New Towns on the edges of London where life appeared to be gentle and serene and families flourished.

Maybe, she thought, that's what we should do after Ray comes out of the Navy, look for housing and a job in a New Town. How lovely it would be to have a proper garden for David, so he could kick a football around with his Dad, and I could grow flowers and perhaps a few vegetables. How lovely to live in the kind of place where fights weren't breaking out every Saturday night and where gangs of rioting youths were unheard of.

'David drink Mummy,' her son said, jolting her back to the reality of the grimy back yard, and she went into the kitchen, poured him a beaker of milk and reached for a cigarette and ashtray.

We need to talk about this when Ray comes home on leave, she thought. Just another five weeks and he'll be here.

But confusingly, this wasn't the happy thought it should have been, and more than anything else it left her feeling unsettled.

* * *

Bobby was wrong about the worst being over; rioting continued the following day, with an escalation because the West Indian community had started fighting back. There were reports of Molotov cocktails being thrown into gangs of Teddy Boys, and more arrests were made.

That evening in Cornwall Crescent Bobby got the record player out again, telling himself that it would help to take their minds off the situation out on the streets, which was now edging its way closer to home.

'How did you learn to dance like that?' Isobel asked as 'Move It' came to an end and they fell, laughing, onto the settee. 'It's crazy!'

'Oh, I learnt a hell of a lot in the Navy – most of which I'm not even going to tell you about!' he replied.

'I hope Ray hasn't learnt too many things he's keeping quiet about,' Isobel said, raising her eyebrows.

Bobby didn't reply, instead turning 'Move It' over and placing the B side on the record player to give them a chance to get their breath back. His music collection hadn't grown, so they only had four tunes to play. As good as they were, this grew tedious after a while and the Dansette was turned off. Isobel switched the wireless on but there was nothing on either the Home Service or Light Programme that they found very diverting. In spite of much concentrated twiddling and tweaking, the reception for Radio Luxembourg proved to be very crackly that evening, so they fell back to conversation and the bottle of cream sherry that wasn't Harvey's (too expensive) but was still drinkable.

Some time later that evening Bobby took Isobel's hand over the table.

'You married the wrong brother,' he said. 'Think how much more fun you could have had with me, we'd have become regulars in the Hammersmith Palais and the Tottenham Royal – they have some great dance bands there, by the way...'

Isobel was stumped for a reply.

'Don't be daft,' she said, pulling her hand away.

'Is it? What's so daft about that?' He picked her hand up again. 'We have fun together, don't we?'

'There's more to life than having fun,' she said.

'Yeah, when you're forty perhaps – but not at our age, Issy.'

'I've got David – everything changes once you become a mother.'

'I wasn't talking about how things are now, just what might have been.'

Isobel flushed. 'I didn't mean...'

'Although that would be nice too,' Bobby turned Isobel's hand over and kissed the palm, 'wouldn't it?'

Something inside Isobel shifted. Yes, it would, she thought.

'You're talking nonsense,' she said, leaving her hand in Bobby's.

'No I'm not. You're lovely, Issy.'

Oh God, thought Isobel, how strong can any woman be expected to be in the face of this?

'Don't tell me you don't get lonely, anyone would.'

'I knew how it would be when we got married.'

'You don't have to be lonely, that's all I'm saying.'

Isobel gazed at Bobby, young and so confident – and most importantly, there. She had to admit to herself that she'd been increasingly attracted to him over the last few days, looked forward to the time they spent together, and secretly blessed the Notting Hill riots for making it all possible.

He leaned across the table and kissed her mouth. Isobel, knowing she shouldn't, enjoyed it and kissed him back. Dangerous ground, she thought, kissing him again, but oh, so nice. And as long as they were discreet – well, who would ever know? In this sherry-fuelled, reckless state of mind it proved to be surprisingly easy to follow Bobby when he took her hand and led her upstairs.

And as she climbed on top of him and guided him inside her Isobel didn't feel the least bit guilty or ashamed. She just felt wonderfully alive, in a way she couldn't ever remember feeling before.

* * *

The rioting continued for several more days. Each morning, Bobby left the house to buy food, or to put in a few hours at the greengrocer's – although business there, as at all local shops, was suffering because people were afraid to leave the safety of their homes. Each evening Bobby and Isobel sat together after dinner, and played their records – now totalling three as Johnny Mathis had joined the collection, crooning 'A Certain Smile' to the only couple on the dance floor. Each night they made love in Isobel and Ray's bed.

David was confused. The screaming tactic, which usually got him into his mother's bed when he woke up in the middle of the night, had stopped working and he showed his displeasure by playing up even more in the daytime. In spite of this, Isobel was happier than she'd ever known.

On the fifth night of rioting, humid and thundery and impossible for normal sleep, they were jolted into wakefulness by a loud bang outside in the street, followed by the sound of breaking glass. Bobby got out of bed and pulled the curtain back a little.

'The family opposite,' he said. 'There's a gang out there, throwing bricks and stuff through the front windows.'

Isobel got up and stood beside him, pulling on her dressing gown as she peeped through the window. From within the house they could see a faint, ominous orange glow. A chant of 'Keep Britain White' laced with obscenities started up, the Teddy Boys in the street getting louder and more menacing.

'There are children in there,' said Bobby, reaching for his clothes. 'I can't just watch this happening and not try to help. If I go along the back alley maybe...'

'No! Bobby, you'll only get hurt – there's nothing you can do...' said Isobel, terrified of the consequences. 'They might already be round the back of the house... please don't go.'

She pulled at his arm. 'Don't leave me,' she said.

Bobby hesitated, and in the few seconds it took for him to make up his mind they heard the clanging bell of a police car approaching at speed. The youths raced off down Cornwall Crescent, their running feet echoing along the pavements, dispersing in all directions at the next junction and scuttling down alleyways.

Bobby pulled a shirt over his head. 'Make a large pot of tea Isobel, and bring it over with as many cups as you can carry.'

By the time she got there a fire engine had also arrived. People stood at their gates, looking fearfully along the road and whispering in groups, but nobody else made a move to help. The damage to the house was slight and there were no injuries, but the black occupants were all in shock.

'They can't be expected to stay in that house tonight,' said Bobby, carrying a small girl towards Isobel. The child's huge, dark eyes searched her face. We must look as strange to them as they do to us, she thought.

'We could let them use my room and the sitting room,' he continued, ignoring the look of horror on Isobel's face.

'What? All of them?'

'It'll only be for the rest of tonight. They've got to have somewhere to go, Issy.'

'But there must be somewhere else – I really can't...'

The child leaned forward in Bobby's arms and reached a hand out to her, touching her cheek. Isobel's heart melted.

'Oh... all right, as long as it's only for one night. God knows what the neighbours will make of this when they find out,' she said.

Most of the neighbours would need no telling as they were either at their front gates or watching from behind the net curtains. Nobody else had come forward to help out, but it seemed everyone wanted a ringside seat.

Two Caribbean families totalling four adults and seven children stayed in Isobel's house overnight, although nobody except the children had any sleep. That night, and the following morning, Isobel learnt that black people were polite and civilised, and they all knew how to use the toilet, including the smallest child. She couldn't be sure about the cat food rumour but she was beginning to think that was fabricated as well, just as Bobby had said.

It took a few more days, but the police finally got the upper hand and life in Notting Hill slowly returned to normal.

And two weeks later, Isobel missed her period.

* * *

Janet's kitchen was filled with the combined smells of mixed spices and stewed apple. With the weather still warm for the time of year, a baking day meant having to keep the back door wedged open a bit to let in some fresh air, but not quite enough to let in next door's cat. A date and walnut cake – Terry's favourite – was already in the oven and Janet was just starting to roll out some pastry when the doorbell rang. She wiped her hands on her apron, headed out into the hall and swung the front door open. She wasn't expecting to see her sister-in-law but was pleased all the same.

'Isobel! How lovely, come in.'

At which point Isobel promptly burst into tears on Janet's doorstep.

Alarmed, Janet bustled her into the hallway, and then wheeled in David's pushchair. He was fast asleep, the teddy he'd been clutching now lying face down on his lap.

'Whatever's wrong? Is it Ray?'

Isobel shook her head and reached into the pocket of her dress for a hankie.

Janet guided her gently into the kitchen and sat her down at the formica table, then turned to fill the kettle and put it on the stove. Thinking it best to disturb him as little as possible, she left David in the hallway – Isobel had made no attempt to bring him through and Janet reasoned that it wouldn't do the child any good at all to see his mother in such a state.

While Isobel mopped her eyes and blew her nose, Janet busied herself making a pot of tea. She'll tell me when she's ready, she thought. I'm not going to push her into it.

'Here we are,' said Janet, putting the teapot on the table and then organising cups, milk jug and sugar.

'I need your help, Janet,' Isobel sniffed.

'You know I'm always happy to help, dear. What's the problem?'

Isobel gulped. 'Ray comes home at the end of next week,' she said tentatively, 'and... I'm pregnant.'

Janet slopped tea into Isobel's saucer, then put the teapot down with a thud before she dropped it.

'*What?*'

Isobel nodded. 'Expecting a baby,' she said, as if she hadn't made herself completely clear. 'Not Ray's, obviously.'

Of all the things Janet might have imagined her saying this hadn't even featured on the horizon, but now that she'd got started Isobel off-loaded the whole story onto her, almost without stopping.

'*Bobby?*'

* * *

There were only so many times they could go round and round discussing the situation. Isobel wouldn't consider getting rid of the baby, nor would she think of leaving Ray.

'Bobby begged me to go away with him,' she said, 'but how could I? What about David? Ray's his father – I can't just take him off somewhere.'

Janet couldn't help but notice that Isobel hadn't said she didn't want to go with Bobby, just that she couldn't do it. Bobby, it appeared, had now gone off to Spain of all places on the pretext of some job opportunity, and wasn't likely to be back – it seemed he'd tried his best to persuade Isobel to go with him but she was determined to stay. Janet was not insensitive to Isobel's feelings, nor Bobby's come to that, but she could envisage a split opening up in the family that would probably never be healed, and she didn't want to see that happen. The shock might even kill old Frank and Rose, and the other three brothers would certainly not want to have anything to do with either Bobby or Isobel again.

'When Ray gets home he'll obviously want to... well... you know...'

'Quite,' said Janet, who had been thinking the same thing. 'But even if you can convince him you've fallen pregnant immediately you're still going to give birth to a baby that he thinks is six weeks early...'

'... but looks like a full-term baby. Yes, that's the problem, except that Ray won't be here to see the baby for several months and by then the six week gap won't show.' Isobel sighed. 'Trouble is everyone else will spot it.'

'I really don't see how you think I can help, Issy. I mean, I would if I could...'

Isobel leaned across the table and took hold of Janet's hands.

'I've got an idea, but for it to work you'll have to go away with me before the baby's born, just the two of us and the children – I can't do this on my own, Janet. We can say that I need to get out of London and into some cleaner air – something like that. If we could go somewhere where nobody knows us, and as long as we didn't register the birth straight away...'

'But that means being away for a couple of months – how am I going to explain that to Terry? He's very easy-going and like most men he doesn't see half of what goes on around him but even Terry will notice that his wife and daughter have gone missing. And anyway, where would we go? And how would we finance this idea of yours?'

Isobel slumped back in her chair.

'I don't know. It's not a complete plan yet,' she said.

'This is never going to work, Isobel, you must see that,' said Janet, as gently as she could. 'I'll do everything I can to help, because we're family and I care about you, but in the end you might just have to brazen it out, you know.'

In spite of her reservations Janet did give some thought to Isobel's ill-judged plan over the next few days. It was true that Terry didn't see his sister-in-law from one week's end to the next, so he wouldn't realise if she wasn't around, but it would be impossible for Janet and Nina to just up-sticks and join her. She couldn't see a way round this.

Ray came home on his fortnight's leave, and Isobel realised in those two weeks just how much more exciting sex was when it was on the forbidden list. But Ray's joy at seeing David again and his attentiveness to her convinced Isobel she'd made the right decision, and she did her best to push all thoughts of Bobby to the furthest corners of her mind. Once Ray was safely back at sea, and the right amount of time had elapsed, Isobel wrote to tell him she was pregnant again.

About once a week, after Ray had gone back to his ship, a letter arrived from Spain, but Isobel never replied. Instead, she gave Bobby's address to Janet, with a request that she let him know once the baby was born. It was several months before the letters stopped, and although she knew it was for the best Isobel was left feeling incredibly sad and even lonelier.

It was in her sixth month, on a cold and foggy Friday morning in February of 1959, that Isobel's salvation came knocking on Janet's door.

'I was in the area and just couldn't pass so close to your house without calling. Hope it's not a bad time!'

Pat Brown and Janet had been best friends in secondary school, but as Janet met Terry and subsequently moved up to London, so Pat met her future husband and moved in another direction to his family's farm in mid-Sussex. Ever since, they'd exchanged Christmas cards but the distance between them being what it was, hadn't seen each other for years.

'How could it be a bad time?' said Janet, holding out her arms to Pat, 'this is such a lovely surprise!'

She ushered Pat into the house, and put the kettle on. Pat immediately swooped on a giggling Nina, cooed over her, and told Janet about life as a farmer's wife.

'Since Les's parents retired it's been non-stop for us, although we're getting some more help in now,' she said, with Nina on her lap gazing up at her. 'In the meantime we've had to use contractors to help us with lambing and harvesting.'

This was a new world to Janet, who marvelled at the change in her old friend.

'And do you have to help with any of this? Don't tell me you know all about farming now – you, a town girl!'

'I help with just about everything!' Pat laughed. 'There's more to being a farmer's wife than cooking breakfasts and making cakes for the WI. You should come and see us one day, Nina would love the animals – we've just had a litter of new pups and there are always cats and kittens about the place.'

'I suppose I could get the train down as far as Haywards Heath...'

'And then I could pick you up at the station. Oh do come, Jan, it'll be such fun. You could even stay overnight if you wanted, there's a cottage on the estate where we used to live before we moved up to the farmhouse. My in-laws have got a bungalow in the village now, makes it easier for them to get to places like the doctor's and so on.'

'And easier for you, I daresay.'

Pat rolled her eyes and nodded. 'They were very happy to have me running them about whenever necessary but I was never really good enough for Les, of course. Not farming stock, you know?'

'But you've learned...'

'Oh yes, I've definitely learned!'

Pat stayed and had lunch with Janet, then went off to the station to catch a train back to Sussex. Later that evening, as Janet was telling Terry all about her visitor, the idea popped into her head, and the following day she sat down in the kitchen to write a letter.

"Dear Pat," she wrote. "I was thinking about your very kind offer..." Janet sat back in her chair. What if Isobel wouldn't stay there without her? Maybe she should have a word with her first... But she knew Isobel had no other suggestions, and as the weeks went on she was getting more and more anxious.

"My sister-in-law is expecting a baby and I was wondering if..."

Janet decided there was no easy way of doing this, and if Pat was going to help she'd have to know the whole story. She tore up the first sheet of paper and started again.

"My sister-in-law has got herself into a bit of a pickle, and you might just be the way out of her dilemma..."

Janet finished the letter, went down to the post office for a stamp and sent it off before she could change her mind, then she wheeled the pram over to Isobel's house.

'A farm? Oh no Janet, I couldn't possibly. Miles from anywhere – from the nearest doctor...'

'Pat's used to delivering lambs, if it came to it I've no doubt she could manage a baby. But that's not likely to happen because they've got a telephone and country doctors are used to driving out to see their patients.'

Isobel looked sceptical and so Janet dealt her ace card.

'Anyway Issy, do you have a better idea?'

And so about a week before the baby was due, Isobel and Janet plus David, Nina and a large suitcase, struggled off a train at Haywards Heath, where Pat was waiting with her station wagon to carry them the rest of the way to Porter's Farm. David, tired, grumpy and all set to scream the place down by the time they arrived, stopped in his tracks when he caught sight of the farm animals, and Pat immediately took him off to meet several sheep, a couple of cows and assorted dogs and cats.

'She'll look after you, Issy. Just keep in touch with me and when you're ready to go back home I'll come down again.'

Isobel looked out onto the garden at the front of the little cottage and wondered if the day would ever come when she wanted to go home. Bearded irises, anemones and a tangle of other flowers she didn't recognise filled the small space, and beyond that wooded hills rose soft and green above the farm. It was quite a contrast to the back yard of her home in Cornwall Crescent.

'It's all going to be fine, you'll see.'

Isobel nodded. 'Yes, I think it is, I really think it is.'

* * *

Nature was kind to Isobel. The baby, a tiny little thing, arrived nearly two weeks late. She managed to hang

244

on until the doctor got there, and it was an easy birth with no complications. Pat kept David occupied over in the farmhouse and provided Isobel with support and a shoulder to cry on, plus plenty of fresh food and home cooking after the event. Right from the start the baby looked exactly like her mother and was placid and quiet – the complete opposite to how her brother had been and consequently much easier. Janet phoned most days and noticed that Isobel's spirits, low at first, did seem to lift as the days went on.

Three weeks after they'd set off for Sussex, Janet took the train to Haywards Heath again and brought Isobel and her children back to London, where David once more set about screaming the place down because he couldn't find any cows, dogs or cats.

Isobel wrote to Ray. "We have a daughter, and she was in a hurry to come into the world – three weeks early but in perfect health."

And Janet wrote to Bobby in Spain. "Isobel has had a beautiful little girl..."

Terry, although he felt instinctively that something didn't quite add up, never commented on it to Janet or anyone else.

They called the baby after the actress Katherine Hepburn. To Ray she was always Katy, but to everyone else, Kate. Her aunt Janet went to the Town Hall in Notting Hill to register the birth and nobody but she and Isobel ever knew that Kate was always ten days late in celebrating her birthday, or that she was actually born not in London, but in rural Sussex. By the time of Ray's next leave, Kate was almost three months old, and the discrepancy in her birth dates was unnoticeable. Ray was delighted with his daughter.

'She's the image of you,' he said to Isobel, 'but she's definitely got the Hatchman chin, no doubt about it.'

When she heard that another little splinter of Isobel's heart broke away. But what was done was done and she was never one to cave in so she just took a deep breath and got on with things.

Isobel was lucky. Thanks to Janet and Pat, she got away with it.

For fifty-two years...

CHAPTER 21

MAY 2011: BRIGHTON

The four of them sat in Janet's living room, and beyond her balcony there was just the sound of waves crashing onto the beach to fill the silence that had settled around them.

'This goes no further than the four of us,' said Janet. 'I can't see any need for your parents to know, Jeremy, or the girls if it comes to that.'

'At least not right now,' said Bobby. 'In time I might speak to Jim and Sue myself, it'd be good to be completely open and honest with them after all these years.'

'And there's no way we can tell Walter, either,' said Nina. 'He'll be devastated if he finds out that in the end Kate and he were only distantly related – half-cousins I suppose if there is such a thing.'

Jeremy nodded. 'Losing her once was bad enough, losing her all over again would just be too much for him to bear.'

'Unless, of course, it all comes out in court...' Nina speculated.

'...which is what we're trying to avoid,' said Janet.

Nina turned to Bobby. 'How old was she when you first saw her?' she asked, gently.

'About nine, I'd just come back from Spain.'

'That must have been so difficult for you...' she said.

Janet cut in. 'We were there that day, Nina, though I don't suppose you'd remember. They were living in Crawley by then and we were already down here in

Brighton so it was easy for us to get to see each other. It was during the school summer holidays and you and Kate were playing in the garden. Bobby turned up unannounced and I thought Isobel was going to faint when she opened the door to him. If I'd known he was coming home I could have prepared her...'

'I can see now how unfair that was,' said Bobby, 'but I didn't think of it that way at the time. She might have refused to see me if she'd known I was coming, and at that moment all I was really thinking about was how badly I wanted to see them both. I never tried that one again, I didn't want to put Isobel through it a second time.'

'What were you doing in Spain for all those years?' asked Jeremy.

'I was a holiday rep. I got in right at the start of cheap package holidays, and as the whole thing took off they flew new reps out almost every week. We looked after all those British holidaymakers who up to then hadn't been abroad.'

Bobby smiled at the memory.

'Not only the holidaymakers either, as it happened. None of us had a clue to start with, most reps had never been to Spain, we didn't speak the language... as time went on we did get a bit more professional though.'

Janet got up to go into the kitchen.

'I'm guessing we could all do with a cup of tea?' she asked, pausing before adding, 'Or there's white wine in the fridge if you'd rather.'

The wine got everybody's vote, not surprisingly under the circumstances.

'We always thought you were really odd,' said Jeremy, 'the way you'd turn up sometimes, out of the blue, and then just drift off again... eccentric, I guess that's how we thought of you. But then, we never knew...'

'Well, that way I got to see Kate occasionally without anyone ever expecting anything from me, or Isobel being embarrassed by the fact I was there.' Bobby paused. 'I paid a high price, losing Isobel, my daughter and the rest of my family in one go. But all credit to Issy, she stuck with Ray, made a go of it and held her family together. If she'd come with me when I wanted her to, what could I really have offered her?'

Nina shook her head. 'But you loved each other, what more could she want?'

Bobby reached across the sofa and took her hand.

'That's not always enough, sweetheart,' he said with a sigh, 'and you've got to remember that fifty-odd years ago things were very different. People didn't have affairs and get divorced as easily as they do now.'

'And all that time you kept in touch with Mum?'

Bobby nodded. 'Yes, from the day Kate was born. She's been my lifeline.'

'You never married and had other children?'

'Never wanted to,' Bobby said. 'It was always Isobel, you see. She was the only one I ever wanted, and I couldn't have her.'

Janet came back into the lounge with a bottle and a corkscrew.

'Jeremy, open this for me will you? I didn't notice it wasn't a screw top when I bought it. At my age you tend to go for the easiest option.'

Jeremy took the bottle and popped the cork, a celebratory sound, and Janet fetched glasses from the sideboard. It felt to Nina as if this was the moment someone should make a toast, but she couldn't think of anything appropriate to say, and nobody else seemed to want to take up the challenge. Perhaps they're all thinking the same, she thought. So there was no chinking of glasses, just a rather subdued 'cheers' from Bobby.

'Well,' said Janet, 'it looks as if the only way we're going to stop David claiming on Kate's will is by revealing the truth to him. Seeing as he's actually only her half-brother I should think that rather limits his chances of success.'

'Plus her closest relative is still living,' added Jeremy, with a glance in Bobby's direction. 'Once he knows all this David will withdraw his claim, he'd be a fool to push it any further, surely.'

Bobby nodded. 'That's what we're hoping.'

'I'll phone Tim Garvey in the morning,' said Nina. 'He can put the situation to David's solicitor and let's hope that will be an end to it.'

Bobby had taken up Janet's offer to stay for a few days, while they waited to see what was going to happen next. When Nina and Jeremy took their leave of them it was still light outside, a fine spring evening – just right for a walk along the seafront – and so they set off westwards, towards Hove.

'Well we didn't see that one coming, did we?' said Jeremy.

'Certainly didn't, but they didn't leave us any clues along the way so how could we? Poor old Bobby, we rather misjudged him, I'm afraid.'

'I think we saw exactly what he wanted us to see.'

'It does kind of explain why Mum was so funny about Walter in the first place – she probably didn't want Kate digging around too much in case something else came to light.'

Nina slipped her arm through Jeremy's.

'I've been thinking,' she said, 'once this business with the will is over, I might go out to Cape Town again. I'd like to see them all and I think it's important that Walter realises he's still a part of the family, even without Kate. If the dates worked, would you come with me?'

Jeremy was quiet.

'Jem? What do you think?'

'Yeah, perhaps I could. You know, I rather wish now that I'd kept in touch with Lebo, but at the time...'

'Well I can't believe she wouldn't want to see you again – if...'

'If she's still there, you mean. Yeah, I know. She might have gone to Johannesburg; they've got quite a vibrant jazz scene going there I gather, maybe more work than in Cape Town.'

Nina gave his arm a squeeze.

'Listen, you'd only have to call into the Green Dolphin, and if she wasn't there someone would know where to find her.'

'You're probably right. Well maybe I could manage a week or so, depending on the timing and if we could get a cheap flight...'

They walked until it was dark, and then Jeremy left Nina at her flat and drove home, wondering how Lebo would react if he did just turn up in the club one night.

* * *

Tim Garvey, used to hearing the unexpected, showed no sign of surprise at what Nina had to say.

'That certainly changes things,' he said calmly, 'especially as her real father is still alive. I'll go back to the other side and see what they've got to say.'

'We're hoping that once David knows, this will put an end to his claim.'

'Well, let's just wait and see. But be prepared for the fact that he might not give in without a fight – people often behave in quite extraordinary ways when large sums of money are at stake. I'll send you a copy of my letter, of course.'

And for the time being, that was that.

Rachel yawned and stretched her arms up above her head. She'd got up early and logged on to the website she'd found previously, knowing that completing their application process would be quite a lengthy job and she'd need to concentrate on it. She had excellent child-care qualifications and was confident that the Wingates would give her a glowing reference, so it was reasonable to assume that her chances of being accepted were pretty good.

She took her mug out to the kitchenette and made another coffee. Rachel had a lazy Sunday in prospect, with the children in their parents' care all day and nothing special to do except make plans for the future. It felt good to be doing something positive about her situation, rather than just floating around in limbo — now she'd taken the first step and could only wait to hear back. In the meantime she still had her job, although with an end to that in sight it was fast losing its attraction.

When her phone rang she snatched it up and answered on the third ring without even checking the number. Recently she'd got out of the habit of doing that although even if she had checked, the caller's number wouldn't have been familiar to her. But if the number was unknown, the voice certainly wasn't.

'Rachel? It's Jason.'

Rachel froze, clicked the phone off immediately and dropped it onto the floor. Then she stood and looked at it for a moment, her hands to her mouth.

It was a very clear line. He could have been across the Atlantic, or on the pavement below. Scary thought. Rachel peeped out of her window and scanned the street in both directions. No sign of anyone loitering outside. There was a phone booth along the road and there was definitely a man making a call from there, but as she watched he walked away – and it certainly wasn't Jason.

The phone rang again. Rachel jumped, then turned away from the window and stared at the handset until the ringing stopped and the call went onto voice mail. Picking her phone up from the floor, and without even checking to see if the caller had left a message, Rachel called Clare.

'Are you busy today?' she asked, in as light a tone as she could manage because Clare was very sensitive to that sort of thing and would pick up the merest hint of trouble in her voice.

'Not especially – what did you have in mind?'

'D'you fancy popping down to see Mum?'

'Sure – what's wrong?'

Rachel sighed. It was impossible to get anything past Clare, who had inherited a lot of her grandmother's traits, although this wasn't something she'd ever admit to. Rachel hadn't wanted to tell her sister about her latest scare with the phone call, but now there was nothing else for it. Clare, as always, was calm and supportive.

'OK, let's get out of town for the day and talk about this on the way down.'

So less than an hour later Clare and Rachel met at Victoria Station, ran together to the platform and jumped onto the Brighton train just before it left.

'Did you ring her to say we were coming?' asked Clare, as they walked through the carriages looking for seats.

'No, did you?'

'No. It'll be a surprise then. We should get her some flowers at the station,' Clare added over her shoulder.

'Hope she's in...'

'If not we'll go to Grandma's – one of them will be at home. Did you switch your phone off?'

'You bet.'

'Did you check your messages?'

'Nope.'

The train was busy with only the so-called first class seats free in most carriages. In the end they had to sit apart until Gatwick Airport, and whilst Clare spent most of the first part of the journey on her phone, Rachel didn't even take hers out of her bag. Instead, she gazed out of the window, mostly unseeing, and contemplated the very different journey she hoped to be taking soon.

At Gatwick there was a surge of activity as people with luggage got on and off the train, and Clare was able to move into the seat opposite Rachel.

'You need to change that phone,' she said.

'I know. It's on my to-do list,' said Rachel, who'd never made a list in her life up to then. 'First thing tomorrow.'

By the time they reached Brighton it was almost two o'clock. They rang the bell at Nina's flat and stood waiting with a bunch of flowers and big smiles on their faces. No reply.

'Looks like Grandma gets the floral tribute,' said Rachel.

'Maybe Mum went round there for lunch.'

'Then we'll have to split the flowers.'

So they set off for the seafront and Janet's apartment block. As they approached it they could see three people sitting on her balcony and once they were close enough they shouted up to them and waved. One at a time the three people turned in their direction, although curiously it took a while for Nina to wave back and the others didn't do so at all. Clare shielded her eyes against the sun.

'Isn't that...' she started.

'Uncle Bobby...' Rachel added. 'How strange is that?'

Janet answered their ring at the door entry and buzzed them up. She was waiting at her door as they came out of the lift.

'You should have let me know,' she said, as she kissed each of them and took the flowers from Clare's hands. 'I could have saved you some lunch.' And saved us all some embarrassment, she thought.

Nina and Bobby were standing around in the living room, looking rather shifty, when the girls went in.

'We didn't expect to see *you* today, Uncle Bobby,' said Rachel. 'How nice.'

Bobby shifted from one foot to the other and glanced at Janet.

'Yes, well... I just thought I'd pop down to Brighton for the day, you know...'

'Rather like us,' said Clare.

Nina stepped forward. 'No, not like you at all actually,' she said, 'there's a bit more to it than that.' Then turning to Janet and Bobby she added, 'I think we've had more than enough secrets in this family, don't you?'

Janet sighed. 'Sit down girls. We've got something to tell you... it's about Kate.'

Clare and Rachel perched side-by-side on the sofa and waited, wide-eyed, for someone to explain.

'Looks like I'd better buy some more wine,' said Janet as she headed for the kitchen. 'The way things are going Jim and Sue will be the next ones to pitch up here – any day now I expect.'

Bobby started off again, back in 1958, but the story took less time in the telling than previously as he edited out some of the details.

'Oh my God!' said Rachel, gulping at her wine. 'So they were both at it!'

Nina flashed a look at her. 'Rachel!'

'And you're not really as weird as we always thought you were,' Clare said to Bobby. 'I'm glad, it was always a bit awkward when you turned up.'

'Clare!'

'Anyway,' said Janet, 'the point is that now we have to try to stop David getting his hands on Kate's money.'

'And this goes no further, girls,' said Nina. 'Promise.'

* * *

Sometime later, Clare and Rachel walked with Nina back to her flat.

'You missed out on the flowers by not being home,' said Clare. 'Grandma hi-jacked them for herself.'

'Doesn't matter,' said Nina, 'it's nice that you thought to buy them. What made you decide to come down here all of a sudden anyway? You're both so busy all the time.'

'Oh just an impulse, you know, on a nice day,' said Clare.

Sounds familiar, thought Nina, but she let it go.

'Well it's lovely to see you even though we were all a bit wrong-footed back there. It was supposed to be just between Uncle Bobby, Grandma, Jem and me for the time being.'

'We can keep a secret,' said Clare.

'I hope so because we definitely don't want Walter or his family to know anything about this,' said Nina as she turned her key in the lock and held the door open for the girls. 'Not that you're likely to meet any of them, though.'

Rachel cleared her throat.

'Actually Mum, I am,' she said, a bit sheepishly. 'Hopefully, I'm going to be working over there quite soon.'

* * *

David's reply, via his solicitor, was not slow in coming back and Tim Garvey rang Nina on the Thursday following Clare and Rachel's visit. Still getting to grips with Rachel's somewhat surprising revelation, Nina was glad of the distraction and something else to concentrate on. She popped in to the office on her way through to the supermarket.

'Mr Hatchman is not pleased,' Tim said.

'We never expected him to be.'

'He seems to think the whole thing is an elaborate conspiracy. Let me read you the letter I received this morning...'

David was certainly put out, that much was clear from the tone of his solicitor's letter, which included the use of strong words such as '*preposterous* '.

' "*... furthermore my client requires proof in the form of DNA tests and unless and until such proof is forthcoming he totally refutes your claim...*" – there's quite a lot more in a similar vein. You can take a copy away with you.'

Tim paused. 'If that's his final position it's going to be very tricky for us. Exhumation is only granted in very exceptional circumstances and disagreements over wills would not normally qualify. Of course we can get sworn statements from your uncle and your mother, they might satisfy a judge...'

Nina felt the tension suddenly slip away, leaving her with an irresistible urge to punch the air in triumph. Or kiss Tim. She did neither.

'If David wants DNA results, then that's exactly what we'll give him,' she said.

'I can't see how we can do that without...'

'We already have Kate's DNA – or at least a lab somewhere has. And we can easily get Uncle Bobby's. We've got him Tim! We've got him.'

* * *

Nina went straight round to Janet's flat after speaking to Tim Garvey. Bobby had been in no rush to return home and Janet in no mood to encourage him to do so, which meant that she was able to tell them both the latest developments at the same time.

'All the paperwork relating to the DNA tests Kate and Walter had were in her filing cabinet at home, Jeremy and I found them when we were looking for her will and solicitor's details. All we need to do now is get you tested at the same lab, Uncle Bobby.'

Janet leaned forward in her chair.

'And that will be an end of it? Really?' she asked.

'I don't see why not,' said Bobby. 'What better proof could there be?'

'And it's exactly what he's asked for – thinking of course that it would be impossible for us to get it.'

'Well,' said Janet, 'I never thought I'd say this, but thank goodness for Walter.'

Nina raised her eyebrows and couldn't resist a wry smile in her mother's direction.

'Yes, yes, all right,' said Janet.

'There's one other thing, though... Tim advises us to put Jim and Sue in the picture, seeing as his DNA was used for the uncle test.'

'There you are – what did I tell you the other day?' said Janet. 'They'll be here before you can say knife.'

'I hope Jim takes it OK,' said Bobby. 'He could never have expected it to turn out like this when he took the test – uncle to both of them, but not quite in the way he imagined.'

'He'll be fine,' said Nina, although in truth she was wondering the same thing herself. The whole difficult experience was proving to be bitter-sweet for Bobby – and to some extent for Janet as well. Jim's disapproval, if that was how he felt, would hurt them both.

Families are so complicated, Nina thought with a sigh. It's every bloody generation too – first there was David kicking up trouble, then we find out his mother had a skeleton in the cupboard, and now, she thought, Rachel's chucking in a brilliant job for no good reason and heading off to look after AIDS babies in Africa.

And suddenly, without warning, Nina realised how much she missed talking things through with Kate. It swept over her like a tsunami, and left her feeling tremendously sad and empty.

Back in her own flat she called Jeremy, got only his answerphone and clicked the phone off without leaving a message because she didn't really know what she wanted to say to him. Sitting back in her chair she flipped open her phone book and opened it at the 'M' page. Like Kate, Nina had fallen into the habit of phoning Walter and Annie on Tuesday evenings and if she called out of the normal routine they'd immediately think something was wrong.

And then while she was sitting there contemplating all of this, her phone rang, and it was Annie.

CHAPTER 22

JUNE 2011: OCEAN VIEW

Annie was just bursting to tell someone and couldn't wait till Walter got home from work, in fact she was so excited that the cost of the phone call to Nina (something they never usually did) hadn't crossed her mind.

'Mandisa has just heard – she's got her first assistant manager's job!'

This was exactly the sort of thing Nina needed to hear to jolt her out of the trough of sadness she'd fallen into.

'That's fantastic news! You must be so proud of her, Annie. Where will she be working?'

'Not too far away, in Somerset West. It's quite a big store – there are three assistant managers there. She's very excited about it.'

Nina tried to remember if she knew where Somerset West was in relation to Ocean View. She vaguely remembered passing signs for it when they were driving somewhere, but that was all.

'Close enough to live at home?'

'Maybe, but only if there's a worker's bus going out that way. That's something she has to look into.'

'Oh. So she might have to find somewhere to live that's closer to work?'

'It could be. I hope not but she isn't going too far away, she'd be able to get back here on her days off.'

Nina, remembering when both her daughters had left home, smiled to herself. That's what they all say, she thought. That's what you think will happen – and it will, for the first couple of weeks, till she finds her feet and makes new friends and life away from home becomes more exciting than it is at home.

'Yes, of course she will. I've got news as well, Annie. But I'm worried about your phone bill, so I'm going to ring you back before we talk too much.'

And in her more leisurely return call Nina told Annie about Rachel's plan to work in an AIDS orphanage.

'It's for six months initially, but if she likes it then I suppose she could extend the time she'll be there. She's been looking on the internet at one of the orphanages this charity runs – it's on a township not far from you, at Hout Bay.'

'Ah, that will be Imizamo Yethus. Where will she live, not there I suppose?'

'I don't think she knows yet, only that accommodation will be provided. She might not get accepted and if she does she might not be sent to that township. They haven't interviewed her yet so I suppose we'll know more once that's happened.'

'You tell Rachel,' said Annie, 'that she is welcome here any time she likes.'

Nina could have cried. The Maketas, constantly struggling to make ends meet, had no hesitation whatsoever in offering to share whatever they had with her privileged daughter, without even meeting her first.

Although she didn't say so to Nina, Annie was thinking that Imizamo Yethus was the last place she'd want one of her daughters to be living.

'We don't know if she would have to live at IY,' said Walter later that evening when she told him. 'Maybe the accommodation will be in Hout Bay.'

'Anyway,' said Annie, 'whatever happens I want her to know that she has a home with us, if she needs it.

And in any case we'll most certainly see her often while she's here. I think it was a relief to Nina, knowing that Rachel has us to fall back on if necessary.'

There was great excitement in the Maketa household that night. Mandisa's promotion had come sooner than anyone had expected it to, and the possibility of one of their English 'cousins' (they had all given up trying to work out the exact relationships) coming to live somewhere close by had thrilled Mandisa and Elana. Even Sele was interested in seeing Rachel.

'Wait till my friends meet her,' he said, clearly thinking this would give him special status in Ocean View.

'Nobody would want to meet your friends,' said Elana. 'That would definitely make her get on the next plane home.'

* * *

Mandisa was sent for a day to the Somerset West store, to see what it was like and meet her future colleagues. There was no company taxi laid on for her that day, unlike when she went on the training course in Port Elizabeth. She left home very early in the morning when it was still dark, took the Volksie bus to Fish Hoek, a train from Fish Hoek to Cape Town and then another train to Somerset West. The journey took almost three hours. By the time she arrived home late that evening she was exhausted, and said the very words Annie had hoped not to hear.

'I can't possibly do this every day.'

As it happened, there was a girl at the Somerset West store that Mandisa knew from her initial management training course and she had mentioned a friend who was looking for someone to share a small flat locally.

'I think I'll get in touch tomorrow,' she said.

'I hope it's a respectable place,' said Annie. 'You don't want to be living somewhere dirty or in a bad neighbourhood. Still, if she's a nice girl...'

He wasn't a girl. But this was no time to mention that and Mandisa wisely kept her mouth shut for the time being. But the next day, during her lunch break, she did call her contact at the Somerset West store, who gave her a phone number for the friend looking for a flatmate. By the time she met Elana at the Volksie bus that evening Mandisa had made arrangements to go and see the flat on her next day off, which was the following Sunday.

'Don't tell Mama it's a boy,' she said.

'Of course I won't! What's his name?'

'Thaba. He sounded friendly and it seems like the flat will be OK. There are two bedrooms, a kitchen and a bathroom. And the rent isn't too bad.'

Mandisa reckoned the flat – or the flatmate – would have to be very bad indeed if she couldn't even stay there for a short time while she looked around for something better. There was a tricky moment over dinner that evening when Annie suggested that she and Walter took Mandisa to Somerset West on Sunday.

'It'll save you a lot of travelling – you know how long it took you to get there before and there aren't so many trains on a Sunday...'

Mandisa thought fast. 'But I want to do some shopping while I'm there,' she said, 'because I need different clothes for work now that I won't be in a store uniform. It might take a while to find the right things, maybe the whole day, and you two will just be sitting in the car waiting for me. Really,' she added, 'it's better if I go on my own.'

'If I can change my day off I could go with you,'

said Elana. 'It's good to have another opinion when you're buying clothes.'

'Well, if you're sure,' said Walter. 'I could use the time to take a look at the car, the suspension's been making a bit of a noise lately.'

That's lucky, thought Mandisa, glancing across at Elana.

* * *

In the end, Walter drove the girls into Fish Hoek, which made the journey slightly easier, but it was still close to midday by the time they arrived in Somerset West.

Although they intended to visit the mall and Mandisa really did want to do some shopping, they made their way first of all to the flat. The directions Mandisa had been given over the phone weren't as easy to follow as she'd thought at the time and they managed to get lost twice. In the end they had to ask in a café for help.

The neighbourhood they found themselves in was definitely not the best, but it had the advantage of being on a bus route that ran straight to the out-of-town shopping mall. Thaba's directions were at least clear about the kind of shop they should look for – he lived above a cellphone shop, only a few doors away from a Spar supermarket. This location was an asset for which it scored extra points.

Once they'd established that they had actually found the right phone shop – there was more than one in the parade of shops – it was easy to locate the entrance around the back of the block. The shop fronts weren't exactly smart and the buildings generally run-down, but hidden around the back things definitely took a turn for the worse. Graffiti had been sprayed over most of the walls, with abandoned televisions and computer screens, rubbish bins and make-shift washing lines forming an obstacle course to the street door. This had been wedged open, although judging by the way the rusted top hinge had parted company with the door frame it wasn't about to close any time soon. Paper packaging and other rubbish had blown in and littered the entrance and the bottom few stairs.

'You'd never be able to bring Mama here,' said Elana.

'It's no worse than some places in Ocean View.'

'She wouldn't go anywhere near them, either.'

Considering he was expecting them, Thaba didn't seem to have made much effort to present the second bedroom at its best. It was hard to see what the furniture was like, because the room was full of cardboard boxes, stacked on and around the bed, some empty and others spilling their contents out onto the floor.

'It's small,' he said, 'but once I get these boxes out it'll seem bigger.'

Everywhere she looked was cluttered and chaotic, from the front door right through, and Mandisa dreaded seeing what the kitchen was like.

'Oh,' she said when Thaba waved an arm at the door to the kitchen and let them go in ahead of him. 'This is quite nice.'

And it was – basic, but clean and surprisingly tidy. Much bigger than the bedroom she'd looked at, there was a table and two chairs in one corner and with a bit of planning it could even double as a living room.

'I only go in there to make coffee,' he said. 'I work in a restaurant so the kitchen is the last place I want to spend my time. There's some equipment in the cupboards, but I've never used any of it.'

Mandisa opened some of the cupboards. There wasn't much, just a few pots and pans and some china, but probably enough to manage on at first. It would all need a good wash.

'Can I see the bathroom?'

'Ah. Just give me a few minutes to clear some things out,' said Thaba, disappearing into the next room.

'What do you think?' Mandisa whispered to Elana. 'I'm not really sure but I don't have anywhere else to look at...'

'It's OK – I think you could live here once you'd cleaned it up a bit. And he seems nice.'

There was a sudden loud knock at the front door, which made them both jump, and without waiting for a reply the door swung open and a young man walked straight in.

'Oh, I wasn't expecting to see anyone else here,' he said, then shouted 'THABA!'

Thaba came out of the bathroom and grinned.

'Hey, man! Didn't think you'd be here so early!' Then he turned to the girls. 'This is my brother Baruti. One of these two ladies wants to rent the second bedroom,' he explained, 'but I couldn't say which one because it's kind of difficult to tell them apart.'

Feeling suddenly emboldened, Mandisa stepped forward and held out her hand. 'It's me,' she said. 'I've just got a job in the shopping mall and now I need a place to live. I'm Mandisa.'

Baruti smiled broadly, a lovely smile, took her hand and gripped it.

'I hope you do decide to move in here,' he said, 'Thaba needs to share with someone nice and sensible for a change, he might keep the place a bit tidier.'

Thaba looked from one to the other. Mandisa said nothing, just gazed into Baruti's liquid brown eyes. He continued to hold her hand.

Elana coughed.

'Well,' said Thaba. 'Let me know what you think, OK?'

No reply. Elana coughed again.

'Erm...Mandi...' she said.

'I'll take the room,' said Mandisa, although she still hadn't seen the bathroom. 'It's just what I wanted.'

* * *

Three weeks later, Mandisa packed her small red and white striped suitcase, and set off for Somerset West. She took enough with her to last the first week, after which she expected to come home for her day off, and refill the bag. Little by little, she was moving out. Annie, if she realised, was surprisingly upbeat about the whole thing. Never a pushy mother, her daughter's sudden promotion had filled her with more pride and optimism than she had thought possible. Now, above all else, Annie wanted Mandisa to succeed, and she was right behind her.

Elana, on the other hand, was thoroughly downhearted. With the exception of Mandisa's training course in Port Elizabeth, the twins had been together their whole lives – now she had the prospect of an empty bed next to hers, and nobody to share conversations or secrets with. In her own quiet way, Elana started to wonder if there was a new direction she could take with her own life.

For Mandisa too it was a strange experience. As excited as she was, it felt unnatural to do things that didn't include Elana. As her world opened up she was painfully aware that her sister's remained just the same and she felt uncomfortable at the thought that she was leaving her behind.

Once I get settled in the flat and at work, it'll be different, she thought. And in any case, I'll be home every week – or maybe Elana could come to Somerset West sometimes.

And Walter, proud of all his children (even Sele, who had after all stuck at his computer course...), just worried that Mandisa would be safe and have enough money for everything she needed. He and Annie weren't able to help her out financially, as he would have liked. So far, no money had come through from Kate's will and although he felt himself under unspoken pressure at home to do so, he hadn't liked to ask Nina about it in case she thought badly of him. If truth were told, Walter would rather have had Kate back for ten minutes than be given all the money in the world, but things weren't getting any easier for the Maketa family and he was essentially a practical man. The prospect of living off Kate's money troubled him, though.

Annie had been to look at a couple of houses nearby, nice one-storey places she told him, with more room than they had ever imagined having, and gardens too. Walter hadn't looked. He couldn't bear the thought that it was only through Kate dying that they were able to consider such things. In his bleakest moments, Walter was deeply ashamed that no matter how things had turned out later, the real reason he had set out to find Kate in the first place was in hopes of getting some money out of her and thereby solving their financial problems. Now that had come true, in the worst possible way.

One Sunday afternoon, while he was tinkering with the car out on the concrete parking lot outside the flats, Sele came down to see what he was up to. Walter wiped his oily hands on a rag, and had the first real conversation he'd ever had with his son.

Sele, his hands deep in the pockets of his jeans, walked around the car, kicked idly at a tyre and then peered under the bonnet alongside his father – as if he had the foggiest idea of what he was looking at.

'I was just wondering...' he started.

'Oh yes? About what?'

'Erm... when will we get the money from Kate?'

Walter sighed, put the bonnet down and wiped oily fingermarks off the edge.

'That's all everyone seems to be thinking about. When I first asked you to find out Kate's address I admit it was money that was uppermost in my mind. But now I couldn't care less about it.'

Sele rubbed a hand over his stubbly jaw. 'I know all of that. But the way I see it – Kate wanted to help us all to get something better and she would have done it herself if she hadn't died. So in case anything happened to her she made sure we'd still get that help by putting us in her will. How can it be wrong if it's what she wanted?'

'It's not wrong, Sele, but I just don't feel comfortable with this rush to spend Kate's money when we don't have her any more. It feels cold-blooded.'

Sele shuffled his feet around in the dirt and Walter leaned back against the side of the car and folded his arms.

'Your mother is looking at houses,' he said.

'That's good,' said Sele. 'Isn't that what Kate would want her to do, so that Grandmama can come and live with us? Like, Mandi taking driving lessons and then buying the car she's going to need for work, and...'

'OK, so what have *you* got planned?'

Sele stuck his hands back in his pockets and frowned slightly, a grown-up look that Walter hadn't seen on his son before. The responsibility of impending inheritance had obviously been weighing heavily on him.

'I've been looking around,' he said. 'College finishes in about a month and there aren't many jobs for people like me who've taken a course on computers but don't have any real experience. Also there are way too many of us with the same qualification. So I was thinking about starting a different course, except that I don't think we'd get help next time, I'd have to pay for it.'

Walter, amazed at what he was hearing, slowly nodded his head and made encouraging noises.

'What is this other course?'

'I've been thinking about accountancy. You often see jobs advertised for accountants and I'm good with maths so I know I could do it. It's on the same campus and I talked to one of the tutors the other day about it. But I'll have to apply very soon and pay the first year's fees straight away. That's why I need to know when...'

'Well,' said Walter, 'I don't know the answer to your question because there is still a lot for the legal people to do. And before anyone gets any money they have to sell Kate's house, although Nina said people have been looking at it. What are the first year fees?'

'About six and a half thousand rand.'

Sele, sensing the disappointment that was just around the corner and heading his way, looked down at the ground and went back to scuffing his trainers around in the dust.

'Then this is what we'll do,' said Walter. 'Enrol on the course if you're certain that's what you want, and I'll speak to Nina. Somehow we'll get the money together.'

Sele looked up at his father and cracked a huge grin.

'You think they'll be able to do it?' he asked.

Walter nodded. 'They're family,' he said.

Sele felt a sudden urge to slap his father on the back and shake him by the hand, but this was obviously a step too far and he managed to stop himself just in time, instead lifting both arms to the sky and clapping his hands together above his head.

'Now,' said Walter,' go in and tell Mama what we just decided. I'll be up there in a few minutes.'

After he'd raced off up the stairs Walter stood for a while and looked across the road at the blocks of flats opposite, identical to their block, and the mountain slopes rising above them, out towards Fish Hoek.

Sele's right, he thought. Kate did have our best interests at heart, and she wanted her money to help us achieve a better life, especially the children. What kind of family would we be if we didn't respect her wishes?

He locked the car and headed for the flat entrance.

I'd better start to show some interest in those houses, he thought. Poor Annie, two shocks in one evening.

Walter smiled to himself, and although the lingering sadness he felt would always be there, he started to feel more comfortable with himself and with a future that didn't include his beloved sister.

CHAPTER 23

AUTUMN 2011: BRIGHTON

David kept them all dangling. Unable or unwilling to accept the proof he himself had asked for, his solicitor was given instructions to 'find a way'. In the end this proved to be impossible, as the family knew it would, but weeks went by with everything on hold before probate could proceed.

Bobby, as Kate's next of kin, then moved centre stage. Still spending a lot of time in Brighton, he was by then thinking of selling up in London and buying a small flat nearby. Janet had put the idea in his head in the first place.

'Why on earth would you want to stay in Ealing, of all places?' she'd said. 'Get yourself a little flat down here, where at least you'll be near some of the family. Anyway, the air's cleaner,' she added.

Over the next few weeks he spent hours down on the seafront, watching the waves rolling onto the shingle and the constant parade of people going by, and gradually the turmoil that his mind had been in for decades began to settle. He found the seaside restorative – and Janet was right, the air *was* cleaner.

Essentially down-to-earth people, Jim and Sue had taken Bobby's news quite calmly – in much the same way as they'd accepted Kate's revelation about Walter. Bobby's first trip to Exeter certainly had its emotional moments, but once that was out of the way things became easier and it wasn't long afterwards that they proved Janet right and came to Brighton for a long weekend.

Over the course of recent events Janet had learned not to bother giving her visitors the option of tea or wine.

'I assumed this would go down better than a cuppa,' she said as she came through into her lounge with four glasses and a rather good bottle of Chablis that Bobby had provided.

'Ooh, lovely,' said Sue, 'and the sun's not even over the yardarm. Still, it's a long time since the four of us were together – just in case anyone was looking for an excuse.'

A lot of bridges were built in that weekend, and a lot of things said that needed to be. The elephant in the room was gradually talked away.

Tim Garvey asked to see Bobby, so that his intentions and wishes could go on the record, and he was quite definite.

'Kate's will stands exactly as she wanted it,' he said, and Tim arranged for the appropriate paperwork to be drawn up that would disallow any future claim should he change his mind.

'You'll get nothing, you know,' said Janet.

'Why would I need anything? I've got all I want already. Let the younger generations have it – that family in South Africa can make much better use of it than I could.'

Meanwhile, Nina reported as much as she could back to Walter and Annie. 'There's still a long way to go but we've got a buyer for the house,' she said in one of her Tuesday phone calls, 'and we're hoping the sale will go through quickly.'

The Maketas, ignorant of the house-buying procedure in the UK, accepted everything she told them at face value, and waited patiently.

By the middle of September Rachel was all set for her adventure. Since leaving the Wingates she'd been living mostly with Nina but dividing her time between Brighton and Clare's flat in London, when her air stewardess flatmate was away. The organising charity was paying most of Rachel's expenses but she'd had to put up the money herself for the flights, using some of the cash she kept after her last aborted visit to Lambeth. As Clare had said at the time, Rachel was making something good come out of it.

At last all the paperwork was in place and it was getting close to the time to leave. She had, as hoped, been assigned to the orphanage at Imizamo Yethus, with (to Annie's relief) accommodation provided in nearby Hout Bay. Rachel – sworn to absolute secrecy by her mother over any issues relating to Kate's real parentage – had been on the phone to the Maketas herself, and was looking forward to meeting them.

'Maybe you could stop overnight – you can share my room,' Elana had said, still not used to the empty bed alongside hers. When Rachel realised that IY's sister community at Masiphumelele was literally just along the road from Ocean View, this started to look like a real possibility.

Nina, Janet and Clare all went to the airport with Rachel to see her off. At Heathrow she met up with another two volunteer workers bound for the same township. Both teachers, of a similar age to Rachel, they were going to work in the primary school at IY and were taking vast amounts of teaching materials with them. Rachel, in comparison, was travelling light. The three of them headed off into departures, Rachel turning round just once to wave to her family, and then she was gone.

'Hope she'll be OK,' said Clare.

'She'll be fine,' said Nina, sounding more upbeat than she actually felt. 'She's not going on her own, after all. And Annie will keep an eye out for her so there's a safety net there if she needs it.'

They left the airport building and Nina went on ahead to the car parking machines, fumbling with the ticket and her purse. Janet hooked her arm through Clare's.

'Let's hope this time away will sort Rachel out and get her life back on track,' she said. 'I haven't liked to see her looking so sad.'

Clare turned to face her grandmother.

'I don't know what you mean.'

'It's all right, Clare, you don't have to break any confidences, I don't need the details,' said Janet. 'It was perfectly plain to me that there was a man behind all this unhappiness, and I knew the best thing for Rachel would be to get right away from him. I read something about overseas voluntary work and just dropped it into a conversation on the phone one day, then left the rest to her. I'm sure she thinks it was all her own idea.'

Clare couldn't help smiling.

'You're a wily old thing!' she said.

'Thank you, dear. It's both a delight and a curse that we oldies see rather more around us than other busier people do.'

'Mum knows nothing about what's been going on,' said Clare.

'I guessed that, and she doesn't need to, either. Let's just leave it like that, shall we?'

'So, Rachel doesn't realise that you...'

'Good heavens, no!' Janet tapped Clare's hand and nodded in the direction of the pay machines. 'Your mother seems to have got the car parking sorted out now – come on, let's get going. And remember Clare, we haven't had this conversation.'

* * *

By the time Nina got home, after dropping Clare off in London then taking Janet back to her flat, it was getting late and she was exhausted. She flopped into an armchair with her jacket still on, prised her shoes off and leaned her head back. It had been a long day. She looked at her watch and thought about Rachel, picturing her settling down for the long flight to Cape Town, seeing which films were on offer and sharing a joke with the two teachers she'd checked in with. Of course Nina hadn't liked saying goodbye to her, but it was easier knowing that Walter's family were there to support her if she needed them.

She reached into her bag and pulled out her mobile, wondering if Clare might have left her a text. There were just two missed calls, both from Jeremy, and as she looked at the screen the phone rang and it was him again.

'Did Rachel get away OK?'

'Yes, and she was so excited – she certainly didn't linger over saying goodbye!'

'Well it's a big thing to do. We were excited too, when we went there and that was just for a holiday.'

'That seems such a long time ago. So much has happened since.'

'Almost a year...where did all that time go to?'

There was something in his tone that made Nina sit up straight, ready for a proper conversation.

'Jem, are you OK?'

'Yeah, it's just, well I was thinking about what you said a few months back about going out to Cape Town again.'

'And?'

'Well I had this rather mad idea about calling the Green Dolphin and maybe getting a message through to Lebo...'

Nina waited. There was no sign of elation in Jeremy's voice, so clearly things hadn't gone as he'd hoped.

'...and the line was dead. So I tried checking the number on the internet and found out that the club had closed earlier this year, which was a shock because it always seemed really busy... Anyway then I talked to one or two people over here and finally got a number for Peter – you remember him?'

Nina flashed back to the Green Dolphin again; the three of them together, Jeremy playing piano, her and Kate at the bar...

'Yes,' she said, 'yes I do. He was really nice.'

'But he couldn't tell me where Lebo is, apparently she left the Cape months ago. He said she went to Johannesburg first and then he thought she might have gone to Namibia but it seems nobody really knows. So I guess that's that.'

'Oh, Jeremy, that's such a shame. I know how much you liked her.'

'It's my own fault, I should have kept in touch. I shouldn't have let her go so easily.'

'But you'll still come with me?'

'If I can. You never know, someone might have news of her by then.'

Nina couldn't help hoping Jeremy would have stopped carrying a torch for Lebo by the time the trip actually happened. Typical, she thought, the first time for ages that a girl really matters to him, and he loses track of her.

'Africa's a big continent,' she said gently, 'probably best not to get your hopes up too much.'

She wished yet again that Kate were there too to add weight to her view. Losing the third point of their triangle had made the whole structure wobbly on occasions and this was one of those times when Nina really felt the loss of Kate's common-sense approach.

'Yeah, you're probably right,' said Jeremy.

CHAPTER 24

AUTUMN, 2012: HEATHROW AIRPORT

Britain was still basking in the afterglow of hosting the Olympic games, the weathered remains of bunting dangling from the occasional lamp post seeming to suggest that people weren't quite ready yet to let it all go. Oscar Pistorius, South Africa's 'Blade Runner' and Olympic poster boy, was everyone's hero and the darling of the running track. Team GB had won over even the least interested TV viewers and the volunteer Games Makers had been good humoured and friendly throughout. The heady atmosphere of summer 2012 lingered.

Heathrow airport had welcomed in athletes, journalists and spectators from all over the world, and waved them off too at the end of the Games. Now, one solo traveller walking into arrivals was about to get her own UK welcome.

It was the red and white striped suitcase on top of a luggage trolley that Rachel spotted first.

'There she is!' she said, moving forward with Clare and Nina close behind.

'Over here!' Rachel called, waving.

Elana saw her and waved back, smiling broadly. She was so tired; it had been a long flight and she hadn't slept at all because she was too excited. She and Rachel hugged each other, and then Nina stepped in for her hug.

'So lovely to see you again,' said Nina. 'Meet Clare, your other cousin. I'm sure Rachel told you all about her.'

'Hope not!' said Clare, smiling. 'Not everything...'

'Those confidential late night chats in Ocean View...' said Rachel. 'No not everything Clare, you're quite safe.'

'Right, let's get you home, you must be exhausted,' said Nina, taking over the luggage trolley and heading for the exit.

'I'm excited about visiting Brighton!' said Elana, hooking her arm through Rachel's. 'Almost as much as seeing London...'

'Tomorrow you'll be able to meet Grandma and maybe Uncle Bobby if he's around.'

They made their way back to the car park, Rachel and Elana arm-in-arm, chatting and giggling as they strolled along behind Clare and Nina, who were left to manoeuvre the trolley then load the luggage in the car.

'We've got so much to catch up on...' said Rachel as they climbed into the back of the car.

'It could take us more than an hour and a half to get down to Brighton at this time of day, so you'll have plenty of time for that once we're on the road,' said Nina, 'but first I need to concentrate on getting away from the airport.'

And so the two-way street of family news was delivered gradually as they sped down the motorway.

'How is your job working out?' Elana asked Rachel.

Rachel's six months in IY had certainly proved to be life-changing, though in an entirely unexpected way. She loved working with the children, and for the first time in her life felt she was doing something that made a real difference. Then, as she came near to the end of her time there, expecting to come back home and start job-hunting, an email pinged into her laptop from the charity headquarters, inviting her for an interview once she was back in London. Rachel's potential had not gone unnoticed.

'The money's not great,' Rachel had reported back to Clare, 'but there'd be expenses-paid trips to visit the orphanages every so often. So I'd be able to get back to Africa and the babies...'

'It's not cheap living in London,' said Clare, 'but I was thinking about that. Maybe if you and I put our money from Kate together we could use it as a deposit on a flat – somewhere in the suburbs where we could both travel in from easily.'

'Would we get a mortgage with that amount?'

'I don't really know – but I'm sure Mum would help out if that was a problem.'

'Well, I haven't got the job yet...'

But two interviews and a lot of nail-biting later, Rachel did get the job. Office-based in North London, she joined a team responsible for recruiting and interviewing people who, just like herself, wanted time out doing something worthwhile. Because she already had experience in the field she was good at evaluating a candidate's suitability, but she was also useful at reporting back from the charity's many projects in Africa because she knew what to look for.

Rachel sometimes thought about her job with the Wingate family; the lovely little flat she'd lived in at the top of their luxury Knightsbridge house, the generous expense account they allowed her, the salary that was way beyond anything she would earn working with a charity. Knowing what she now knew, it all seemed rather shallow. It was like looking in on a different world, but one she had no desire to step back into.

Now, hurtling down to Brighton with Elana wide-eyed and excited next to her on the back seat of Nina's car, she could only wonder at how much her life had changed.

'The job's great,' she said. 'I really love it. I may be going to Botswana soon, we've got an orphanage near Gabarone that's just started up.'

'You won't be going while I'm over here, I hope...'

'No, I won't be going anywhere for at least a month,' said Rachel, 'and I've taken the rest of this week off work to show you as much of London as we can fit in.'

'And after the weekend I've got some time off and I'm taking you back down to Brighton for a few days,' said Clare, 'and then maybe the two of us can go off somewhere different for a couple of nights.'

Elana was visiting England for two weeks, taking over her sister's long-held desire to travel – and along with it her suitcase. When Mandisa left Ocean View, Elana's cosy world crashed in on her, and she realised that no matter how much she tried to come to terms with it, life at home as the remaining twin was never going to be complete. Rachel was around for six months, and that helped, but once she'd gone Elana felt that she also needed to do something of her own, something radical, but what? Unlike her sister, Elana didn't want promotion at work, she didn't even like her job particularly, it was just a means of earning money and she had no real interest in selling shoes.

One evening, partly out of boredom, she took Mandisa's book on Southern England down from the shelf and started reading. That night Elana couldn't sleep. She remembered clearly when Mandisa first brought home her new red and white cabin bag and said '*one day this suitcase is going to fly to England*'.' But her life had moved on and it was clear by then that her sister wasn't going to fly anywhere – her career was taking off, she was seriously dating Baruti and the suitcase had ended up back at Ocean View. In the early hours of the morning Elana got up, pulled it out from under Mandisa's bed and wondered if she dared take it to England herself. By morning the slightly scary notion of the night before had tentatively become a plan, and in her lunch break she called into a travel shop in the mall and made some enquiries about flights to London.

Walter and Annie had been taken aback at first by Elana's announcement that she planned to visit England.

'On your own?' asked Annie, surprised that of her two daughters it should be this one that was taking the plunge. Elana had never been a trail-blazer.

'Of course – who else would I go with?'

'Well,' said Walter, 'I think it's a great idea.'

Annie saw the excitement lighting up her daughter's face, and knew she would never be able to talk her out of this trip. But Annie viewed a good many things differently by then – and even though she was certain to worry constantly about Elana while she was away, she didn't want to stop her from going.

'I can see that you've made up your mind to go,' she said. 'Have you spoken to Nina or Rachel about it?'

Elana shook her head. 'I wanted to talk to you first, in case...'

'Then you'd better give them a call,' said Annie, adding, 'in case of what? Did you think we would not let you go or something? You're very lucky to have relatives in England who you can stay with, how many other girls round here can say that?'

Walter, sitting behind Annie, hid a smile behind his hand, and winked at Elana.

Now, here she was, looking out of the car window on a bright morning in late September, at traffic and roads that weren't so very different to those at home. But beyond the fringe of the motorway a glimpse of something else rushed past: fields, cows, sheep, an occasional church steeple – England!

Elana put her head back and smiled sleepily. Later she would make a quick call to her parents, but she knew that Nina would be phoning them anyway that evening. It was Tuesday, and some things never changed.

CHAPTER 25

2013 – A GOOD YEAR

Kate would have been happy to see how her family fared in 2013. If she was looking down on Cape Town she would have seen Walter and Annie settling into their new home in Muizenburg (an easier journey to her mother, who stubbornly refused to move in with them), and cheered when Walter found work in a garage close by which paid him more than he'd been earning in Ocean View, for fewer hours. Annie's previously unsuspected talent at gardening worked a little magic on the scrubby, untended patch at the back of the house, and that would have impressed Kate, especially the vegetable plot and the bed where she initially struggled and then succeeded in growing typical English flowers – always referred to by the family as 'Mama's Surrey garden'.

She'd have been proud to see how Sele applied himself to his accountancy studies, sailing through the first year exams with distinction. Mandisa and Baruti's wedding would probably have made her shed a tear or two, and Elana's decision to return to the UK with a work permit and a job offer tucked into her handbag would have delighted her.

Closer to home, it would be a relief to Kate to know that Jeremy finally met the love of his life, living in the same village as him all the time, and when all the legal work on her estate was finished she'd have been thrilled that Tim Garvey asked Nina out to dinner, and hoped it was the start of something special. As Clare and Rachel's careers blossomed, Kate would have loved seeing them holidaying together in Cape Town and spending time with their African family. It was just what she'd hoped for, from the day she and Walter first met.

She'd have watched Bobby changing his lifestyle completely by moving down to Brighton, and perhaps she quietly had some of the conversations with him that they were never able to have in real life. And maybe that was why he woke some mornings after vivid dreams in which he sat and talked with his daughter. At those times Kate would have been grateful for Janet's sensible presence, as she listened patiently to his account, gave him tea and biscuits, and then gently talked him back into the real world.

And when Walter and Annie finally made the trip to the UK, Kate would have cried, and wished so much to have been there with them.

Maybe she did see it all. Maybe.

* * *

In June 2013, Bheki Msonga died for the second time. With the identity and a few bags of drugs he'd stolen from the doomed man in Mitchell's Plain he'd been able to follow Mandisa's advice and get far away from the Cape Flats. After a couple of false starts he found a niche for himself in Port Elizabeth – but never in a million years did he expect to run into Mandisa that day in the shopping mall, and it unsettled him almost as much as it did her. Unfortunately, Bheki's new life didn't have long to run after that as he was the victim of a mugging incident which left him with a fractured skull. He never regained consciousness, dying three days later between crisp white sheets in Port Elizabeth's Livingstone Hospital.

In October 2013, the British government belatedly made moves to introduce a life sentence for human trafficking. Too late for the Grey Man – six months previously he'd been convicted and jailed for five years for his part in what became known in the press as the 'Lambeth Slavery Ring'. Rachel was right; there was no paper trail, and she never had that knock on her door from the police.

Meanwhile Jason continued to live undetected in the USA on the proceeds of his care homes, although when he read about the government crackdown it did cause him a few days of concern and he was even more scratchy than usual with his family for the rest of that week. Unbeknown to him however, the Grey Man had only been the start of it, and back in the UK investigations were quietly gathering pace, with justice waiting patiently in the wings.

* * *

On Thursday 5th December, Nelson Mandela died, aged ninety-five. The world went into mourning and black South Africans celebrated his life in the traditional way, with singing and dancing. A memorial service, held in pouring rain at the FNB Stadium in Johannesburg, was attended by tens of thousands of ordinary people, as well as the great and good from across the globe. The crowd's biggest cheers were reserved for President Barack Obama and Archbishop Desmond Tutu, but when President Jacob Zuma spoke, sections of the crowd booed him.

Watching the proceedings on television from the comfort of his living room, Walter's comment on the crowd's disapproval was as succinct as always.

'I never liked that man.'

Annette Keen lives on the south coast, where she spends her non-writing time as a jazz promoter, quilter, yoga enthusiast and seafront-walker.

Distant Cousins is her second novel. Her first (*The Generation Club*) is also published by Sunbird Publishing and both are available via her website or from Amazon.

www.annettekeen.co.uk